BY DEATH DIVIDED

Laura Ackroyd, journalist girlfriend of DCI
Michael Thackeray, becomes drawn into the
plight of Julie Holden and her daughter
Anna when she writes an article about
domestic abuse. Julie takes flight to a
women's refuge, but her dreams of safety
are shattered when Anna goes missing...
Meanwhile Mohammed Sharif is trying to
keep the balance between his traditional
Muslim family and his job as a policeman.
When his newly-married cousin Faria Aziz
disappears, his private enquiries soon
become a police matter, and Thackeray and
his team must tread a careful path to avoid
upsetting Bradfield's Muslim community as
they investigate.

BY DEATH DIVIDED

BY DEATH DIVIDED

by

Patricia Hall

Magna Large Print Books
Long Preston, North Yorkshire,
BD23 4ND, England.

British Library Cataloguing in Publication Data.

Hall, Patricia
    By death divided.

    A catalogue record of this book is
    available from the British Library

    ISBN   978-0-7505-2973-0

First published in Great Britain in 2008 by Allison & Busby Ltd.

Copyright © 2008 by Patricia Hall

Cover illustration © Brighton Studios

The moral right of the author has been asserted

Published in Large Print 2008 by arrangement with
Allison & Busby Ltd.

Magna Large Print is an imprint of Library Magna Books Ltd.

Printed and bound in Great Britain by
T.J. (International) Ltd., Cornwall, PL28 8RW

PREFACE

The splash when her body touched the water would have disturbed no one. The place had been carefully chosen, a stretch of the river that ran deep between embankments in the old industrial heartland of Milford, where the mills had long ago closed down and only a small beginning had been made on replacing them with anything new. All was in darkness at that time of the night.

The woman slipped easily into the deep fast-running water. Heavy rain for days the previous week on the high hills to the west had left the river in spate. If God had chosen destruction for her, this was the perfect place. The water was dark and peaty and carried the accumulated debris of its tumbling course down from the moors, fragments of grasses and brittle bracken and heather, the occasional tree branch tufted with hanks of greasy wool left by the hefted sheep still late grazing on the unfenced land between Yorkshire and Lancashire.

The woman slipped beneath the surface of the rushing water, invisible and anonymous as the river took her past the confluence of the Maze and the Bradfield Beck, and the channel widened out slightly but barely slackened, its flood waters

7

breaching the banks here and there and spreading into the scrubby fields and woodland along the river's edge beyond the town, creating a morass only the most fool-hardy walker would venture into for days. The banks of the Maze would be no place for dogs or children or small boats for a while. She would be carried a long way, far from home, by this implacable accomplice to whatever had happened that night.

And so it proved. For days she slipped down the river unnoticed, half submerged in the deepest water furthest from the bank, through the ever-widening valley, past villages, under bridges, unseen by the few intrepid walkers who ventured near in the still pelting rain, ignored by the most venturesome animals who tried to drink in the shallows, floating alone, her trailing garments taken for a dislodged tangle of weed if they were spotted at all, Ophelia with nothing at all for remembrance.

But eventually she came to rest as her clothes became entangled with a branch torn from a tree, which itself had lodged firmly under the arch of an old stone bridge spanning the river in the village of Ingleby, an ancient hamlet in the flat, open farmland where the river began its long slow meander across the plain towards the Ouse and, eventually, the sea. It did not take long for her remains and the branch, inextricably meshed, to collect more debris, pushing the flow of the river into unexpected eddies, sending ripples and even small waves lapping across the

8

riverside path. And there she lay for days, no more than a single part of the natural wreckage from the week's storms, wreckage that lashed and lacerated her remains. Only her long scarf was visible on the surface as the tumbling water tried to wrench it from her body like a dirty white streamer and sent it downstream beyond the shadow of the bridge, a silent, tugging, tattered signal of distress. The fish found her body first, and then a dog, which stood, ears pricked and tail stiff, barking excitedly until at last someone came to investigate.

CHAPTER ONE

Rage overtook him like a foul fog, filling his mouth with bile and squeezing his chest like a vice, forcing breath from his lungs with a harsh rattle. There was never any warning. One moment he was calm and in control, and the next filled with this murderous madness, which he only half-remembered after it had abated. But more and more when he returned to his normal self he was aware of the havoc it – or was it he? – had created. Today it was the traffic. Just the common or garden everyday traffic. He had left his trip late and on the way back had hit the gridlock of parked cars outside the schools, and had only been able to inch his way along the normally quiet suburban roads of Southfield towards his home. Inevitably, his fury centred on the small blue car in front of him, inching through the stream with the heads of two children just visible through the rear window.

Close to the shops, breathing heavily and grinding his teeth, he saw his chance to overtake. Foot down, barely seeing where he was going, he swung out, crashed his foot hard on the accelerator and felt the satisfying surge of power through his spine as he began to pass the small blue car. Only then did he see another vehicle pulling out of a side-road into his path. He pulled the wheel viciously to the left and cut in on the blue car with a howl of rage. He was not conscious of the impact, not conscious of anything except the fact that he had swerved in time to avoid the vehicle coming towards him and that the road ahead of him was miraculously clear. He put his foot to the floor and accelerated away and the surge of speed began to soothe the flames of his anger. By the time he arrived home his heart rate had returned to normal and, on auto-pilot now, he put the four-by-four in the garage and dropped down the door, unaware of the smear of blue paint on the bull-bar, or even what it signi-fied. His voice, when he opened the front door and sang out 'I'm ho-o-o-me,' was completely normal, cheerful even. He had already blotted out that brief visit to his other dimension. But his voice faltered as no reply came to his greeting, and after a brief and increasingly angry look round, he realised the house was still empty. They had not come back.

Back in Southfield, a crowd had already gathered around the small car slewed across the pavement in front of the shopping parade when the Panda car pulled up at the kerb. PC Ali Mirza, who had only been a couple of streets away when he was told to attend the incident, could see a woman in jeans and a fleece leaning against the front door of the blue Nissan, which, if it had skidded any further, would have crashed through the plate-glass window of the hairdresser's, A Fine Cut, where customers and staff in pink overalls were staring through the window in some agitation. The woman was shouting and gesticulating angrily, and Mirza made his way cautiously through the bystanders to confront her. Only just out of his probation, he felt less than confident amongst the wealthy white residents of Bradfield's most exclusive suburb.

'Is this your car, madam?' he asked, in a voice husky with nervousness. He could see two children still strapped into their seats in the back of the blue Nissan and the woman followed his gaze. School run, second family car, he told himself, hardly unusual up here, and undoubtedly a woman who would be confident of her rights.

'My God, they could have been killed,' she half-screamed, and promptly burst into tears.

'Is anyone hurt?' Mirza addressed his question then to the small crowd that was watching him, faces impassive, but got only negative shakes of the head in return.

'So can anyone tell me what happened?' He glanced at the driver who had by now pulled open the back door and was undoing the seatbelts of a boy of about eight and one slightly younger, both in the uniform of the primary school half a mile away. He walked to the front of the car and pulled out his notebook to jot down the registration number. The front offside wing of the car was badly scraped and dented and the lights had smashed. There had obviously been some sort of a collision but there was no sign of any other vehicle that might have been involved. He turned back to the woman, who was now half into the back of the car, comforting the two children. Careful, he told himself, she must be in shock.

'I can tell you what happened, Officer,' a tall elderly man in a military-looking overcoat offered. 'It was an atrocious piece of bad driving. If I'd been a bit quicker I would have taken the number of the other vehicle, but he was away so fast I didn't manage it.'

The driver of the car, tear-stained but calmer now, let go of her children and turned back towards Mirza, pushing her tangled hair out of her eyes.

'The bastard ran me off the road,' she said. 'He could have killed us all, people on the pavement, anything could have happened...' She waved her hand around at the small crowd of shoppers and at the prosperous-looking hairdresser's salon and the baker's and the delicatessen behind them, and then leant back against the side of the car again, shivering.

Mirza stood with pen poised over his notebook.

'Perhaps if you give me your details, madam, then you can tell me exactly what happened. Do you have your driving licence with you?'

The woman shook her head vaguely, but managed to offer her name and address.

'I picked up the boys from school,' she said. 'There was a lot of traffic coming back up the hill.' She waved back down towards the main road, which led into Bradfield town centre. 'Then I was aware of this four-by-four very close on my tail. Too close, obviously wanting to get past. But he couldn't. There was too much traffic coming the other way.'

'It was a man driving?' Mirza asked.

'Yes, I think so, I could see him in my mirror. And then when I turned off to come up here, past the shops, he turned as well and then pulled out very fast, but he didn't notice another car coming into the main road from the turning over there...' She waved vaguely again to a junction on the opposite side of the road. 'So before I knew what was happening he'd cut in in front of me and clipped my wing and just pushed me over, onto the pavement. There was nothing I could do.' She searched Ali Mirza's face desperately for understanding.

'Did he stop at all?' the constable asked.

'Of course he didn't,' she said, angry suddenly. 'He shot off like a maniac.'

'Could you describe the car? Colour? Make? Anything at all?'

'Big, dark, blue or black, I suppose, four-by-four, with a spare tyre on the back. Like bloody tanks, aren't they, those things? I don't know why they need to be driving them in town at all. They're a menace.' She shuddered suddenly and glanced at her small blue Nissan. 'My husband will go crazy,' she said. 'I've only been out ten minutes and this happens.' She glanced at her watch. 'I must get back,' she said. 'I've left my daughter with a friend...'

Mirza closed his notebook.

'I suggest you drive home with the children now, Mrs Mendelson, and I'll arrange for someone to contact you later to take a proper statement from you. Luckily no one's been hurt, so no serious harm has been done.'

'You'll try and find that lunatic, though?'

'I'll put in a report, but without a registration number he may not be easy to trace.'

'He could kill someone next time.'

'Yes,' Mirza said. 'I'm sure he could.' And after taking the names and addresses from half a dozen of the witnesses, he got into the Panda car with a feeling of satisfaction that he had handled that well enough.

Laura Ackroyd glanced at her watch, logged off her computer and ran her hands through her unruly cloud of copper hair. It had been a good day for once, with her boss, Ted Grant, thankfully out of the office at a conference of the local newspaper groups' editors. Slightly ominous, that, had been the consensus round the water cooler that morning. They all knew that the position of many local newspapers was potentially dire as crucial advertising slipped away to new media, and circulations dipped because the younger generation seemed not to have inherited their parents' interest in parochial news. Stories of belt-tightening and redundancies were the stock-in-trade of the media columns these days and the staff of the *Bradfield Gazette* knew that they would not be immune to the chilly winds blowing through the company. But even so, Laura refused to feel too despondent. For the first time in many months she felt that life was good and could get better.

She spent five minutes in the cloakroom repairing her make-up, giving her reflection a quick smile in the mirror, and then left the office and drove up the long hill out of the town centre, through the thickening early evening traffic, and parked outside a substantial house in a leafy avenue in Southfield. This was the time she enjoyed visiting her friend Vicky Mendelson best, the hour or two after her two older boys had arrived home from primary school and the youngest child, Naomi Laura, named after her mother's best friend, was having her tea and being prepared for bed. She had known Vicky and her husband David since they had all been students together at Bradfield University and, lacking children of her own, although she still nurtured hopes that might be put right, she relished the chance to take even a small share in Vicky's slightly chaotic teatime rituals. But when Vicky opened the door this particular evening she did so with an anxious air, and gave Laura a hug that lacked its usual enthusiasm.

'What's the problem?' Laura asked, sensing trouble. 'You look shattered.'

'It's been an awful day,' Vicky said, obviously close to tears. 'Some lunatic bashed my car when I went to pick up the boys from school. And then drove off without a bloody word. I've had the police taking details, everything.'

'My God, were you hurt?'

'Fortunately no one was hurt and the boys took it in their stride, as kids do. But I feel a bit shaken up. And I've also got an unexpected visitor. Sorry,' she whispered as she led Laura down the hall to the kitchen, where she saw a pale, thin woman in jeans and a loose, long-sleeved shirt, sitting at the table with her hands clutched around a mug of coffee, as if for warmth. The stranger looked up as Laura came into the room and gave a tentative smile.

'This is Julie Holden,' Vicky said.

'Hi, Julie,' Laura said cheerfully before she crossed the room to give Naomi, who was sitting in her high chair, a kiss. 'Where are the boys?' she asked.

'They're watching TV with Julie's little girl, Anna,' Vicky said.

Laura put her head round the sitting room door and saw two dark heads and one blonde one on the sofa in front of CBBC.

'Hi gang,' she said but got only the briefest murmur in exchange from Vicky's two sons, who were immersed in their programme. Back in the kitchen she accepted a cup of coffee gratefully and took a seat next to Julie Holden.

'Is Anna at school with the boys?' she asked. But to her horror Julie shook her head violently and her eyes filled with tears. It was obvious that Laura had touched a sensitive nerve with what she had thought was an innocuous question.

'She used to be, but she's not going to school at the moment,' Julie said. 'We've got a bit of a family problem.'

Laura glanced at Vicky, who was busy wiping her daughter's sticky hands and face.

'Julie's just left her husband. I've been telling her to do it for ages, and now she has,' Vicky said.

'I'm sorry,' Laura said, her tone cautious. If she had interrupted an informal marriage guidance session she was not so happy about her unannounced intrusion. She, of all people, was the last person to offer advice on relationships. And at a point when she was beginning to think that maybe she could look forward to a family of her own, she was not keen to immerse herself in other people's disasters.

'Vicky makes it sound easy, but it's not,' Julie said, her voice thick with emotion.

'It is when he's been treating you like he's been treating you,' Vicky said angrily. 'It's a no-brainer. You can't possibly stay with him.' Laura looked from one woman to the other, Julie clutching her mug, pale and scared-looking but now with two vivid red blotches of colour in her cheeks, and Vicky, standing above her, flushed with indignation, but plump and beautiful and, the accident not-withstanding, a golden picture of content-ment, and she wondered at the contrast. She felt her usual prickle of jealousy and tamped it down firmly. There was no need for jealousy now, she thought, with the future looking good.

'I'm sorry, perhaps you don't want me here just now,' Laura said, finishing her coffee quickly and glancing from one woman to the other.

'No, no,' Julie said quickly. 'You might be able to help. Vicky says your partner is a policeman. I think I might need some advice.'

Laura hesitated. Michael Thackeray, she knew, would not welcome being dragged into a stranger's domestic affairs, even at second hand. But catching the desperation in Julie's eyes, she knew that she could not refuse at least to listen.

'Tell me about it,' she conceded, hoping her reluctance did not appear too obvious. By way of reply, Julie rolled up the sleeve of her shirt to reveal a series of blue and purple bruises the length of her arm.

'This time he threw me across the room,' she said quietly. 'If I stay with him I think he'll kill me in the end. It's been going on for months. I've lost track of how long.'

Laura drew a sharp breath.

'Have you been to the police?' she asked. 'They have special departments these days to deal with this sort of thing.'

Julie shook her head.

'Then you must do that,' Laura said. 'You can't let him get away with behaviour like this. It'll only get worse.'

'I've already told her that,' Vicky chipped in. 'She can't let this go on. Anna's at risk as well.'

'No, no, he'd never hurt Anna,' Julie said sharply. 'He wouldn't lay a finger on her. He adores her.'

'You can't be sure of that if he's so violent,' Laura said. 'What does David say about it?' she asked, turning to Vicky, whose husband was a Crown Prosecution Service lawyer and, she thought, far better qualified than she was to give advice to a battered wife.

'I don't want to bother him,' Julie said, her voice dull.

'You need a solicitor who specialises in family law,' Vicky said. 'I'm sure David could recommend someone.'

'Oh, they have all those sorts of details at the place where I've arranged to stay,' Julie said.

'Julie's got a place for herself and Anna at the refuge in town...' Vicky began to explain, only to be interrupted.

'But I can't stay there long,' Julie said, her voice strained. 'It's too close to home. He'll find me. I can't let him find me. I don't know what he'll do.' Laura could see that the woman was terrified and on the edge of panic.

'Surely you can get an injunction to keep him away,' she said tentatively, dredging her mind for anything she had ever written in the *Gazette* about domestic violence.

'I don't even know where he is,' Julie said. 'I've been ringing him at home since we left

21

this morning but he's not answering the phone. I don't even know if he's still there, but I daren't go round in case he is.'

'Doesn't he have a mobile?' Laura asked.

'No, no, he hates mobile phones. He thinks people can spy on him if he carries a mobile.'

'Sounds a bit paranoid,' Laura said.

'He is,' Julie snapped. 'He is. I really think he's going mad.'

Laura had driven Julie Holden and her daughter back to the refuge in the centre of Bradfield and watched them scuttle into the dilapidated old house with the unexpected signs of twenty-first century security precautions only too clearly visible: the wire mesh over the downstairs windows, the CCTV cameras observing the scruffy garden from every angle and the answer phone system not just on the front door but also on the high iron gate. It looked more like the entrance to a prison than a refuge, she thought, and she wondered what effect it had on the no doubt numerous children who were forced into its confines by dangers in their own homes she could not even begin to imagine. She sighed. She knew, from what little Michael Thackeray had told her about his own marriage, which had ended in tragedy, how overwhelming passion could transmute into a species of war. And she had learnt, since she had known him, how difficult he found it to deal with these issues at work, as he frequently had to. And yet her imagination still could not stretch to any scenario where such anger could affect her own life.

Tiredly, she pulled away from the kerb and made her way through the rush hour traffic in the direction of home, relieved to escape the atmosphere of fear and tension her two passengers had carried with them like an echo from a dark place. For all the ups and downs in her relationship with Michael Thackeray, who carried a weight of guilt she could only dimly begin to comprehend, she had never felt physically threatened by his periodic descents into depression and the ever-present threat of a drink-fuelled binge. For a man so burdened he was remarkably gentle, and for that she was thankful and had begun to hope that the long shadow of his troubled marriage was lifting at last.

When she had eased her way out of the traffic and into the leafy avenue where the two of them shared a flat in a tall Victorian house, she was surprised to see his car already parked outside. They both started work early but she was generally home first, not subject to the vagaries, in terms of time or emotion, that the daily battle against crime implied. She found Thackeray watching the television news.

'Good day?' she asked, as she took off her coat and leant over the back of the sofa to kiss him. He laughed.

'I spent the afternoon at County listening to the latest on the amalgamation of the Yorkshire forces. People already complain that we're not close enough to the ground so I don't really understand how these new massive organisations are going to help. I wouldn't be at all surprised if it all ran into the ground eventually.'

'It's all about serious crime and terrorism, isn't it?' Laura asked. 'Isn't this new FBI-style organisation supposed to do all that nationally anyway?'

'I thought that was the general idea,' Thackeray said.

'I'd have thought for the rest of it, it would be better to be close to the ground. It'll be like trying to run the *Bradfield Gazette* from Leeds or Manchester.'

'Supposedly there are things small forces can't do, but as we're a big force we'll have to go through the pain for no particular gain, as far as I can see. I expect it's all about saving money in the long run. Fewer chief constables can't be bad, can it?'

'It's fewer editors I could do with,' Laura said with a grin. 'But I can't see any chance of that. Will it affect CID?'

'Probably not,' Thackeray said, turning the television off. 'We've already got as many specialist units for serious crime as anyone could possibly need. So let's not worry about it. How was your day?'

Laura's face clouded as she told him about visiting Vicky and meeting Julie Holden and her pale-faced, anxious daughter.

'She should first of all report it to us,' Thackeray said. 'And then get an injunction to stop him coming anywhere near her and the child. There's nothing we can do unless she takes the first steps and make a complaint.'

'That's what I thought,' Laura said. 'How can a man...' She started the sentence and then bit her tongue, though Thackeray was looking at her calmly enough.

'Count yourself lucky you can't comprehend what anger can do,' he said quietly. 'You don't want to go there.'

'No,' Laura said. 'And you're not going there, either. Ever again.'

CHAPTER TWO

Detective Constable Mohammed Sharif stared out of the CID office window, lost in thought as he gazed across the windswept square flanked on one side by police HQ and on the other by the Italianate Bradfield town hall which looked even more out of time and place than usual on this grey and gusty winter morning. Born and bred not a mile away amongst the close-knit stone terraces off Aysgarth Lane, he should be used to this climate, he thought. For him there were no childhood memories of blue skies and dusty villages to idealise of an evening, as his father and uncles often did. On family visits to Pakistan, he had concluded that it was hot, dirty and anarchic, and he had always been pleased when the plane bumped its way down through the cloud cover into Manchester airport. But he still hated the British winter and longed for a sight of the sun.

Sharply intelligent, Sharif had clawed his way from an impoverished home life after the textile mills had closed, plunging Bradfield's immigrant population into long-lasting unemployment, and made it through indifferent schooling and the local university, and then into the police force. His choice of career had not pleased his parents. They would have preferred the law or a business career for their first-born, who had achieved the almost impossible in their eyes by going to university at all, but Sharif, when he had eventually made CID, had been content. It was what he wanted and he had withstood the sullen racism he had met every day on the streets and even within the police force itself, to follow his dream, self-confident enough in the end, with his sergeant, Kevin Mower's backing, to give evidence at a tribunal that put an end to the careers of two officers who had indulged in particularly blatant acts of prejudice a year or so earlier. That had not endeared him to many of his colleagues. That was the downside. The upside turned out to be a new respect from most of his colleagues, and even a wary acknowledgement by a hostile minority that he should not be messed with.

But now he faced a dilemma, a conflict of loyalties that had been creeping up on him for weeks and which he knew he had to resolve soon. It was a problem which brought his membership of his own community and his obligations to the job into a stark and very personal confrontation. He glanced across the office and caught Kevin Mower's eye. If any of his colleagues could understand his problem, it had to be Mower, who was still felt to be something of an outsider here himself: a Londoner of less than pure anglo-saxon parentage, who was still regarded with a certain amount of suspicion by his clannish Yorkshire colleagues. But Sharif had not felt able to confide his worries even to him.

'OK?' Mower asked across the room.

Sharif glanced at his computer screen, where he was supposed to be searching the records of known offenders whose modus operandi might link them to a spate of street robberies carried out in broad daylight in the bright new shopping centre on the edge of the town.

'A couple of possibles, Sarge, going on the victims' descriptions,' Sharif said. 'Give me ten minutes.'

'Fine,' Mower said and returned to his own screen.

But Sharif could not concentrate on the task in hand. Unlike most young unmarried Asian men, he had not been content to stay in the family home. As soon as his income allowed, he had chosen a small self-contained flat several miles from the Aysgarth area, a flat where he could indulge his passion for rock music and entertaining friends, even, occasionally, women friends, away from the censorious eyes of his own community. As a non-observant Muslim he felt no shame in what he was doing, but for his parents' sake he kept quiet about his lifestyle when he visited them, and he tended to frequent clubs and cinemas when he was with white friends, and especially young women, sufficiently far away from Aysgarth Lane to protect his family from any hint of scandal. Recently, since he had acquired a more serious girlfriend, Louise, a local girl who had come back from college to teach in one of the town's secondary schools, he generally went out in Leeds to avoid adverse comment on their relationship from either side of the racial divide. The disadvantage was that he was increasingly less well informed about what was going on in the heartland of the Punjabi diaspora around the Lane, and, he feared, less useful in the job as a consequence.

The previous evening he had visited his parents on the way home from work and had found them both slightly abstracted. They had been that way the last time he had seen them a week or so previously and he had not had the curiosity then to wonder why. His mother had plied him with huge portions of traditional food, never convinced that he could possibly be having enough to eat when out of her care, and filled him in on the charms of various eligible young women she had just happened to come across in the community, and his father had discoursed vaguely about politics in Pakistan and, much more interesting to Sharif, the activities of various solemn-faced and bearded young men at the mosque.

'They're not dangerous,' his father had opined, his own face serious. 'We do not have crazy men here.' But, conscious of recent events, Sharif wondered how his father could possibly know and tried to prise a few names out of him.

His mother had changed the subject quickly to her usual run-down on the activities of his younger brothers and sisters, all married and living locally, and then began to run through the litany of his aunts and uncles – getting older and more difficult – and his cousins, their behaviour apparently more modern and scandalous by the day. He had no doubt that his own idiosyncrasies, not least his determined refusal to take a wife yet, would be recounted endlessly amongst the rest of the family in exactly the same way. He never left home for his own place without silently congratulating himself on his decision to move out and escape the clammy clutches of the clan.

But there had been one jarring element in this rare family visit. When he had inquired, without great enthusiasm, about his young cousin Faria, who had been married off, he suspected reluctantly, to a distant cousin in Pakistan, his mother's comments turned unusually angry.

'She never visits her mother,' Ayesha Sharif said, lips pursed in her plump face. 'Not for months has she visited home. I don't understand that in a daughter.'

'They moved away from Bradfield, didn't they?' Sharif had said mildly. 'Does she drive a car?'

'No, she doesn't drive, but Imran Aziz could bring her to Bradfield. It's not very far. Milford is not very far. And there are no children coming, as far as I know.'

Sharif opened his mouth to speak and then instantly thought better of it. The idea that a young bride in her late teens might not yet want children would not only not cross his mother's mind but would deeply offend her ideas of what was right and what was wrong. He smiled faintly but even so he determined to call his young cousin, in whom he had always taken an older brother's interest, as she had no brothers of her own.

'Married two years now and no children,' his mother went on, irritating Sharif with the censoriousness of her tone, and as soon as he decently could he made his escape.

But when he called the Milford number which he had for Faria on his way home he got only Imran Aziz, who told him that Faria was not at home. Imran hung up quickly and did not elaborate on where a young Muslim wife might be without her husband at ten o'clock at night, a fact that Sharif found faintly disturbing. He had tried the number again the next morning before setting off for work, reluctantly leaving Louise still getting dressed in his bathroom, and this time he got no reply. Should he worry? he wondered, recalling the lively eyed girl and her two sisters who had been regular visitors to his home when he was a boy. He had lost touch as they had all grown up and he had gone his separate way, but Faria had been his favourite and he determined to make a visit to Milford as soon as he had the time. He had no intention of allowing his parents to arrange a marriage for him, and Faria had been very young when hers was set in train. Perhaps it was not working out well, he thought, and resolved to find out.

'Just about to print out the details, Sarge,' he said guiltily in response to Mower's increasingly impatient query. 'Give me ten seconds.'

Feeling slight anxiety that he had dismissed Laura's concerns about her brush with a battered wife the previous evening too easily, not least because he had been determined to make the most of a rare long evening with her, DCI Michael Thackeray took the trouble to wander casually into the domestic violence unit at police HQ that morning. Most of the desks were empty, but he found the head of the unit, DS Janet Richardson, in her tiny glassed-off office, surrounded by heaps of files. She glanced up at him anxiously with tired eyes.

'Morning,' she said. 'We don't often see you down here. We don't have a body for you – not yet. Though I know a few men doing their best to oblige.'

Thackeray nodded, accepting the justice of her implied criticism. Crime prevention was meant to be a priority but as money was poured into higher and higher-tech policing, intelligence gathering, surveillance, rapid response units, armed response units and efforts to combat the threats of terrorism and organised crime, he knew Janet felt increasingly under-resourced and neglected in the wider scheme of things. Yet the most usual murder was the result of a common or garden domestic dispute.

'My girlfriend ... partner, I mean, came home last night very upset about some woman she'd met at the refuge in town who's being harassed by her husband. I wondered if she'd made a complaint.' Thackeray's faint grasp of the politically correct still left Laura amused at times.

'What's her name?' Janet asked, turning to her computer screen. But when Thackeray told her, she scrolled through her data and then shook her head.

'No record,' she said. 'Has she been

seriously hurt? We can prosecute off our own bat now, you know, but it's difficult if they won't give evidence.' She pushed a sheaf of photographs across her desk towards him. 'Look at those,' she said. He glanced at pictures of a woman whose face and upper body were shown in colour, covered with a lurid mass of cuts and bruises, and drew a sharp breath.

'Not only will she not go to court but she's bloody well gone back to the bastard,' Janet said wearily. She pushed the photographs back into a folder and put it in a wire tray.

'Case closed,' she said. 'CPS won't look at it without her.'

'Will you let me know if Mrs Holden comes in?' Thackeray said. 'Laura and her friend Vicky Mendelson are very worried about her. And there's a child involved. A little girl.'

'I'll have a word with social services,' Janet said. 'They may have had some involvement. Is Vicky David Mendelson's wife?'

'Yes. The CPS lawyer.' It had been at David and Vicky's house, soon after arriving in Bradfield, that he had met a redheaded young woman who had occupied his thoughts and emotions, not always comfortably, ever since. But Thackeray kept his private life determinedly private, still scarred by the pain of having his disintegrating marriage the focus of vicious canteen gossip years before.

'Right,' Janet said. 'David's been very helpful on some of these cases. Unlike some lawyers and coppers I've come across. There are still some male dinosaurs around who won't take it seriously, over here and at the CPS.'

'You can count on me, Janet, if you need back-up. You know that,' Thackeray said mildly.

'Yes, I know,' she said. 'My major worry at the moment is that I don't think we're getting anywhere near knowing what's going on under the surface with the Muslim community.'

'Ah,' Thackeray said. 'You'll be treading on eggshells there, then?'

'You have to believe it. Some of the brides who are still coming from the sub-continent speak no English at all when they arrive. They're incredibly isolated.'

'But there are fewer of them now, surely?'

'Yes, it is changing, but very slowly. There are still imams who insist the Koran allows men to beat their wives. It's bloody medieval, like those veils a few of them wear over their faces, the niqab. They give me the creeps. But don't let the community relations people hear me saying that. Anyway, I'm sure if there is domestic violence in Muslim families, we'll never hear about it. It's not part of the women's culture to complain.'

'It doesn't look as if it's part of our culture either, from what you say,' Thackeray said, a hint of anger in his voice too. 'This Julie Holden. She's an educated woman, for God's sake. Why on earth isn't she in here raising hell if he's knocking her about? She's letting him get away with it, covering up for him, effectively.'

'Relationships are not rational,' Janet said, seeming slightly surprised at his vehemence before she turned back to her files. Her expression jolted Thackeray back to more than one relationship of his own that had been very far from rational. Painfully he pushed the monsters back into the dark pit from which they thankfully crept out less often since the death of his wife, knowing that in Janet Richardson's world he could not count himself amongst the innocent, and sighed.

'Let me know,' he said as he turned away, but she did not even bother to reply.

Vanessa Holden unlocked the bathroom door very gently, aware that on the last fraction of its turn it tended to click. She hoped he was asleep, or if not, was too far away to hear her moving. Once it was open she kept her hand on the lock for a long minute, listening hard, but she could hear nothing.

Before she switched the light off and inched the door wide open, she glanced one last time in the mirror and flinched. For all her efforts with foundation and face-powder she had not succeeded in hiding the darkening bruise down her left cheek where he had hit her. Nor had she completely disguised the purple circles beneath her eyes, the result of several nights now spent barely asleep, wondering whether he would come back and terrified of what would happen to them both, whether he did or whether he didn't.

She had taken her outdoor coat and her handbag into the bathroom with her and intended to creep down the stairs now and out of the front door before he realised she had moved from her bedroom, where she had locked the door in his face after he had attacked her, hours ago now. But she had no real idea where she would go if she got out of the house, her house, that he had invaded like some unpredictable incubus days ago when Julie had first left him.

He had come home tonight in a towering rage again and then slumped in front of the television, with the sound turned so high it made her dizzy, while she put together an evening meal with shaking hands. It had not been to his liking. Her food never was. Even as a little boy he had been a picky eater and as a teenager he had almost given up eating at home, preferring the bright lights and noise of fast-food restaurants and pubs.

Once, when she asked him whether the food was better than her own offerings he said, bizarrely, she thought, that the food wasn't what he went for. He liked McDonald's, he said, because no one could hear him thinking.

If she was honest with herself, she had been relieved when he went away to university and even more relieved that he successfully completed his course, got a job as a manager in a high-tech company in Lancashire, and announced, soon afterwards, that he was to marry a young woman called Julie whom Vanessa had barely met, but who seemed pleasant enough when she did. Gradually, her memories of the erratic teenager she had lived with faded as her time and attention were taken up with her husband, who developed cancer in his sixties and died before his seventieth birthday. After gruelling years, Vanessa tentatively hoped for some calm and even happiness. She found herself pleased when her son and his family eventually moved back to Bradfield and she invested in a smaller house, one of a Victorian terrace, deliberately chosen to be close to her son and his growing daughter, Anna, whom she idolised.

But she soon learnt only too bitterly that her respite had been brief and her modest ambitions hopelessly optimistic. The marriage, she soon discovered, was on the rocks, and although Julie said little and Anna, increasingly pale and silent, even less, she guessed that it had become violent. To her horror, a couple of days earlier, he had arrived on her doorstep with a large suitcase. Julie had left him, he said, and taken the child with her. He could not stay in the family house on his own, he said, it was too quiet, and had decided to come 'home' for a bit. Only when Vanessa began to protest mildly and try to persuade him to go back to his own place did she realise exactly why Julie had given up on the marriage in despair.

Bruce, it appeared, had not only lost his wife and daughter but also his job, although the firm had allowed him to keep his four-by-four, which he had been using to visit the sites they had been working at all over the north of England. He could barely afford the petrol for it now, Vanessa realised, and he spent most of his time in the house, either with the television turned up to full volume, or pacing restlessly around, talking to himself. When she suggested that he should see a doctor he screamed and swore at her. And any innocent query about his welfare, like tonight when she asked him if he wanted anything to follow his main meal, could be met with a sudden eruption of violence. She fingered the gash on her cheek, where the blood was slowly congealing, as she inched down the stairs, her arthritic knees making progress slow. He had thrown his empty plate at her, spinning it like a frisby, before hurling his chair back and careering drunkenly out of the room and into the kitchen, where she heard him throwing crockery about in a frenzy. As she closed the front door behind her she felt tears cutting channels through her newly applied make-up as despair overwhelmed her. With her coat collar turned up she hurried away from the house, feeling the sharp wind on her wet face. She had absolutely no idea where to go.

Vicky Mendelson turned the DVD player off and stretched lazily. David was out at a lawyers' dinner with his father, the children were all sound asleep upstairs and the only decision she had to make now was whether or not to wait up for her husband and hear the latest legal gossip over cocoa tonight, or go to bed and follow up in the morning over breakfast. She was sleepy, but guessed that conversation tomorrow would be as difficult as two small boys getting ready for school and a hungry toddler to feed and David himself in a distracted state after a late night could make it, so she determined to wait up and wandered into the kitchen to get herself another glass of the wine she had opened to dissipate the solitariness of her own supper. Wives were not expected at her father-in-law Victor's little get-togethers, and knowing her mother-in-law's lack of interest in the law she was not surprised. Anyway, she had chosen to be a full-time mother, at least until all the children went to school, but she still envied her friend Laura Ackroyd's independence almost as much as she guessed Laura envied her her family life. The grass on the other side, she thought wryly as she went back into the sitting room and glanced at the TV schedules. But then she froze as she heard an unexpected noise outside the house, not at the front door where David could well have been arriving, but at the back of the house from which french windows led into the garden where flower beds and a worn lawn struggled for survival amongst the children's play equipment.

Her heart thumped as she listened intently. The curtains were tightly drawn so she could not see out and she knew that it would be pitch black out there with all the lights at the back of the house switched off. She glanced round anxiously, realising that her mobile phone was upstairs in her handbag and the only other phone downstairs was in the study, where, if she switched the light on, she would be instantly seen by anyone in the back garden. Her ears straining against the silence, she could hear nothing.

'I must be imagining it,' she told herself firmly, but she knew she wasn't, and was acutely conscious of the three children sleeping upstairs. Then it came again, a slightly different sound this time, which she knew was someone trying the handle of the back door. Swallowing down panic, she ran out of the room, flicking light switches as she went, and stumbled up the stairs to fumble frantically for her phone. Whoever was outside would know they had disturbed someone now and, as she called David's mobile, she peered out of the uncurtained bedroom window into the shadowy half-lit darkness of the garden. There was someone there, she decided with absolute certainty, although she could not make out exactly where amongst the shadows of the trees and bushes moving and rustling in a stiff breeze.

To her immense relief David answered quickly.

'Call the police, now!' he said when she had explained what was happening. 'I'll be there in fifteen minutes, max. Dial 999 now, Vicky. Don't take any chances. I love you.' Her hands trembling on the keys, she did as she was told.

The call came just as Laura, already in silky pyjamas and with her hair in a loose copper cloud around her shoulders, was thinking about enticing Thackeray to bed and wondering, when she got him there, whether she dare broach her near obsessive wish to come off the pill.

'Damn and blast,' she muttered, struggling up from the sofa where she had been leaning amorously against her lover to pick up the receiver on the other side of the room.

'Hi,' David Mendelson said, and she caught the tension in his voice immediately. 'Is Michael there?'

She handed the receiver to Thackeray and watched anxiously, seeing his face tighten as he listened for a couple of minutes without saying anything.

'Are uniform with you now?' he asked at length, and Laura's heart lurched as she heard David respond.

'Do you want me to come over?' Thackeray asked, and when he obviously got an affirmative answer, he cut the connection and turned back to Laura.

'It's nothing too serious,' he said, seeing her panic-stricken face. The Mendelsons were Laura's closest friends in Bradfield, and David had also been the first friend Thackeray had made himself when he arrived in the town as the new DCI, a friend who had gradually encouraged him back from the frozen emotional state he had arrived in into a semblance of a normal life. He had also, most memorably, and as a deliberate ploy in his campaign to restore Thackeray to normality, introduced him to Laura.

'What's happened?' Laura asked.

'Vicky was there on her own with the children and heard someone snooping around in the back garden. The local car got there pretty fast but as far as David knows they haven't picked anyone up yet. I think if I make an appearance it might just stiffen their resolve a bit, take it a bit more seriously than they might otherwise.'

'I'll come with you,' Laura said flatly, hurrying into the bedroom to pull on jeans and a sweatshirt over her pyjamas.

Thackeray knew better than to argue and they drove the mile or so to the Mendelsons' home in Southfield in an anxious silence. They found the house lit up, the patrol car still parked outside, and Vicky and David in the sitting room with the two boys, who had been wakened by the excitement. Laura flung her arms round Vicky.

'You must have been terrified,' she said.

'A bit,' Vicky admitted, her eyes full of tears.

'It's good of you to come. The officers are out at the back,' David said, taking Thackeray's arm and leading him out of ear-shot of the two confused and sleepy children. 'An attempt's definitely been made to force the back door.'

'Even though the house was obviously occupied?' Thackeray said. 'That's not your everyday opportunistic burglar. They want to avoid people as much as possible. Let's

44

have a look, shall we?'

He led the way into the back garden, where two uniformed officers were shining their flash-lights into the bushes and around the back of the garage. They looked startled to see Thackeray.

'Sir?' the older man said.

'Mr Mendelson is a good friend,' Thackeray said. 'I'm not here officially. Just as a friend of the family. Wilson, isn't it?'

'Sir,' the officer said in acknowledgement. He did not look particularly happy at this unexpected interruption of a routine chore by a senior officer.

'Two of you?'

'That's Ali. Ali Mirza. Just finishing his probation and doing a bit of overtime.' Wilson's face, in the dim light from the kitchen door, was impassive, but Thackeray could feel the undercurrent of resentment. Why, he wondered angrily, why the hell, after all this time, couldn't they just accept people? But the middle-aged copper, his girth stretching his uniform to its limit, was still talking.

'Someone's had a go at the kitchen door,' he said. 'But he's done more damage to the woodwork than the actual lock. Looks like an amateur job to me. Could be kids. It's easy enough to shin over the back gate, even though it's locked.'

'Let's make sure we have a good look

round in daylight, shall we?' Thackeray suggested. 'There may be some prints on the door, or the gate, if you think that's the way he got in. He, they, whoever.'

'Yes, sir,' the constable said without enthusiasm, and Thackeray knew he had pushed his influence as far as it would go. This was not CID business, much more likely to be a case of anti-social behaviour by local teenagers high on drink or drugs, and he and PC Wilson both knew that. He ushered David back into the house and left the two officers to their desultory search. He knew that they would find nothing in the dark and they wouldn't be looking very hard for fingerprints or DNA in the morning.

'I don't think it's anything to worry about, David,' he said. 'They're very unlikely to be back.'

'I'll look at the security at the back of the house,' David said. 'I hate having to turn the place into a fortress but maybe security lights out there, or an alarm on the back gate? Vicky was terrified.'

'I'm sure,' Thackeray said. 'I suppose there's just a chance it could be someone with some personal grudge, someone you helped put away. I'll make sure the forensic people do a thorough check for prints tomorrow, just in case it's anyone we know.'

'I'm grateful, Michael,' Mendelson said. 'If anything happened to the children...' He stopped suddenly, realising he was treading on delicate territory. 'You know?' he said lamely.

'I know,' Thackeray said, and turned away.

CHAPTER THREE

'Morning, guv,' Sergeant Kevin Mower said cheerfully as he stuck his head round the DCI's door. His love life had recently taken a distinct turn for the better and the swarthy Londoner, still not entirely at home amongst the dour Yorkshire coppers he worked with, had even been heard whistling around the CID office recently. Seeing his boss also sitting at his desk in a more relaxed frame of mind than had been apparent for months, he smiled even more broadly. Michael Thackeray, he reckoned, was getting it a bit more regularly too, although he knew better than to ever comment on the DCI's personal life. He had fancied Laura Ackroyd himself when he first met her and still reckoned she had made the infinitely more demanding choice. But he wished them well, especially now that he had found a dishy and sexually athletic partner he could envisage spending some serious time with. He straightened his multi-coloured silk tie, which set off a sharper suit than most detectives could muster for Sunday best, and tried to temper the smile that kept breaking through as he contemplated the previous night's adventures with his foxy lady.

'Anything I should know about?' Thackeray asked, not wondering too hard what had made the sergeant so cheerful. It did not take a very skilled detective to work it out. Mower enjoyed a sudden vivid mental image of Jess slowly lowering her generous breasts towards his face. But he suffocated the thought as soon as it had been born.

'Odd case up at Southfield overnight, guv,' was all he said. Thackeray looked slightly surprised.

'You mean the Mendelson intruder?'

Mower looked blank.

'No,' he said. 'The woman a patrol car found up by Forster Park. Looked as if she'd been mugged, but she doesn't seem to be saying anything yet. She's in the infirmary. Mild hypothermia, they say, elderly and very confused. But someone had hit her quite hard. Her cheekbone is broken.'

'Nasty,' Thackeray said. 'Best have a word yourself when the doctors say she's fit enough. A description would be good. The number of street robberies is creeping up again after all the hard work we did last year to get it down. Doesn't make the crime figures look good. I'll raise it when I see the super to review the state of play.'

'And what's this about a Mendelson intruder? This is David Mendelson, I take it?' Mower asked.

Thackeray described the events of the previous night and the sergeant's face darkened.

'Nasty,' he echoed Thackeray. 'Do you want me to chase up uniform? Make sure they've actually sent someone up to look for prints?'

'You could do. It would be better coming from you than me. I got the distinct impression that Derek Wilson, who took the shout, resented my involvement.'

'He would. He's as unreconstructed as they come, is Derek,' Mower said. 'I've come across him before, blundering about on Aysgarth Lane with all the sensitivity of a rhinoceros. I wouldn't be surprised if he voted for the blasted BNP.'

'I wonder who teamed him up with the new Asian probationer last night, then,' Thackeray said. 'He hardly sounds like the best mentor we could come up with.'

'Ali Mirza? He'll be fine. He's a bright lad and knows where he's going. Actually, it's our Sharif I'm worried about at the moment. He seems seriously distracted and I don't know why. He's lost his focus, somehow. He's not married, so it can't be that sort of trouble.'

'Maybe it's the fact he's not married,' Thackeray said. 'Maybe his family's putting him under pressure.'

'Maybe,' Mower said. 'I've got the feeling

recently that there's someone serious in his life, but whether she's white or Asian I've no idea. But he's got real potential, has Omar. I'd like to see him succeed, go for sergeant in a while, maybe, and not just to prove what idiots bigots like Derek Wilson are. I'll see what I can suss out over a pint of orange juice with him. Unless you want to volunteer for that honour?' The oblique reference was as close as he dared get to the fact that Thackeray did not drink – ever.

'I'll pass,' Thackeray said dryly, glancing at the heap of files on his desk. 'Now, as it looks like there's a lull in serious crime, I'll get on with the crime figures, with my crime manager's hat on. Though that may be tempting fate. But I wasted a whole day yesterday at county with the super, listening to how wonderful our new enlarged force is going to be. The only thing they didn't tell us was how much money they're going to waste on yet another reorganisation. But have a word with uniform about the Mendelson inquiry, and with your mugging victim, when she's fit. While we've got the time, we might clear up a few minor issues, which are actually the ones that scare people half to death.'

His image of Vicky Mendelson, traumatised in her own home the previous night, was still vivid. He had promised David some help and even if he could not be seen to be leaning too heavily on his uniformed colleagues, he was determined to provide it.

'And see if someone has time to check on other attempted break-ins in Southfield. There might be a pattern there we've not noticed.'

'Guv,' Mower said cheerfully. With a following wind, he thought, he just might be able to catch Jess for a drink at lunchtime, a luxury in CID, and the thought filled him with a sudden pang of desire.

Laura Ackroyd rang the bell at the women's refuge, a five minutes' walk from the *Gazette* office, talked her way through that obstacle and then through the solid front door which was reinforced with plates of heavy metal. She grimaced slightly as the door swung open. She had thought that only drug dealers up on the Heights, the town's most dilapidated estate, now in the throes of demolition, went in for this level of fortification, in their case against raids by the police.

'It's like Fort Knox in here,' she said lightly to the woman in jeans and sweatshirt who opened the door for her, but there was no answering spark of amusement in her eyes.

'You have no idea what we put up with,' she said, pushing untidy hair away from her unmade-up face. 'I'm Carrie Whittaker, by the way. I work here.'

The house was early Victorian, a mill-owner's stately pile, no doubt, in those days of frantic industrial expansion when towns like Bradfield metamorphosed from weaving villages to booming mill towns in less than fifty years. The house would have been handily placed for the master's access to the burgeoning warehouses and factories on the seven hills rising above the Beck, its heyday as a family home long before the town's more affluent residents took flight to less sooty residences in Ilkley and Harrogate. Many of the solid stone mansions had been converted into flats or offices, others demolished in the Sixties and Seventies to make way for new development. But this one had evidently stood still, gently decaying, until the women's refuge had taken it over and packed in as many women and children as the space would allow, and then some.

Laura followed her guide up the broad staircase to the first floor, where at least the windows were free of wire mesh, and faint sunlight filtered across the broad landing.

'If you write anything about this place, please don't mention anyone by name,' the woman said. 'What Julie says is up to her, but no one else's confidentiality must be breached. You do understand that, don't you? It can be dangerous. Most of their partners don't know where they are.'

'Of course,' Laura said. 'I'll be careful.'

It had taken her a good portion of that

morning's editorial conference to persuade her editor, Ted Grant, to allow her to embark on a feature, or maybe a series, on domestic violence at all, and she knew that unless she could come up with some pretty sensational case histories her investigations might get no further than the now merely proverbial spike, where unused articles used to be physically impaled. These days a click of a computer key could consign reams of unwanted material to the bin in a second.

'See if you can find a battered husband, too,' Ted had growled before reluctantly approving the project. 'It's not all one way, you know.'

'I'll look for a battered granny if you like,' Laura had come back, with an unwary flash of anger. 'They say that's getting more common, too.' But it was Julie Holden's desperate eyes, and the way the child, Anna, had clung to her mother as they scuttled into this building, that had haunted her.

Julie answered the door of her room quickly, and offered Laura a wan smile.

'Come in,' she said. 'I don't know whether I should be doing this, but come in anyway.'

It was a small room, sub-divided from a larger one, and was over-filled by two single beds and a bleak minimum of other furniture. Julie waved Laura into the single wooden chair and sat on one of the beds beside Anna, who barely glanced up from

54

her book as Laura arrived.

'Should she not be at school?' Laura asked.

'I can't take her back to Southfield Primary. Bruce would ambush us up there too easily. And I've not got her in anywhere else yet.' The child glanced at her mother with eyes full of tears, but she said nothing, turning back to Harry Potter in silence. Laura took her tape-recorder out of her bag.

'Do you mind?' she asked. 'I want to get it right.'

'Fine,' Julie muttered, her voice low. 'Though I hardly know where to begin.'

'At the beginning,' Laura said gently. Somewhere in the building a baby began to cry. 'When did you get married?'

'Anna, why don't you go downstairs and see if you can help get lunch ready,' Julie said suddenly. The girl looked at her mother mutinously for a moment before putting her book face down on the rumpled bed and rolling herself to the floor.

'Don't be long,' the child said. 'You know, I really, really hate it here. I really, really want to go home now.'

Anna closed the door with a bang that reverberated around the high ceilings of the hallway outside and sparked renewed howling from the baby close by. Julie sighed but said nothing, clearly close to tears herself.

'Are you up to this?' Laura asked, suddenly feeling guilty at intruding on this private tragedy. 'I can come back another time if you like.'

'It's not going to get any better, is it? Let's do it,' Julie insisted and Laura, not for the first time, nor inevitably the last, felt surprised at how readily people under stress proved willing to discuss their most intimate problems with complete strangers. Reporter as therapist, she thought wryly, and knew that few of her friends would take that concept seriously.

Julie began slowly, almost hesitantly, as Laura switched on her tape recorder. She had met Bruce, she said, in Blackpool, where she had been brought up and was working as a teacher. He was an IT trouble-shooter for a local company. He had been good-looking and charming and, she admitted, swept her off her feet soon after she had broken up with a previous partner. They had married within six months of meeting and without Julie even having met Bruce's parents. And soon after that, she was pregnant and they settled in Lytham close to her family home, coming back to Bradfield, which was Bruce's home town, years later when and where he had found a better job. With his father dead and his mother alone, she had not argued against the move, knowing that she could probably find part-time teaching work there as easily as in Blackpool.

But almost as soon as Anna had arrived, eight years ago, things had already begun to change, she said.

'I know a lot of dads get jealous of the baby, because they're not the centre of attention any more. But she was a quiet baby, not much trouble, and I knew enough to try to include Bruce in everything we did, to make a real family. But every now and then he would get really angry, explode almost, with rage. Not often, but often enough to make me quite careful of how I behaved, and wonder how far I could trust him with Anna. I thought it would pass. I loved him very much, and I really thought it would pass as she got older and more independent. But I didn't suggest having another child. I could see that one was as much as he could cope with. Probably ever.'

'But it didn't pass,' Laura prompted, uncomfortably aware of how personally interested she was in this woman's experience.

'No,' Julie said softly. 'It didn't pass. And since we came to Bradfield his rages have been getting more frequent and more violent. And it's been getting harder and harder to cover up. I was terrified he would begin hitting Anna as well as me.'

'Has he?' Laura asked.

'No, I've always managed to protect her. Quite often she's been in bed asleep when things have got bad. I tried to leave him once before but he begged and begged me to go back. He seems quite normal, you see, most of the time. Loving and so ashamed of what he's done. And I let myself be persuaded. In fact, I generally end up comforting him. Stupid I know, but I did love him once. But recently, since we came to Bradfield really, he's been flaring up more often and I've got completely frantic with the worry. Even in between the rages he's been moody and distant, not his normal self. I thought this time if I didn't get out I'd be the one to crack up completely, so a few days ago I packed up and went out as if I was taking Anna to school as normal. But we came here and I've not been back.'

'He's no idea where you are?'

'Not at the moment but I don't think it will take him long to find this place. We'll have to move on. The husbands and partners do turn up here, that's why there's all the security. To keep fathers out.' Suddenly Julie was in tears and Laura switched her taperecorder off.

'I'm sorry,' she sobbed. 'I just never thought I would be in this situation. It all started so well. We were so in love. We had good jobs. We weren't short of money. Anna was a very much wanted baby. Where did it all go so wrong?'

'Who have you talked to about it, apart

from Vicky?'

'No one really. I went to the doctor and said I was stressed and he gave me some tranquillisers.'

Laura looked at her aghast for a second.

'I would have thought it was your husband who needed pills, not you,' she said.

'He won't go near the doctor,' Julie said. 'He's got quite a phobia about the medical profession. I think he had some sort of bad experience before I met him. He never talks about it. And he won't go near marriage counsellors. I've suggested it but he says he doesn't want anyone interfering in his private life, asking questions, demanding explanations. He seems quite frightened of that.'

'I think you ought to see your doctor again and be honest with him this time. I don't know much about mental illness but it sounds as if your husband could be suffering from some form of it. And talk to the police. If you don't do something pretty dramatic, you or Anna could get seriously hurt.' Or worse, she thought, and she knew that Julie could recognise the unspoken thought only too clearly.

'That's what Vicky said,' Julie said dully. 'But I don't want him locked up. That would destroy him. I just want it to stop.'

Mohammed Sharif, known at work happily

enough as Omar, but not here, felt the familiar sounds and smells of Aysgarth Lane enfold him, the Punjabi chatter, the spicy aromas, the car horns of impatient young drivers and every now and again the beat of a Bangla rhythm. It felt like home and for a fleeting moment he regretted having cut himself off so completely from it. He had parked in one of the narrow streets of terraced houses nearby and joined the early evening crowds making their way from one Asian emporium to another. He inched through the door of the Punjab Bazaar, a gloomy cluttered store where women in brightly coloured *shalwar kameez*, headscarfs worn loosely around their hair or shoulders, gossiped amongst the crammed shelves. He had promised Louise, who did not realise how unusual it was for an Asian man to be seen in a kitchen, that he would cook her a curry that night, and he spent some time selecting large plastic packets of coriander, cumin and red pepper for his store cupboard on the other side of town, where such things only appeared on the supermarket shelves in minute and highly priced jars. He slipped easily back into Punjabi at the checkout, where he was greeted by name. This was a tight-knit community, which did not lose track of its sons if it could help it.

He dropped his shopping into the boot of his car and then made his way up the hill, not this time to his parents' home but to the house of his aunt and uncle, Faria's parents, and knocked lightly on the front door, which opened directly onto the street. It was opened by his cousin Jamilla, a few years younger than Faria. She was a young woman now, he noticed with approval, elegant in her traditional dress but with her headscarf only loosely furled around her shoulders revealing glossy black hair cut short in a fashion which he did not think her parents would totally approve of. She looked instantly pleased to see him, but he could see an anxiety in her eyes that worried him.

'Are your parents at home?' he asked. She shook her head and ushered him in. The proprieties were not offended by the visit of a cousin, even an unmarried one. She led him into the living room, where they found her sister curled on the sofa. The younger girl, Saira, turned the television off with a guilty look.

'It's all right, it's only Mohammed,' Jamilla said. 'We were watching a Bollywood video. My father doesn't like it. He says it's far too modern.' She laughed. 'If he only knew what went on out of sight these days. There's no way we're going to marry backwoodsmen from some dusty village.'

'Good for you,' Sharif said, aware that perhaps they regarded him and his less than traditional choices as some sort of role model, and knowing that it would be much harder for these young women to break free than it had been for him as a male in a strictly paternalist community. 'Are you staying on at school, Jamilla?'

'I'm doing A levels. I'm going to university, whatever they say,' she said.

'Me too,' Saira said. 'I want to study law. Perhaps I'll join the police like you.'

'Perhaps you will,' Sharif said. 'Your parents should be pleased. But watch your film if you like. I enjoy the music and dancing, though I can't say the plots appeal much. I really came to see your father.'

Jamilla looked at her cousin for a moment thoughtfully.

'Did you want to ask him about Faria?' she said quietly at last. 'He won't talk about her, you know, even though she hasn't been to see us for ages.'

'My parents told me that,' Sharif said, wondering how much these two smart young women had kept in touch with their older sister. 'Have you spoken to her at all?' He knew a lot of the girls had mobile phones their parents did not necessarily know about.

'Not for weeks,' Jamilla said. "When I call, Imran Aziz answers so I hang up. The last time I spoke to Faria she seemed fine.' She glanced at her sister for a second and the younger girl nodded imperceptibly, as if giving her permission to go on.

'You mustn't tell anyone, Mohammed,' Jamilla said. 'But the last time we spoke she seemed really excited because she said she was pregnant, but it was very early and I wasn't to tell anyone except Saira because she wasn't sure yet. She sounded really happy about it. But since then I haven't managed to get through to her.'

'If she was really pregnant surely she would have let your parents know?' Sharif said.

'I know, I know, so maybe it was a false alarm. She doesn't seem to have told my mother yet. False alarms happen, you know,' she said seriously as if Sharif might be unaware of such female mysteries.

'I know,' he said gravely, suppressing a smile.

'And we think it's happened before,' Saira said.

'You mean the false alarm?' Sharif said. 'She's lost babies?'

Saira nodded, her face serious.

'I'm only guessing,' she said. 'But she always sounds very sad about not having children yet.'

'So how long ago did you speak to her?'

Jamilla glanced at her sister again as if for confirmation. 'About two months ago maybe. My mother's very upset because she doesn't come to see her any more.'

'And you haven't been over to Milford to

63

see her? It's not very far.'

'We thought when school finishes we might go on the bus to visit her, didn't we, Saira?'

'We don't like Imran Aziz much,' Saira said. 'But Faria is working all day in some travel agent's, so we could only really see her in the evening when he would be there too.' Sharif guessed that the girls' new-found determination not to marry anyone from a Pakistani village had been reinforced by the arrival of Imran Aziz in their lives, the proverbial cousin from the old country, though not in this case, he believed, a country bumpkin.

'Perhaps I'll go over and see her myself,' Sharif said. 'Do you have her address? Or do you know where she works, perhaps? It might be easier to catch up with her there.'

'Oh, would you?' Jamilla said fervently, and Sharif realised just how seriously anxious she was about her sister. She went over to a small bureau on the other side of the room and rummaged through a drawer. She came back with a small notebook of addresses and phone numbers from which Sharif copied Faria's details into his own notebook.

'I'm not sure where she works, but it's some sort of travel agency. Surely you could find it, Mohammad. You're a detective.'

'I'm sure I can,' Sharif said. 'No problem.'

'I know my parents are worried about her,' Jamilla said quietly. 'They won't admit it but I think they are afraid that she has run away from Imran Aziz. But she wouldn't do that if there's a baby coming, would she? I really wanted to tell my mother, but she made us swear not to.' Saira gave her sister an anxious look and Sharif knew the scandal a runaway wife would cause in the family and the wider community and hoped for Faria's sake her parents' fears were not true.

'Did she agree to this marriage?' he asked. 'I was never sure.'

'Nor was I,' Jamilla said quietly. 'My father wanted it, I know that. But Faria would never talk about it. Like you, I was never sure.' Her dark eyes filled with tears.

'I'll see what I can find out,' he said, his stomach tight with foreboding. And when he left and glanced down the narrow, almost deserted street, few cars here, where many of the men were out of work, he wondered if he risked precipitating a family crisis by pursuing his cousin. But as he hurried back to his own car, close to the still bustling thoroughfare of Aysgarth Lane, he concluded he would have to risk it. The three sisters had always been close and if Jamilla and Saira were so worried about Faria then the least he could do was try to set their minds at rest. He would take a chance and track her down in Milford. It was, he thought, the least he could do. In the meantime he would cook for Louise, a simple thing that would shock his father and uncle to their core, but which in the new life he had created for himself seemed quite normal. He was, he thought, further adrift from his roots than anyone in his family could imagine.

CHAPTER FOUR

Sergeant Kevin Mower walked the short distance from police HQ to Bradfield Infirmary and presented himself at the ward where the night's apparent mugging victim had been found a bed. The doctor treating her had reported that she was now fit enough to be questioned, but showed few signs of being able to explain who she was or how she came to be lying on a patch of waste ground, battered and bruised about the face and at serious risk of hypothermia.

She was, Mower thought as the nurse showed him to her bed, a good-looking elderly woman, in her seventies, he guessed, with almost white hair and intelligent blue eyes. But the gash on her cheek, which had been stitched, had caused the left side of her face to swell and discolour, and her hands, which clutched at the sheets nervously, were also bruised, although her nails were clean and carefully trimmed, not the hands of anyone who might have collapsed after an evening's binge drinking. He introduced himself and was sure that he saw a flash of consternation in her eyes.

'I'm sorry about your accident,' he said.

'Mrs...' The woman licked her lips and then set them in a straight line.

'I think I must have had a dizzy spell,' she said, her voice husky but perfectly clear, her accent only faintly local. 'The doctor tells me there's nothing serious to worry about. I don't think you need to waste your time with me, Sergeant. It's very kind of you, but there's no need.'

'The doctors were concerned about you,' Mower said. 'You seemed not to know your name, and they suspected a crime might have been committed. They were quite right to call us. Have you forgotten your name?'

The woman hesitated for a moment and then shook her head slightly, wincing with the pain.

'Of course not,' she said. 'I was just a bit confused when I woke up here.'

'So you are?' Mower prompted firmly enough for her to be clear he was not going to be fobbed off.

'My name is Holden, Vanessa Holden.' And she gave him an address in Southfield.

'Do you have a husband we can contact, Mrs Holden?'

'No, no, I've been a widow for years,' she said and hesitated, as if she had been about to say more and had changed her mind. Mower wondered for a moment if she had a boyfriend she was reluctant to admit to, but dismissed the idea with the arrogant contempt of youth.

'No one else we should contact for you? Other family...'

'No thank you,' Vanessa Holden said with finality.

'So can you remember what happened last night? We've had a series of muggings of elderly people in your area, that's why CID is so interested. If you can remember any-thing, give us a description of an assailant, that would be very, very helpful.' Mower knew that someone of her class and gener-ation would generally help the police will-ingly enough if they could, but Vanessa Holden shook her head again.

'I can't remember what happened,' she said firmly. 'The doctor says it might come back to me but it certainly hasn't done yet, so perhaps it never will.' Mower wondered whether he was imagining the note of certainty in her voice again, as if a decision not to recall anything about her injury and what led to it had already been taken and she was merely confirming it now.

'Do you live alone, Mrs Holden?' he asked, and again heard that slightly odd hesitation, and a flickering of her eyes, which told Mower without doubt this time she was lying.

'Yes,' she said. 'But I'll get someone – a friend with a car – to come round later and take me back. I don't walk very fast now, you know. Arthritis. The doctor says I can go after lunch. I'll be fine.'

'Well, I'm pleased to hear that,' Mower said. 'But if you do recall any more about what happened, I'd be grateful if you'd call me.' He handed her a card. 'It's often difficult to get a clear description of these young muggers. I'm sure yours would be more accurate than most.' But he could see he had lost her. She glanced away towards one of the nurses as if for help and Mower guessed that she had no interest in muggers because there probably had not been one. If someone really had assaulted Vanessa Holden she probably knew, but did not intend to tell him, who it was.

On his way out he met a white-coated young woman doctor he vaguely recognised and asked exactly when Mrs Holden would be discharged.

'There's no reason to keep her,' she said. 'And, as always, we need the bed.'

'Is there any indication what caused that gash on her face?'

'Not really. It could have happened if she felt faint and fell, although it's quite deep and there wasn't any sign of mud or gravel in it, apparently, which is a bit odd if she fell out of doors. But it's really not serious. We only kept her in overnight because of the risk of concussion. We've told her to see her own GP about any dizzy spells she might be having, if that's what it really was.'

'You sound doubtful,' Mower pressed.

'Well, I was a bit surprised she had forgotten so completely after such a relatively minor injury. But at her age, you never know.'

As Mower came out of the hospital entrance he pulled out his mobile and thumbed in a text to Jess. The swift and explicit answer made him grin exultantly as he strolled across the town hall square in the watery sunshine that had followed the previous night's heavy rain. Promises, promises, he thought happily, as he put Vanessa Holden's problems onto the mental back burner. He would get no information from that source, for whatever reason, he thought: there was no assailant, no witnesses and no real evidence of a crime having been committed, and CID really had more important things to think about.

DC Mohammed Sharif drove back from Milford to Bradfield that evening feeling extremely uneasy. He had driven the seven miles to the smaller town after work and found his way to the address which Jamilla had given him for her sister Faria. It proved to be in a narrow street of stone terraced houses not far from the town centre, each one set back behind a wall and a tiny patch of garden, some well-tended, but most, like

71

that at number 41, cluttered with wheelie-bins and assorted rubbish that had missed its target. In the fading light there were few people around, and few lights on in this or any other house. He knocked a couple of times, without really expecting an answer. And when he peered though the downstairs window, where the curtains were only half drawn, he could see very little of the gloomy interior at all.

There was absolutely nothing that his detective's nose could pin down as suspicious but still something about the evidently empty house disturbed him, and when a male voice spoke immediately behind him he gave a start that to an observer must have looked uncannily like guilt.

'Ah said, what d'you think you're up to?' The voice was broad Yorkshire and the tone distinctly unfriendly but when Sharif turned he found himself looking down at an elderly man in a flat cap and threadbare sweater, who had apparently stepped out of the house next door and was speaking to him from his own gate, leaning his full weight on it to keep it firmly shut.

Sharif smiled faintly and, he hoped, reassuringly. The man was small and wiry, coming barely up to the tall Asian's shoulder, but he radiated determination like a small bantam cock, alert for any intruder on his territory.

'I'm looking for my cousin who lives here,' he said. 'Don't worry, I'm not a burglar.' He hesitated to admit to being a policeman but guessed that, if it came to the crunch, it might take his warrant card to remove the suspicion from this next-door neighbour's sharp eyes.

'Oh aye? And what's your cousin's name then?'

'Faria,' Sharif told him. 'She's the wife of Imran Aziz. Have I got the right house?'

Sharif watched a range of emotions flicker across the old man's weatherbeaten, deeply wrinkled face as he looked him up and down before he nodded slightly, his expression marginally more friendly.

'I don't know her name, that one,' he said. 'I hardly ever see her. She sometimes hangs t'washing out in t'back yard but that's about it. But he's Imran, I do know that. I took some package for him one time, months back, summat from Pakistan. There were nobody in that day either so the van left it wi' me.'

'They moved here about two years ago, after they got married,' Sharif said.

'Aye, that'd be right. He's quite a bit older than she is, real May and September job, that.'

'Quite a bit older,' Sharif agreed non-commitally, although he knew that he was not the only one in the family to wonder at

73

the twenty-year age gap between bride and groom, something he had almost had his head bitten off for when he raised the issue with his uncle on the plane to Lahore for the wedding. 'I don't suppose you know where they are? If they're away, anything like that? I really need to speak to my cousin and there's been no answer to the phone for a few days.'

'I wouldn't know owt about their comings and goings,' Faria's neighbour said dismissively. 'We keep ourselves to ourselves.' I bet you do, Sharif thought, guessing why without any difficulty at all. This was not a predominantly Asian area, like Aysgarth Lane in Bradfield, and he knew that an Asian family buying into a white street would not be greeted enthusiastically by many of the local families. Local lore had it that brown faces reduced property values and that often became a self-fulfilling prophesy as the whites began to move out in a torment of anxiety and prejudice. He turned away from the front doorstep with a sigh.

'Course, they might have gone away after being harassed like that,' the neighbour conceded reluctantly.

'Harassed?' Sharif said.

'Brick through t'window a week or so back.'

'BNP thugs, you mean?' Sharif snapped. 'Did they report it?'

'Not BNP. No way. A couple of your kind – long white shirts and beards, like summat from bloody Afghanistan on t'telly.'

'Muslims?'

'Aye, Muslims.'

Sharif shook his head angrily, not sure what this bit of information might imply.

'I'll have to come back another time then,' he said. He hesitated for a second and then pulled his wallet out of his inside pocket.

'I'll just leave Faria a note, I think,' he said. 'Ask her to call her mother.' He was conscious of the old man's bright birdlike eyes watching him suspiciously as he scribbled something on a page from his diary. 'Maybe their phone's out of order,' he said inconsequentially, knowing that was untrue, but he wanted to give this curious observer as little to gossip about as he could. He slipped the page through the letter box and closed the dilapidated gate carefully behind him.

'Thanks for your help,' he said as the old man turned on his heel and closed his own front door with a sharp bang that said more than words could about his resentments, and Sharif wondered, for the hundredth time, whether the two communities that lived so uneasily side by side in these small Yorkshire towns, could ever learn to coexist without friction. It was without surprise that he noticed a tattered British National Party election sticker in the window of number

43. It was in sad and neglected streets like these, he thought, that the racists gained ground, not in the vibrant multi-cultural enclaves of the big cities where a rainbow nation seemed to thrive. And the difference, in the end, came down to money, or the lack of it. Faria and Imran had little enough, he thought, but judging by the state of the street, their white neighbours had even less, and probably much less chance of escaping their poverty. An Asian like him, western-ised, confident and turning up in smart clothes and an almost new car, would only feed the old boy's sense of injustice.

He had turned back towards Bradfield, driving unusually slowly to give himself time to think. There was no evidence that he could see that anything was wrong at the house in Milford, no reason to send in the uniforms to break down the door. But even so there was this knot of fear in his stomach. On the way into the centre of Bradfield, where he coexisted happily enough with white neighbours in his flat in a warehouse building, he turned again into the warren of streets around Aysgarth Lane where Punjabi immigrants had created over forty years as near a replica to a village society as the old men had been able to impose on the unyielding grid of Yorkshire millworkers' houses.

He pulled up close to the mosque, an

imposing structure that had been paid for by the long and painstaking accumulation of cash from pockets that could ill afford it. But he was not here to pray. He rarely observed the strictures of his religion these days and his father had despaired of turning him back into Islamic paths, failing to understand how thoroughly the young men who had recently become strict observers of their faith alarmed him. Instead, he turned to one of the identical stone houses in the shadow of the minaret and knocked again on a solid frontdoor. This time his knock was answered promptly by a stocky middle-aged man in a white *shalwar kameez* and skull cap, his grey-flecked beard reaching comfortably to his chest.

'Mohammed,' he said with a welcoming smile. 'We don't often see you here – or at prayers. Come in.'

Ignoring the implied criticism, which was only to be expected from the Bradfield mosque's imam, Sharif followed Achmed Siddique into the dark living room of the small terraced house, where he had to move piles of books and papers from chairs before both men could find anywhere to sit. When the ritual pleasantries had been completed, Siddique looked inquiringly at the detective.

'So, is this an official visit or are you looking for a little spiritual guidance at last?'

'I'll skip the guidance, but I'm not here on

official business,' Sharif said carefully. 'It's a family thing.'

'Good,' Siddique said. 'There's enough of the official business going on already. Most of it unannounced. I suppose we have to expect it in the circumstances but it gets a little wearisome being regarded as an emissary of that lunatic in the mountains at every prayer meeting when what I am preaching is the precise opposite of his ravings.' He glanced away as if to hide the anger in his eyes.

'It's that bad?' Sharif asked sympathetically.

'We're all being blamed for what those misguided young men did,' Siddique said. 'I had thought things were getting better but now people spit at us in the street and abuse the women. It is a bad time, Mohammed. Maybe you're insulated from it, but here in Aysgarth Lane, it's a very bad time.'

'I know,' Sharif said, knowing that far from being insulated he was in the front line, part of a police service horrified and disgusted by the effects of terrorism, which reached them on the grapevine in detail far more graphic than ever reached the public. He was lucky that his nickname had not been transformed into Osama by now, he thought bitterly. Maybe in his colleagues' private conversations it already had.

'So what is your family problem?' Sid-

78

dique asked quietly. 'Are you thinking of marriage at last? To someone your parents have difficulty accepting?'

Sharif laughed.

'Not yet,' he said. 'Although I'm sure the time will come. No, what I wanted to ask was whether you have any contact with the imam in Milford. My cousin Faria – you remember – married Imran Aziz and went to live there. For some reason she has lost touch with her parents and I've not been able to contact her for a while, either. It's been a couple of months since anyone has spoken to her and everyone is very worried. I remember when I went to the wedding I was told that Imran was a religious man, very traditional, and I wanted to find out if he was still observant and whether the imam there had contact with either of them.'

'They have a new young man at the mosque there,' Siddique said slowly, looking unhappy. 'I've only met him once and I was surprised at how poor his English was. His name is Abdel Abdullah. They recruited him in Pakistan and he preaches only in Urdu.'

'Special branch will be taking an interest, then,' Sharif said.

'I'm sure.'

'Do you think he's a serious menace?'

Siddique looked even more unhappy at that, but he shook his head slowly.

'You know it doesn't work like that. After

everything that's happened, the most dangerous people are working very quietly, in the youth clubs, the gyms, the bookshops, or simply in their own houses. They don't raise their heads over the parapet if they can help it. The mosques don't know who they are, if they ever did. I don't think there is anyone dangerous in Bradfield, but I can't really know for sure. Some of the young men shout a lot but I think that's all they do. But there's no doubt the anger grows all the time, even amongst the most peaceable people, and with some justification. Not just Palestine, but then Iraq and Lebanon on top of that. Your security friends will have a better idea than I do what's going on but there's no doubt that times are getting more difficult. As for Milford,' he shrugged. 'I think my new brother is just not very experienced, that is all. He should learn the ways of the mosques here soon, God willing. Tone down his passion against sin, adultery, homosexuality, all that. This is not a fanatical country.'

'Could you ask him if he knows Aziz?'

'I could,' Siddique said. 'If Aziz is as devout as you say, I'm sure he will know the name. I'll see what I can find out, Mohammed, but I can't make any promises. But there's probably some innocent explanation. Perhaps your cousin has been ill.'

'According to her sisters, she may be

expecting a baby. But that's no reason not to contact her parents. Quite the reverse.'

Siddique nodded. 'Perhaps her husband is of such a traditional mind that he dislikes her travelling alone.'

'Perhaps,' Sharif said, his expression hardening. 'I always thought that she had been persuaded into this marriage. Forced, maybe, though I hate to say that about my uncle and aunt. It seems unlike them.'

'Ah,' Siddique said. 'That would be...' He hesitated, choosing his words carefully. 'That would be unfortunate. Change takes a long time.'

'Too long,' Sharif said, not hiding his own anger. 'We bring much of the dislike and suspicion on our own heads by clinging to old customs that are not required by the Koran.'

'It's not all on one side,' Siddique came back quickly. 'What's that English saying? Six of one, half a dozen of the other? I think that's right, you know.'

'Maybe,' Sharif said. 'All I know is that if you make an effort you can succeed in this country. It's not impossible. How is it that the Indians do so much better than we do here? Are they better? Brighter? Or just more adaptable?'

'Well, you've done it, you've succeeded in a most unlikely profession,' Siddique said soothingly. 'But you don't bother to come back and show these angry young men at the mosque your success. You should think about that, maybe.' Sharif got to his feet and turned to go, not wanting the imam to see that his last comment had hit harder than he liked. 'Maybe,' he said again.

He walked slowly back down the narrow street to where he had left his car, but before he got there he was aware that he was being watched by a group of young men, bearded and in *shalwar kameez* rather than the jeans and sweatshirts worn by most of the teen-aged youths around the Lane. They clustered on the corner where the road swung round to rejoin the main road and its bustling shops. He avoided their eyes as he flicked open his electronic lock and made to open the driver's door of the convertible that was his pride and joy. The young men had been chattering in Punjabi as he approached but they fell silent as he got within ear-shot, until one suddenly spat in his direction, narrowly missing his shoe, and followed with a flood of invective aimed at the antecedents of policemen in general and himself in particular. Sharif could feel the anger surge like a tsunami from his stomach but, gritting his teeth, he slid into the driver's seat and started the engine. Another gout of saliva hit the windscreen and without thinking he switched on the screen-wash and was slightly surprised when it showered the nearest of the group with a mixture of dirty water and more.

The young men drew back, shouting furiously as Sharif slammed the car into gear and pulled away from the kerb as fast as he dared. Safely round the corner he slowed again and stopped, clutching the steering wheel with trembling hands, taking deep gasping breaths for a moment until his rage subsided. He was, he thought, stretched on a rack not of his own making in his chosen profession, eternally marked out as some sort of traitor even by those in his own community who seemed genuinely to want peace and harmony, and watched at work with cold-eyed suspicion by those few of his colleagues who wanted – and expected – him to fail.

Ten years ago as an enthusiastic recruit he had truly believed he could make it work. Now, after all that had happened since at home and abroad, he was beginning to suspect he was losing everything, his own culture, his prospects of promotion, his peace of mind and his chances of happiness. He no longer prayed, as the Prophet (peace be upon him) instructed, but he certainly cursed, regularly every day, with multi-cultural enthusiasm. But he cursed George Bush, bin Laden, Tony Blair and the Saudis, the Palestinians, the Israelis and the Pakistanis indiscriminately and with vigour for the destruction of his hopes and dreams.

He had always thought of Bradfield as his home, had balanced nimbly between two cultures and, he thought, made a success of his life, and had begun to hope recently that he might even be able to pull off a marriage that flew in the face of tradition, but it was getting harder. The tightrope felt as if it was fraying fast.

Michael Thackeray opened the door of the flat he shared with Laura Ackroyd and sniffed the air, surprised not to identify the cooking smells that greeted him more often than not. He tried his best to be the modern man Laura expected but cooking was not a skill he had ever acquired and she seemed happy enough to reign as queen of the kitchen when they ate at home, veering between experiments in fusion food and plainer fare, only a cut above the canteen fodder he had survived on for most of his adult life and that, if he was honest, he still preferred.

Laura was not in the living room and he found her in the bedroom, brushing her copper red curls and wearing very little, a sight that filled him with urgent desire. He slipped his hands around her breasts and kissed the back of her neck, and she responded with a long lingering kiss. But then she glanced at her watch and pushed him away.

'There isn't time,' she said regretfully. 'We're due at David and Vicky's at seven-thirty.' She smiled at him mischievously. 'I did remind you this morning. Had you forgotten?'

'I had,' he said, not bothering to hide his disappointment. 'Do we have to go?'

'Vicky says – though honestly I can't remember – that it's the anniversary of the night I met you at their dinner party. You can't have forgotten that, surely?'

On that unexpectedly significant previous occasion, David Mendelson had been intent on introducing Bradfield's new DCI to his father Victor, one of the town's longest serving solicitors from its most eminent law firm, to a member of the town council and to a journalist from the local paper who, to Thackeray's surprise, turned out to be young, beautiful and red-headed.

If Vicky had harboured an ulterior motive for introducing her oldest university friend to an apparently eligible single man she had had no intention of admitting it back then and had often wondered later, as Michael and Laura's stormy relationship progressed, whether such a thought should ever have entered her head at all. But there was no hint of those doubts in her eyes as she opened her door tonight to her guests, both of whom, she was relieved to see, appeared unusually contented with each other.

'Come in,' she said. 'It's just the four of us. Or at least it will be when I've got my demon boys upstairs to bed.' Right on cue, her two sons tore out of the sitting room and flung their arms around Laura whom, they obviously hoped, would save them from banishment for at least a few precious minutes more. Laura followed Vicky into the sitting room with a hand on each boy's shoulder, followed by Thackeray, his face impassive as he came to terms once again with a family life he bitterly envied and feared he would never now reproduce, having lost his chance so catastrophically the first time around. He took a proffered soft drink from David Mendelson with a nod of thanks and sank into a chair beside him, leaving the women and children chattering on the other side of the room. He greeted his host's immediate launch into a discussion of a recent case they had both been involved in with guilty relief.

When Vicky had finally filled Laura in on Daniel and Nathan's continuing achievements in primary school, and persuaded the boys in the direction of their bedrooms, Laura turned to the two men again and picked up the thread of their conversation.

'The last I heard the stupid woman had gone back to the bastard,' David said. 'She'll end up one of your murder victims, you'll see.'

'I'm sure you're right,' Thackeray said. 'But if the combined persuasion of the police and the Crown Prosecution Service can't get a woman to give evidence, I don't see what else we can do. According to our domestic violence people, there was no corroboration from anyone else with the Robinson woman. No neighbours, no frequent visits to A and E, nothing you could have proceeded on without her testimony. She just turned up the one time at the infirmary, beaten half to death, said her husband attacked her and then changed her mind and withdrew the complaint.'

'What's all this?' Laura asked. 'Battered wives? I'm supposed to be writing something about that. I suggested it to Ted Grant after Vicky's friend Julie turned up here. She won't make a complaint about her husband either. Says it would be bad for the child.'

'Well, anything you can do in the *Gazette* to make people take it seriously would be good,' David said. 'It really isn't easy to launch a prosecution never mind get a conviction. And there's always that fear at the back of your mind that it's going to end up with someone dead.'

'I haven't trawled through our archives yet,' Laura said. 'Can you remember any cases from the last few years that I should look at, cases where the husband has ended up in court?'

'Not offhand,' David said. 'I think there was something in Leeds about ten years ago where the wife ended up killing her abusive husband. There was a great furore about whether she could plead provocation even if he hadn't been attacking her at the precise moment she took a knife to him. I think he was asleep when she actually stabbed him.'

Laura shuddered, avoiding Thackeray's eye. She found it difficult to comprehend the curdled emotions that polluted and destroyed relationships which must have started off in harmony, although she knew he understood some of it only too well.

'I'll look it up,' she said. 'I do remember it vaguely.' She glanced up as Vicky came back into the room, glad of the opportunity to change the subject.

'So how is Naomi Laura?' she asked brightly after the child the Mendelson's had named after her. 'I'm sorry we missed her bedtime.'

CHAPTER FIVE

'Are we completely crazy?' Vicky Mendelson asked Laura Ackroyd the next day as they pulled up outside a neat and tidy semi on the cheaper side of Southfield, close to the primary school that Anna Holden no longer attended.

'Probably,' Laura admitted as she turned the engine off and peered at the anonymous modern house. 'But as Julie says, he can be charm and consideration itself if he chooses. I think in most cases like this the violence is only directed at one person.' She fervently hoped she was right, knowing that she faced Thackeray's justified wrath if this un-announced visit went pear-shaped.

'I hope you're right,' Vicky said. 'Anyway, perhaps he's out.' But Bruce Holden was in, unshaven and in his dressing gown but awake enough to recognise Vicky and offer her a shamefaced smile as he held the door open. He was, Laura thought, a normal enough looking man, attractive even in a slightly overweight way, with clear blue eyes and tousled fair hair, nothing like the monster she had been half expecting to confront.

'Come in,' he said. 'Did Julie send you?'

'She asked me to pick up one or two things for Anna,' Vicky said. 'This is Laura, another friend.'

Holden's eyes flickered in Laura's direction without interest. He waved the two women into the sitting room, where a thin veil of dust over every flat surface indicated as clearly as anything the abandoned state of his home.

'I want her to come home,' he said thickly, not sitting down himself but beginning to pace around the room with a sort of restless irritation. 'She knows I love her and Anna to bits. Will you tell her please to come home? I need them here.'

'I'll tell her,' Vicky said. 'But that's something you'll have to resolve between you. In the meantime, she wants this stuff for Anna.'

She handed Holden a list handwritten on a sheet torn from an exercise book, which he glanced at cursorily. For a moment Laura thought he was going to screw it up, but he seemed to overcome whatever surge of emotion the list had prompted and nodded dully.

'Most of it's in her room,' he said. 'Do you want to go and look? I don't think I can.'

Vicky nodded and made for the door.

'I'll wait here,' Laura said quickly, thinking that would give her a chance to talk to Holden privately. She guessed that he did not trust Vicky but might regard her as a more or less unknown quantity in his marital war. And that he might be looking for allies.

Holden kept on pacing for a moment as they listened to Vicky going up the stairs and opening the door of Anna's room. Then he flung himself down into a chair opposite Laura and closed his eyes, apparently oblivious to what was happening around him. He was a tall man, carrying his superfluous weight easily, but now she could see that the skin around his eyes was slightly puffy and putty coloured, and he constantly licked dry lips.

'Has she persuaded you to put her up then?' he muttered resentfully. 'Given poor little wifey sanctuary, have you?'

'Not in my tiny place, even if my partner would put up with it,' Laura said.

'So where the hell is she? I know Vicky knows, though she won't bloody tell me, will she? I never liked that woman, chattering away about my affairs at the school gate. She put Julie up to this nonsense. She's got a vivid imagination, has Julie. Makes things up a lot.'

Laura opened her mouth to protest that bruises could not be imaginary when she had seen them with her own eyes, and then thought better of it. It would do no good to provoke Holden, she thought, and in spite of his relatively normal demeanour he might actually be dangerous. But it seemed to be too late. Her scepticism must have shown in her eyes.

'Do you know where they are?' he shouted suddenly, his colour rising.

'She and Anna are safe enough,' Laura said. 'I don't think they feel safe here at the moment.'

'I haven't even been here much,' Holden said, his face as sulky now as a spoilt child's. 'I've had to go to my mother's to get a square meal. Anyway, it's Anna I want to see. That bitch has no right to keep my daughter away from me. I'd never hurt Anna. I love her to bits. I have rights too, you know. I'm her father.'

'You would need to talk to a solicitor about that,' Laura said.

'Has she gone to the bloody police?' Holden asked furiously. 'Why do I need a solicitor, for God's sake? They're all bloody sharks.'

Laura floundered for a moment, unable to grasp how thoroughly Holden seemed to have blanked out the implications of his recent behaviour.

'When a marriage breaks down you usually need a lawyer,' she offered feebly. 'Perhaps an advice centre... Or your doctor, maybe, could help with your problems.'

But if the suggestion of a lawyer had enraged Holden the word 'doctor' seemed to turn him incandescent. He jumped up from his chair and for a moment Laura froze, thinking he was going to attack her, but instead he lurched across the room and took hold of a photograph of Julie that had been standing on a low table and hurled it into the fireplace, where the glass and frame disintegrated with a crash.

'That cow,' he spat. 'What's she been saying about me? Why would I need a doctor? I hate doctors. I never want to see another bloody doctor in my life, investigating, prying, spying, trying to get inside your head.' As he ranted, Laura got up and sidled towards the living room door, relieved to see Vicky coming back downstairs carrying a carrier bag full of the books and other items Anna had asked for. Vicky glanced into the sitting room and seemed shocked by the change in Holden's mood.

'Time to go, I think,' Laura said quietly, heading towards the front door, but as she opened it Holden followed them into the hall.

'Tell that bitch I want to see my daughter,' he yelled. "Tell her I've got rights. She can't just take Anna off like that without a word. Tell her if she doesn't arrange for me to see her I'll organise it myself. I'm not stupid. I'll find them. Believe me.'

Laura pulled the door shut with a feeling of relief and followed Vicky back to the car.

'Well, that wasn't a triumph of diplomacy,

was it?' Vicky said with a tight smile. 'What did you say to him?'

Laura shook her head. 'Not a lot,' she said as she pulled away from the kerb, the quiet suburban street almost deserted in the pale sunshine, and she wondered how many other well-kept façades hid horrors like Bruce Holden. 'I suggested getting help – a lawyer, counsellor, doctor, and he went mad. I really thought he was going to hit me. I think Julie's right and Bruce Holden is seriously dangerous.'

'We could have got him done for assault if he'd touched you,' Vicky said. 'That might have been quite a good thing. We could have given evidence then.'

'Well, thanks,' Laura said dryly. 'I'll do a lot of things for battered wives but I don't think getting battered myself is one of them.'

'He's going to keep looking for her, isn't he?' Vicky said.

'Yes, I'm sure he is. He asked me if she was staying at my place.'

'I think she needs to get out of Bradfield for a bit,' Vicky said. 'It won't take him long to find the refuge and he's mad enough to try to break in to find them.'

'I think he's mad, full stop,' Laura said. 'He made some seriously odd comments about doctors.'

'Well, it'd be a lot easier to get him for assault than get him treatment for mental illness,' Vicky said seriously. 'David always says madmen have to kill someone before anyone takes their problems seriously.'

'I can believe it,' Laura said.

'Why don't you discuss it with Michael. He might have some ideas without making it official.'

'Mmm,' Laura prevaricated. 'Did you say his mother lived in Bradfield? He said he'd been blagging meals off her.'

'Julie has talked about her mother-in-law. I think she gets on quite well with her.' She glanced at her watch. 'But I can't come detecting again with you again just now. I left Naomi with David. He's working at home this morning but he has to be in court later so I must get back. Would you like to drop in for a coffee?'

Laura shook her head.

'No, I must get back to the office before Ted Grant fills my desk with some bright young recruit willing to work for half the salary – or on work experience for nothing at all. It's not safe to venture out for long the way things are these days. Redundancy's hanging over the place like a big dark cloud.'

'What's caused this crisis, then? Is the *Gazette* in trouble?'

'It's not just the *Gazette*. Fewer and fewer people seem to want to read local papers any more,' Laura said. 'They're all glued to the Internet and reality telly. It's the curse of

Big Brother. Our readers are all in their fifties and sixties and rising. You can tell from the ads: lots of walk-in baths and stair-lifts, while the world of all-singing and dancing mobile phones passes us by.'

Vicky glanced at her friend curiously. She knew that she had put some of her ambitions on hold to stay in Bradfield with Michael Thackeray and she wondered how much that still frustrated her. As Laura pulled up to drop her off she kissed her quickly on the cheek.

'Maybe you should take a break,' she said, but then wished she hadn't as Laura looked stricken.

'Maternity leave, you mean?' she said. 'In your dreams.' She did not tell Vicky of the few days she had spent recently wondering whether her carelessness had led in that direction anyway, sleepless and unwilling to confess to Thackeray why she was tossing and turning all night. It had been a false alarm but had confirmed what she had known in her heart for years: if she and Michael were to have children she would have to persuade him first, and she was not at all sure that she would be successful.

'I meant a holiday,' Vicky said lightly.

'Yes, of course, that might be a good idea if I can prise my overworked copper away from his job for a while,' Laura said. 'I'll see you soon.'

'You were right to tell Kevin, and Kevin was right to insist that you pass it on,' DCI Thackeray said, taking in both the officers who had come to see him together that morning. 'It may be nothing, but it may be something. No one should take chances in the present climate.'

'And no one's free of suspicion,' DC 'Omar' Sharif muttered resentfully.

He had gone to Sergeant Kevin Mower that morning to ask for his advice but had been hustled into the DCI's office against his better judgement when Mower heard what he had to say. Sharif had been up early and had driven quickly against the commuter traffic back to Milford to knock again on his cousin's front door. When once again there had been no response, he had headed into the centre of Milford and parked out side the mosque, which was housed in a converted Victorian chapel. As he arrived he could see a few men leaving after attending morning prayers but by the time he had taken off his shoes and gone inside he found only a handful still present, surrounding a heavily bearded man who was talking to them in Punjabi. Abdel Abdullah, the new imam who preached only in Urdu, glanced at Sharif, clearly taking in his jeans and bomber jacket without approval, and greeting him in the traditional way.

'Can I speak with you privately?' Sharif asked, in English first, to lay down his own ground rules, and then repeating himself in Punjabi. The imam nodded and the other men moved away.

'I'm trying to make contact with Imran Aziz, who's married to my cousin Faria,' Sharif had said bluntly. 'She's not been in contact with her family for a couple of months and they asked me to visit her. But there's no one at their address, and I wondered if her husband had been to the mosque recently. I am told he is very devout.'

'I do know our brother Imran,' Abdullah said in Punjabi. 'I have not been here very long but I think it is true he is very devout. But I have not seen him at prayers this week. Not at all, which is a strange thing.'

'Did he say they had plans to take a trip? A holiday in Pakistan perhaps? Maybe Faria has travelled out in advance. He answered the phone a couple of nights ago but simply said she wasn't there.'

'As I say, I am new here,' Abdullah repeated. 'So I know nobody very well. I have heard nothing about his plans. But if you like, I can ask some people who might know him. Do you have a telephone number?'

Sharif reached automatically for one of his cards, but then hesitated, and pulled a pen and notebook out instead, transcribing his mobile number carefully and handing it over. He could not explain the sudden hesitation to let this man, who was watching him with unsmiling intensity, know he was a policeman. He just guessed that he would get more cooperation if he kept his profession private.

'I'm sure there is an innocent explanation for my cousin's silence,' he said. 'If they have gone to visit his family I know it can be difficult to make international calls sometimes from parts of Pakistan. But it is strange she didn't let her parents know and they are concerned.'

'She is part of her husband's family now,' the imam said flatly. 'He will decide these things.'

Sharif opened his mouth and then thought better of contradicting this version of a wife's status, but he was surprised at how much he was repelled by it. It brought to mind images of burkas and the Taliban and reminded him of the outrage of one of his girlfriends years ago, a North African woman who had lived many years in France, when film of women in Afghanistan had been appearing on television screens every evening.

'I hope to hear from you, then,' he said, swallowing down the urge to argue with this man, every inch of whom radiated self-righteousness. 'Thank you,' he said, and spun on his heel and left the mosque quickly, knowing he was being watched all the way by some of the young men who had moved away when he came in.

He glanced at his watch as he walked back to his car, and wondered if there was time to try to discover where Faria worked. But he was due in the CID office at nine, and guessed that the various travel agents who had offices in the town centre would not be open so early. He would have to come back another time.

All the way back to Bradfield he wondered whether he had over-reacted. But it was crazy, he thought, for small mosques like Milford's to still be recruiting imams from Pakistan. Surely the Muslim community in Britain was big enough to be able to train its own teachers and scholars and ensure they had a reasonable grasp of English. By the time he got to police HQ in Bradfield he had worked himself into such a suppressed fury that Kevin Mower soon spotted his abstraction and crossed the room to ask him what was wrong. And when Sharif told him, he offered neither comment or advice, but insisted that he repeat his story to the DCI.

'It may be nothing, Omar,' he had said, leading the way to Thackeray's office. 'But report it to the boss and then if this imam turns out to be dodgy they can't accuse you of failing to act.'

'Cover my back, you mean?' Sharif muttered, not hiding his bitterness.

'You'd be a fool not to,' Mower said, looking grim.

But then, face to face with the DCI, Sharif felt foolish. Part of his strategy for success in the police service had always been to play down his difference from any other officer and this sudden catapulting of his private concerns into the official arena bothered him more than his colleagues could have been aware.

'There was nothing there to pin down, sir,' he said. 'It's odd that Imran and Faria are not around, but not unheard of for people to go on long visits in our community. She may have gone ahead and now he's gone to join her.' The other alternative that haunted him, that Faria might have run away from an intolerable marriage, he did not want to raise in this company. The shame and embarrassment that would cause his family was too personal to be broached to non-Muslims of even the most sympathetic kind. And sympathy only went so far in the police service before suspicion inevitably kicked in.

'As for the imam, Abdel Abdullah,' he said, 'it was just a feeling. A few bearded young men hanging about and an obviously pretty traditional imam. But a fanatic? No, I've got absolutely no evidence for that at all. It would be a travesty to say I had.'

'I'll pass your impressions on to special

branch,' Thackeray said. 'They may want to talk to you. It may well be an overreaction but you know how it is. We all need to be ultra careful.' He shrugged slightly wearily. Like everyone in Yorkshire, he was appalled that young suicide bombers could have emerged from the tightly packed streets of a local Asian community without any serious suspicion beforehand.

'And as far as your cousin is concerned, if you can't track down her or her husband soon, I suggest you or her parents try to make contact with her husband's family in Pakistan before you panic. As you say, there could be an entirely innocent explanation.'

'Sir,' Sharif said. 'It would be embarrassing for us all to report a missing person when there is nobody missing.'

But if Faria was in Pakistan, he thought, why had her husband not told him that when he had spoken to him a few nights previously? Even so, he had to admit that Thackeray was right in principle. The family had not done enough investigation itself to locate Faria. His mind flew back to the hot and humid days he had spent in the family's ancestral village in the Punjab at her wedding and he wondered whether the marriage he had witnessed had been arranged, in the traditional way, or actually forced on the young woman who had certainly not looked particularly happy as the ceremonies proceeded. Nothing had been said by his own parents, but he recalled his own slight sense of surprise that Faria had agreed to marry her distant, and much older, cousin. But he had never raised the issue. Notorious for his more relaxed lifestyle, he hesitated to be seen to be questioning such a sensitive area within the family. He had no reason to suppose that his uncle did not have Faria's best interests at heart, nor the slightest real evidence that she had objected to the match. If she had done, surely her ambitious young sisters would have known and had some views on the matter. But they seemed content with what had happened.

He sighed heavily as Thackeray turned back to the paperwork in his desk. But as he followed Mower back to the main CID office, the sergeant stopped and turned to face him.

'I've got a mate in special branch,' he said. 'I'll see if I can get any hint of what's going on in Milford if you like. They're keeping a close eye on comings and goings to Pakistan, obviously. They may even have your cousin's husband under surveillance.'

Sharif froze, the anxiety gnawing again at his stomach, like a hunted animal alert to the slightest hint of danger.

'You mean he might have used the marriage to get into the country for all the wrong reasons?' he said, his horror apparent in his eyes. 'But that would have meant my family being involved. That's inconceivable. My father and my uncle were incandescent after the London bombings, especially when it turned out that the bombers were local boys, from Yorkshire. You have no idea how betrayed most people in the community felt. Suddenly all the yobs in town felt they had good reason to abuse us, spit at women, provoke young men...' His voice trailed away, close to despair.

'That's as may be,' Mower said grimly. 'But these people don't go around wearing little labels saying "I'm a Terrorist". Or at least, the successful ones – in their terms – don't. If the imam in Milford's a bit dodgy, as you obviously think he might be, your cousin's husband may be a suspect too. And you'll get nothing back through official channels, for obvious reasons.'

'Because I'm Asian, too,' Sharif said bitterly.

Mower looked at him with some sympathy in his eyes.

'You know the way it is now,' he said.

'Oh yes,' Sharif said. 'I know the way it is.'

CHAPTER SIX

Laura Ackroyd waited for Michael Thackeray to come home that evening with increasing impatience. She had left the office early and driven back up to Southfield after Vicky had telephoned her to give her Bruce Holden's mother's address, but when she had knocked on the door of Mrs Holden's neat Victorian house she had got no reply. Standing back from the front door she realised that the curtains were closed on all the downstairs windows but upstairs she thought she saw the faint shadow of a movement at the window. Never one to give up easily, she rang the bell again, more insistently this time, and eventually she had heard a shuffling movement behind the door and a voice asked who was there, without any attempt being made to undo the locks.

'My name's Laura,' she said. 'I'm a friend of Julie's.' She knew she was stretching the truth but only, she thought, in the interests of Julie and Anna themselves. And when Vanessa Holden eventually opened the door, with much unbolting and unbarricading, she felt vindicated as she took on board the elderly woman's bruised face with a long line of stitches down the cheek.

'Mrs Holden?' she asked gently. 'Can I come in? I don't want to intrude but I did see Julie and Anna yesterday for an article I'm writing about violent relationships and I thought you might be able to help me too. And help Julie, as well, maybe. You do know her husband – your son – has been hitting her?'

Vanessa Holden shuffled backwards into the shadows of the hallway, offering no objection to Laura following her, and allowing her to close the front door behind her.

'Pull the bolts,' she said, her voice faint, and Laura did as she was told although she did not think that the cheap bolts on the door, top and bottom, would resist a determined intruder for very long. When Vanessa opened the sitting room door, allowing a little more light into the hall, Laura could see that she was in her dressing-gown, as if she had just got out of bed when she had disturbed her.

'I'm sorry,' she said quickly. 'If you're not well...'

'Come in,' Vanessa said, her voice slightly firmer. 'I was just resting. As you can see, I've had a little accident. They only sent me home from hospital this afternoon. It's nothing serious but I still feel a bit shaky.'

'I'm sorry,' Laura said again, accepting the chair the woman waved her into. Vanessa put on the lights, though she did not pull the curtains open, before lowering herself down on to the edge of an armchair, with a wince of pain.

'Did you have a fall?' Laura asked.

'Not exactly,' Vanessa said. 'My memory's a bit hazy, but I think I was pushed. I went out for a walk, to get away for a bit, and I know there was someone else there when I fell over. I'm not sure who it was. I can't walk very quickly these days. My knees are bad. But I do like to get out for some fresh air when I can. I don't like to use the car all the time.' She glanced away and Laura could see that her eyes were full of tears.

'Do you live here alone?' Laura asked.

'I did,' Vanessa said. 'I'm a widow. My husband died some years ago and I thought I'd got some sort of life back together. You never really get over it after a long marriage, but I was coping.' She hesitated.

'And then?' Laura prompted.

'My son, Bruce. Have you met him as well?' When Laura nodded Vanessa Holden shrugged and gazed silently at a fading bowl of flowers on a side table. 'When they came back to Bradfield I was really pleased, but it wasn't long before I realised that his marriage wasn't going well. Last week, when Julie finally left him, he arrived on the door-

107

step and announced he wanted to move in with me – just until she came back, he said, though I guessed that she wouldn't come back. I already knew he'd been hitting her, you see.'

'So your son's been living here?' Laura said, surprised. She had had no reason to assume that when she saw him earlier in the day he was not living in his own home.

'Just for a few days. But I don't want him here. He was out when I came home this morning. Maybe he went back home, I don't know. That's why I locked all the doors. I can't have him here any more.' A shudder suddenly went through her body. 'He's been hitting me, too,' she said in a whisper that Laura could barely catch. 'When he loses his temper he's like a madman. In fact, a doctor might say he is mad, I think. I can't have him near me any more. If that's what's been going on with Julie I can understand why she left with the child. I knew something was dreadfully wrong, but she never told me exactly what.'

'And he's been hitting you too?'

Vanessa glanced away and then nodded almost imperceptibly, putting a hand to her damaged face.

'He threw a plate at me, because he didn't like his meal,' she whispered, almost as if ashamed. 'That's why I went out on my own last night. It was quite late but I thought I had to get away. I think I must have fallen. I really can't recall. It's all a bit hazy.'

'But you weren't mugged?' Laura asked. 'It was your son who hurt you?'

Vanessa nodded silently.

'How long has this been going on?' Laura asked angrily. 'With you, I mean. Julie's already told me about her experiences.'

'Oh, only just these last few days. He's never had the opportunity before, I suppose. It's so strange. He seemed a normal enough little boy. That's him there, in a school photograph.' She waved to a picture of a sunny looking child in school uniform. 'He must have been about twelve then. Quite a happy child, really, but he became a very depressed teenager. Though not unusually so, I didn't think. All my friends used to say that their teenagers were the same: sulky, long silences, outbursts of fury. He went to college, got a job, and then another job in Blackpool.' She hesitated before deciding to go on.

'We didn't see much of him while he was over there. I think there were girlfriends before Julie. And he did say one time that he had been in hospital, though he was a bit vague about why and for how long. But by then my husband was ill and I was preoccupied. I suppose I didn't have time to worry about him as much as I used to. When he got married his father was too ill to go to the wedding. But I was pleased for Bruce. I thought a wife and family were what he needed. And when they came back to Bradfield I was delighted. I was on my own by then and was anxious to see more of them, Anna especially. We only ever had the one child so there were no other grandchildren. Not like some of my friends, who seem to be surrounded by them.' As Vanessa went on she seemed to become more and more forlorn, twisting her hands in her lap and occasionally fingering the stitches in their zigzag pattern on her cheek.

'I know it's difficult,' Laura said. 'But you really ought to report him to the police if he's abusing you. I said the same thing to Julie. He needs to be stopped before he causes someone some serious harm.' The knowledge that battered wives very easily become murdered wives hovered at the back of her mind like a dark cloud and she wondered if it applied to battered mothers too. But she did not want to panic this frail woman who seemed to be having difficulty in coming to terms with what had already happened to her to blight what should have been an enjoyable old age.

'The police have special units to deal with cases like this,' Laura insisted. 'It doesn't have to go as far as a prosecution if he's willing to accept some help to control his temper.'

'I can't do that,' Vanessa said. 'Julie must do what she has to do. She has a child to care for, but I can't complain to the police about my own son. I'll just tell him he can't stay here any longer. He must live in his own house.'

'Do you think he'll listen?' Laura asked sceptically.

'I don't know,' Vanessa said, and with that Laura had to be content. But by the time she got home half an hour later she found that she was seething with suppressed anger herself, and when Thackeray finally arrived home she poured out everything she had uncovered about Julie Holden's situation. Thackeray listened tolerantly enough but when she had finished he shook his head in exasperation.

'I know it's infuriating,' he said. 'But unless these women make a complaint it's almost impossible for us to do anything. We were aware of Vanessa Holden's alleged accident. The hospital alerted us. But according to Kevin Mower she couldn't – or wouldn't – remember what happened, so we didn't even know if a crime had been committed. She could simply have had a fall. It's not unusual at her age.'

'So that's it, is it?' Laura said. 'She's sitting in her own home, terrified of her own son, and no one can do anything to protect her?'

'She tells you that now, but it's not what

she said yesterday and it may not be what she'll say tomorrow. She has to make a complaint. Of course, if you can persuade her to do that, we'll take it seriously.'

Thackeray put an arm round her and pushed her unruly hair away from her face as if about to try to kiss her, but she pushed him away, her face flushed.

'Don't you dare say "I love you when you're angry",' she said. He smiled faintly and pulled away.

'I wasn't exactly going to say that. But I do think that you're in a better position to do something about all this than the police are. Just for once, and don't ever quote me on that. Write your story, why don't you? Do your campaigning. It can't do any harm and it might actually do some good, if not for the Holden family then for some other battered woman who reads it and makes the decision to take a bully to court.'

'Hah,' Laura came back, not mollified, but slightly encouraged to find that for once Thackeray allowed that her work might be useful. 'I'll talk to Ted again in the morning,' she said. 'I'll see if I can widen my brief to include battered mothers.'

'And talk to your Asian contacts as well,' Thackeray said thoughtfully. 'There are more ways than one in which wives can be bullied. I suspect some young women are still being bullied into marriage, one way or another. And I'm not sure how that works out in the long run.'

'What do you mean?' Laura asked quietly.

'I can't tell you anything specific,' Thackeray said. 'Not without breaking a confidence. Let's just say that young women are still going back to the subcontinent to marry and I reckon that some of them don't go very willingly. How are they treated when they find the marriage is not going well? What do they do? Where do they turn for help?'

'That sounds like a hornets' nest,' Laura said. 'And one Ted Grant may not be very keen to poke a stick at.'

'And when did that ever stop you?' Thackeray asked. And Laura grinned wickedly before she kissed him.

For the second time that week Mohammed Sharif drove slowly towards the network of terraced streets off Aysgarth Lane on his way home from work. If he had been reluctant to knock on his uncle's door the last time, he was ten times more reluctant now. He knew that his news would not be welcome and his inevitable questions resented bitterly where they touched on family honour. Even if he had attended the mosque five times a day for prayers, for as long as he had lived, he would not be greeted with any warmth now, and as someone who had obviously abandoned most of the traditions his uncle and his father held dear, he would be doubly resented.

His tentative knock on the street door was opened quickly by his uncle himself, who greeted him with obvious coolness. He led him, unsmiling, into the cramped living room, where his wife and his two younger daughters were sitting, almost as if they had expected him.

'Jamilla has told me that she spoke of Faria,' Faisel Sharif said curtly, obviously angry that Mohammed had visited his young cousins when he had not been there himself.

'My parents told me that you were worried because she hadn't been in touch,' Sharif said. 'There's nothing the police can do unless someone reports her missing – you or her husband preferably, so this is not official yet. It can't be. But obviously I'm anxious too. I've tried to contact her but apart from a brief phone call to her husband, who just said she was out, I've not been able to speak properly to either of them. It does seem very odd. I wondered if you'd heard from her yet? Have you spoken to Imran Aziz?'

The question hung in the air as his uncle lapsed into a brooding silence before glancing at his two younger daughters and then waving an angry hand towards the door.

'Go upstairs while I talk to your cousin,' he said. Jamilla looked for a moment as if she might protest but then thought better of it and the two girls left, closing the door behind them. Sharif's aunt said nothing, her hands twisting her long scarf compulsively between her fingers, her dark eyes opaque. Sharif waited. Whatever his uncle wished to tell him, he could see that it was causing him great distress and there would be no hurrying him. Eventually he glanced at his wife, whose eyes filled with tears, and they both sighed.

'It is a long story and God willing it will have a happy outcome,' Faisel said at last.

Sharif waited again, his stomach churning, but well aware that the older man would not be pushed and that his wife would not pre-empt anything he wanted to say. But the longer he waited the more he was certain that he would not like what he was about to be told.

'It goes back more than twenty years, to the year Faria was born,' Faisel Sharif said at last. "The family was already well settled in England. I came alone originally, to join your father, and we had good work at Earnshaw's mill. My wife came later, and soon after that our first child arrived.'

'I remember all that,' Sharif, who had been about ten at the time, said quietly. 'I remember when Faria was born.'

Faisel nodded impatiently, clearly not wanting to be interrupted.

'But I began to get letters from my father about a dispute in the village between him and his cousin, Imran's father. There was trouble over some land that no one disputed belonged to the family but which my uncle wanted to sell and my father did not. My father prevailed but there was bad blood remaining with this cousin, a lot of bitterness, and he suggested that we promise my daughter to his cousin's young son Imran in marriage, if he had not already married by the time she was old enough. There was such a gap in their ages that I thought it would never happen. God willing, it was just a sop to a disgruntled old man.'

'So you agreed?' Sharif said quietly, trying to hide his shock. 'I was far away. It seemed like a gesture, a way to ease the relationship that had been soured.'

'But the debt was called in?'

'Imran wanted to come to England and had not been able to get a visa. The marriage offered a way. He already had a wife but he divorced her. There were no children.'

'And Faria agreed to this...?' Sharif hesitated, trying to conceal the anger which threatened to overwhelm him as he thought of the pressure which must have been brought to bear on his beautiful, intelligent young cousin. 'She agreed to this arrangement?' he asked at last, keeping his voice level.

'In the end,' his uncle said. 'She could see that this was a debt of honour that her grandfather could not deny.'

'Do her sisters know?' Sharif asked, thinking of the two younger girls with their ambitious plans for the future and a more liberated lifestyle and wondering how bitterly they might be disappointed.

'No, Faria simply told them that she accepted my choice of husband for her in the traditional way.'

'I don't think they believed her,' Sharif said flatly.

'That is not important,' Faisel Sharif said, although his nephew thought he could hear a lack of conviction in his voice. The younger girls would not be so pliant, he thought, and guessed that Faisel knew that already. He was sure that there would be storms in this family for years to come.

'So do you know where Faria is now?' He knew now why his uncle had remained silent about Faria's unexplained absence but he wanted to hear him spell out his fears himself. 'Has she gone to Pakistan for some reason? Just what is going on?'

'I don't know,' Faisel said. 'Neither of them has said anything to me. Everything seemed normal, although there were not children yet, which grieved us. And then

Faria lost contact. She used to telephone her mother every week or so.' Faisel glanced at his wife, who nodded in confirmation. 'And she came to see us regularly. But for two months now – nothing.'

'And Imran Aziz has offered no explanation?'

'Imran Aziz answers the telephone and says Faria is not there at that moment and he will ask her to telephone. But she does not telephone. This has happened three or four times now.'

'You haven't been to Milford to look for her?'

Faisel shook his head and Sharif suddenly realised the extent of the older man's impotence in the face of this disaster. Having acceded to his own father's demand that the long-ago arranged marriage should be implemented, in spite of being aware that it was no more than a convenient way around the immigration rules, he felt unable to confront Imran Aziz, no doubt afraid that whatever he did would re-ignite a quarrel half a world away between two old men over a patch of dusty earth.

Controlling his anger carefully, Sharif took a deep breath and broached the question he knew was tormenting his aunt and uncle.

'So you're afraid she has run away from this marriage?'

His uncle shrugged helplessly.

'It is a possibility,' he conceded. And obviously one which Faisel could not bear to contemplate, Sharif thought. With two more daughters coming up to marriageable age, the scandal would reverberate around his family and the community, in Bradfield and Pakistan, damaging their prospects of a good match and no doubt encouraging Imran Aziz and his dishonoured family into taking whatever steps they could to find the runaway wife and deal with her. He shuddered.

'I realise she may have run away of her own free will,' he said carefully. 'And that is bad enough. But there are other possibilities.'

Faisel nodded and his nephew almost had the feeling that he might prefer any other possibility – even Faria's death – to the dishonour of her deserting her husband.

'There are a lot of questions you should be asking, and I should be asking not just as her cousin but as a policeman. We need to know she is safe. Just because she is married doesn't break all Faria's ties with our family. I want to see her, or at least speak to her on the telephone. I'd also like to know a bit more about why Imran Aziz was so desperate to get to England that he would divorce one wife and take another. And I may not be the only one asking that question. Did it never cross your mind that there might be something odd about that? That he might have an ulterior motive in coming here?' Sharif refrained from spelling out his worst fear of what that ulterior motive might be, but he knew his uncle understood him very well when he saw the flash of alarm in his eyes. The older man licked his lips while his aunt stared at him as if mesmerised by a snake.

'He is from a very respectable family,' Faisel said.

'So is bin Laden,' Sharif snapped. The two men stared at each other, both outraged, until the younger Sharif gave a shrug.

'I'll make more inquiries in Milford,' he said. 'Do you know where Faria was working? I've not had time to track down her employers yet. She may have talked to someone at work about going away.'

His uncle shook his head.

'A travel agent's. That's all I know.'

'And will you contact Imran's father back home? We'll all look foolish if Faria is safe and sound there on a visit to her mother-in-law.' But he knew that was a forlorn hope. There was no reason why Imran Aziz should not have told either him or Faisel if Faria had gone to Pakistan. The situation was a whole lot more threatening than that.

'I will speak to my father,' Faisel said, and his nephew knew how much that concession cost him. 'God willing, she is there.'

'God willing,' Sharif said grudgingly.

He turned his attention to his silent aunt.

'Did Faria ever give you a hint that the marriage was an unhappy one for her?' he asked more gently. 'Could she have run away from Imran, do you think?' But when his aunt shook her head he did not think she was simply lying to avoid the shame that would bring on the family, although he doubted very much that she would tell him all she knew.

'She said nothing,' she said. 'Nothing like that at all.'

Sharif turned back to his uncle.

'I will have to talk to my boss about this,' he said

'Why?' his uncle came back angrily. 'This is a family matter.'

'It may be. But Imran is behaving very strangely. Perhaps he just doesn't want to admit that his wife has deserted him. Or perhaps there's more to it than that. I got the impression that there were some wild young men at the mosque in Milford. I have to report things like that. I have no choice.'

'You were a fool to join the police,' his uncle said bitterly. 'It will pull you in two eventually.'

'Perhaps,' Mohammed Sharif said. 'And perhaps you have pulled Faria in two your-self by insisting on this marriage. You chose to come here and produce British children.

You can't expect them to live by the rules of some backward village in Pakistan. It's not reasonable and it's bringing us nothing but trouble.'

Sharif had never spelt out his feelings so clearly to his uncle and he could see how unwelcome the message was. But his own anger made him bold.

'I will speak to your father,' Faisel Sharif said through clenched teeth.

'My father is not responsible for me any longer,' Sharif said, realising how absurd this conversation would sound to his white friends and colleagues. 'I live in another world,' he muttered. 'I have to.' And with that he left, closing his uncle's front door carefully behind him. He doubted that he would ever be invited to cross the threshold again.

CHAPTER SEVEN

Julie Holden flung open the office door at the women's refuge, startling the two women inside.

'Have you seen Anna?' she blurted, oblivious to the frosty looks that greeted her. Carrie Whittaker, whose interview with one of the refuge's clients had been interrupted, shook her head irritably.

'Isn't she with Polly in the kitchen? She enjoys helping her.'

Julie turned on her heel, unzipping her jacket as she hurried down the corridor to the kitchen where an evening meal was being prepared, only to find it deserted, a few pans simmering steamily on the stove. Still clutching a chemist's bag in one hand she rushed back up the stairs calling for her daughter. Anna had promised to stay in her room finishing her Harry Potter book while her mother went out for half an hour or so to do some shopping, but when Julie had returned she had found the room empty and now, as she stood between the two narrow beds, her heart thumping, she realised that Anna's coat, which had been hanging on a hook on the door, was missing. When she looked round more carefully, she could see that Anna had taken her book and that some of her other most precious possessions – her teddy bear, her school pencil case and a battered old briefcase of her father's, which she loved and had carefully arranged around her bed – had also disappeared.

Julie's heart felt as if it had frozen and she began to shake. She sat down heavily on her bed and tried to swallow down the panic that threatened to engulf her. But even before she had managed to collect her whirling thoughts, Carrie put her head round the door.

'Did you find her?' she asked. Julie felt the tears coming.

'She's gone,' she said. 'She's taken some of her things ... her precious Harry Potter book, her pyjamas, her teddy bear... She must have slipped out while I was out shopping. I was only gone twenty minutes.'

'Are you sure?' Carrie said, putting a hand on Julie's shoulder. 'Have you been round to ask everyone? She might be with some of the other children.'

Julie shook her head vehemently, knowing that Anna was uncomfortable with some of the younger children, some still in nappies, who seemed to spend most of their time grizzling and squabbling in the communal rooms downstairs, but she followed Carrie on a tour of the building which, as she expected, failed to find anyone who had seen Anna recently.

'Surely the doors were locked?' Julie protested as the two women stood in the hall facing each other impotently.

'Anna would probably be able to reach the lock,' Carrie said. 'They're fitted too high for small children but not for a child of her age. We're not in the business of locking people in, after all, only keeping unwanted visitors out.'

'I must ring the police,' Julie said urgently. 'They must start a search.'

'Are you sure you need the police?' Carrie said quietly. 'Isn't it quite likely that she's headed off to see someone? I know she's not been very happy here, has she? You'd only to look at her to see how fed up she was. These things take it out of kids, you know that. Could she have gone to see her father?'

'No,' Julie almost screamed. 'After the way he's treated me? She couldn't have gone to see her father. Don't be stupid.'

'Look,' Carrie said quietly. 'We're not going to get anywhere like this. Just sit and think calmly and rationally for a moment. You say she's taken some of her stuff so she must be heading somewhere she thinks she can stay. Has she got any money?'

Julie swallowed hard and tried to concentrate.

'Not very much. A couple of quid maybe,

saved from her pocket money.'

'So enough to take a bus but not enough to get out of town. She hasn't taken any more out of your bag?'

'No, of course not,' Julie snapped back, but then calmed down enough to check.

'I had my bag with me when I went shopping,' she said more calmly. 'There's nothing missing as far as I can see.'

'So she obviously knows she can't go far. She's a bright girl. If she waited until you left her on her own, she must have planned this quite carefully. Would she know which bus to get to get to your family home?'

'She might do,' Julie conceded, feeling sick. 'If she could find the right bus stop in town. I don't know, do I? I simply don't know.'

'Calm, calm,' Carrie said. 'Has she got a mobile?'

'No,' Julie said. 'She was badgering us to get her one, but I thought she was too young. She didn't need one yet. She's only eight.'

'Has your husband got a mobile?' Carrie persisted.

'No. He hates them. Won't carry one.'

'So come down to the office and we'll call him from there. Is he likely to be at home?'

'Yes, no, I don't know,' Julie muttered but she followed Carrie downstairs and dictated the number to her, but it was obvious after they had both listened to the ring tone for several minutes that there was not going to be a reply.

'Is there anyone else Anna might have decided to visit?' Carrie asked. 'A school-friend, maybe? Any other relations?'

Julie ran her hands through her hair, close to desperation now.

'Her grandmother, maybe.'

'Then let's give her a call, shall we?'

Julie pulled out her own mobile and called her mother-in-law, and this time the phone was answered quickly.

'Vanessa? Is Anna with you by any chance?'

There was an unexpectedly long silence at the other end before Vanessa Holden spoke.

'No,' she said slowly. 'But Bruce called me. He says Anna has turned up there saying she wants to stay at home. He said you're not to worry. She's fine. She's with her daddy now.'

'Oh no,' Julie said, tears coursing down her cheeks now. 'Please, no.' Vanessa began to say something else but Julie broke the connection abruptly.

'I've got to get her back,' she sobbed. 'She's not safe with that man. No one is.'

'It may not be so easy.' Carrie's arm was around Julie's shoulder now. 'You can't report her missing if she's with her father and seems to have gone to him of her own free will. Has he ever hurt her?'

'What?' Julie looked aghast.

'Has he ever hurt her? Physically, I mean. Has he ever hit her?'

'No,' Julie said. 'I swear I'd have killed him if he'd tried.' Carrie drew a sharp breath.

'Not a good idea to let anyone hear you say that if you're going to get into a custody battle with your husband.'

'Custody battle?' Julie said, appalled. 'The man's mad. Mad and violent. Anna's not safe with him for a moment.'

'That's something you may have to substantiate before you can get Anna back,' Carrie said. 'Believe me. I've seen it all before. This may not be easy.'

'Oh, Anna, Anna. What have you done, you silly, silly girl?'

'I think you need a solicitor,' Carrie said. But Julie just stared at her, still in shock, each coherent thought a massive effort.

'I'll go up there,' she said eventually. 'I'll talk to Anna. She'll come back with me if I explain to her why she can't stay with Bruce.'

Carrie glanced at her watch.

'I'd come with you but I've got a meeting of the trustees shortly. This place is going to have to close if we can't raise some more money soon. I daren't skip the meeting. But honestly, Julie, it's not a good idea rushing about banging on doors and having a public row with your husband. It will only make the situation worse and damage your chances of keeping Anna with you. Believe me. I've seen so many of these cases. They don't always work out well for mothers and kids.'

'I'll keep calm,' Julie said, her face obstinate. 'I'll see if I can get a friend to go with me. We'll have a rational discussion.'

'With an irrational husband? I don't think so.' Carrie's patience was obviously wearing thin. 'Look, I really have to go. Why don't you stay here until I get back and then I'll find time to drive you up to – where is it? – Southfield? Keep on trying to contact them by phone by all means, but don't go steaming up there in a fury, please. It won't do you or Anna, or your chances of getting her back, any good at all. Believe me.'

Julie nodded dully and turned to go back up to her room. She sat on her bed for a while until she heard the heavy front door close and she guessed that Carrie had left the building. She tried her home number again but when it rang unanswered she tried Laura Ackroyd's number instead and explained what had happened.

'Do you have time to come up to Southfield with me?' she asked. 'I need to go. I need to see Anna. But I think Carrie's right. I need a witness and I can't think of anyone better than you.'

Michael Thackeray sent for DC Sharif

halfway through the morning. With a dry mouth and thumping heart which he feared might be heard as he opened the DCI's door, the young detective was not surprised to find a man he had never seen before closeted with the DCI.

'This is Doug McKinnon from the new anti-terrorism unit in Manchester,' Thackeray said by way of introduction. 'He'd like you to go through what you've already told me about your cousin and her husband, and your trip to Milford.'

Somewhat hesitantly, Sharif did as he was told, hoping that his lack of enthusiasm was not obvious. This interest from MI5, because although that had not been spelt out, he was sure that McKinnon was one of the 'spooks' given the unenviable task of working with specialist police officers and trying to anticipate terrorism, was not unexpected. But Sharif still hated exposing what might still be merely a family problem to this level of official scrutiny. Once a name was on MI5's radar, he was quite sure that it would never be eradicated and he still felt he had little real reason to suspect his cousin's husband or the intense young imam in Milford of anything criminal at all. Even worse, if their names went into the intelligence files, he had no confidence that some sort of question mark might not be inserted into his own record too. Guilt by association, he thought bitterly, was what this was all about, if your skin was the wrong colour and your religion, however nominal, suspect.

McKinnon listened sympathetically enough to Sharif's tale, making a few notes as he went along. When he had finished he glanced at Thackeray, an impassive presence on the edge of the conversation.

'There's no record of your cousin or her husband leaving the country in recent weeks, for Pakistan or anywhere else,' he said, turning back to the detective constable. 'For what that's worth.'

Sharif nodded, not knowing quite whether this was good news or bad and unsurprised that passenger lists were being closely monitored. During a relatively sleepless night after he had dropped Louise back at her own flat, he had considered taking some holiday and booking a trip to Pakistan himself to visit family members there, but that idea seemed pretty pointless now. And the last thing he wanted to do was turn up on the anti-terrorist radar himself. He had absolutely no faith that being a copper would protect him from suspicion now attention had been drawn to members of his family.

McKinnon was looking at him speculatively.

'I understand you don't live with your parents any more,' he said. 'That's pretty unusual, isn't it?'

'I'm thirty-two,' Sharif said. 'Would you live with your parents at thirty-two?'

'But in your community...?' McKinnon said blandly.

'I have my own flat and my own life,' Sharif said. 'That's my choice.'

'Did the family approve of your choice of career?' McKinnon persisted. Sharif flashed a look at Thackeray, a covert appeal for support, but he was gazing studiously out of the window and did not meet his eye.

'I don't know what that's got to do with anything we're discussing,' Sharif protested.

'It has if we're to make use of your contacts in the Muslim community,' McKinnon said. Sharif froze.

'Are you suggesting that I spy on my own family?'

'Not your own family specifically,' McKinnon said. 'But you've already reported your concerns about the mosque in Milford. You could be very useful to us if you kept your eyes open, got involved a bit more in community life...'

'My cousin is missing, Mr McKinnon,' Sharif said quietly. 'That's what concerns me.'

'And if that turned into a more serious inquiry I would certainly not expect DC Sharif to be involved in the investigation,' Thackeray broke in sharply at last. 'He's much too close to it to be objective.' Sharif made to protest but then thought better of it, turning back to McKinnon, who was still watching him with chilly eyes.

'I am not known as a religious man, Mr McKinnon,' he said. 'I'm not an observant Muslim. If I suddenly started attending prayers and asking questions I would arouse suspicion immediately. I'm sorry. Of course, if information reaches me from my family or anyone else, I'll pass it on. That's my duty as a citizen and a police officer. But I won't be your spy. I'm sorry.'

'So you'll do no more than the minimum?' McKinnon said, not concealing his anger.

'That's not what DC Sharif said,' Thackeray broke in.

'It's as good as,' McKinnon snapped back.

'Thank you, Mohammed,' Thackeray said firmly. 'I'm sure you've plenty of work to be getting on with.' Sharif nodded and left the office, closing the door gently behind him, and leaving Michael Thackeray shaking his head at McKinnon.

'I told you he wouldn't buy that,' he said. 'He's an excellent officer with a serious future ahead of him. But in present circumstances, Muslim officers walk a tightrope. You were trying to push him off.'

'We need intelligence,' McKinnon said.

'We all need intelligence,' Thackeray said. 'And Sharif will provide it. But not by pretending to be what he's not. That would destroy his credibility in the community and I won't have that. And anyway, as he rightly says, it couldn't possibly be effective. He would fool no one.'

'He's ambivalent, like a lot of them.'

'No,' Thackeray said flatly. 'He's not. He's as appalled as anyone by terrorism, as are most of the Muslims in this town. I won't have him tainted by these fanatics who were so secretive that their own families didn't know what they were planning. If you want intelligence from the mosques you'll have to find another source. Sharif's not the man you need.'

'If you say so,' McKinnon conceded, still not looking convinced. 'But I'll make a note of it.'

'I'm sure you will,' Thackeray said grimly.

Laura Ackroyd reluctantly drove Julie Holden up the long hill to Southfield when she finished work at four that afternoon. The trip was against her better judgment, but Julie had insisted that she would tackle her husband alone if she had to, and eventually Laura had caved in to her frantic entreaties. She had picked Julie up from outside the women's refuge, where she had been standing on the pavement, a forlorn figure in jeans and a bedraggled red fleece, trying to shelter from the drizzling rain that had been gusting across the town from the

Pennines all afternoon.

'Sorry to keep you waiting,' Laura had said as she pushed open the passenger door to let Julie in. 'I couldn't get away quite as soon as I hoped.'

Julie nodded as she fastened her seatbelt.

'I'm glad you could help. I thought of Vicky but she can't leave Naomi easily, and anyway, I reckoned a reporter might give Bruce pause for thought.'

'Maybe,' Laura said non-committally, uncomfortable with the idea that her profession might be used as a bargaining chip in this marital war. 'But there's one thing I have to say. I'm not going to get involved in snatching Anna by force. If she's gone to see her father and wants to stay you'll have to use legal means to get her back.'

'I don't know that she went there voluntarily, do I?' Julie said, her expression mutinous.

'From what you say about her packing her favourite things it looks pretty obvious to me,' Laura said bluntly. 'She wasn't happy at the refuge, was she?'

Julie shook her head, looking so desolate that Laura felt for a moment that she was being unnecessarily unfeeling. But then she hardened her heart again, knowing from her research how easy it was for family disputes like this to tip over into appalling violence against spouses and children alike. She had seen Michael Thackeray devastated by scenes of family violence too recently to want to risk that – for him or anyone else – again.

She drove soberly through the thickening traffic, to the modest detached house on the edge of Southfield, that she had last visited with Vicky. They sat for a moment gazing at Julie's home, where blank widows showed no sign of life.

'Perhaps they're not there,' Laura said, almost hoping she was right. The nearer she got to this proposed confrontation, the more unhappy she felt about it.

'Where else would they be?' Julie snapped. 'Anna wouldn't have gone anywhere else.'

'Bruce could have taken her somewhere else,' Laura said. 'To keep her out of your way. Which is his car?' There was no car on the short drive leading to the Holden's garage and only a few parked on the quiet suburban street outside.

Julie shook her head.

'It must be in the garage,' Julie said. 'He won't have gone anywhere. One of our problems was that he wouldn't make decisions. He says he needs thinking time, but in fact he just broods on things and works himself into a fury if he doesn't like the answers he comes up with. Then I get the blame.'

And the bruises, Laura thought, wondering again why Julie had not left her husband years ago.

'Well,' she said. 'We'll only find out where they are if we knock on the door.' Julie nodded, looking wan and uncertain now the moment had come, but she followed Laura to the front door and waited as the bell sounded inside the house. For a long time there was no response to Laura's repeated rings, but finally they heard sounds inside, a child's voice and then a man's, and then a looming presence visible through the frosted-glass panel in the door.

Eventually it opened a crack and a face appeared, no longer boyish but haggard and unshaven, with disheveled hair and bleary eyes. Bruce Holden looked as if he had just got out of bed, and Laura wondered if he had been drinking.

'Is Anna here?' Julie asked, her voice shrill with suppressed tension. 'Have you got Anna?'

'She came to see her dad,' Holden said. 'What's wrong with that?' his gaze fixed on Laura.

'Who's this? Your sodding friend again? Can't you do anything without someone to hold your hand?'

Irritated, Laura gave Bruce her full name this time, but that was not enough for Julie.

'She's a reporter from the *Gazette*,' she said. 'She's writing about domestic violence.'

'Well, she can sod off, then,' Bruce said,

his scowl darkening. 'There's nothing for her here. I wouldn't have let her in with Vicky bloody Mendelson if I'd known.'

'Where's Anna?' Julie cried, putting her foot in the door as Bruce made an attempt to close it. 'I want to see her.'

'Well, you can't, you bloody can't,' Bruce shouted, not concealing a fury that Laura guessed would have ended in physical violence if she had not been there. 'So now you know what it feels like.' And he pulled the door back a foot and then slammed it, making Julie pull her foot away sharply to avoid serious injury. She staggered backwards, grabbing Laura for support, her face ashen and her eyes filling with tears again.

'You can't deal with this on your own,' Laura said. 'I did warn you. You have to get help.'

'Who from?' Julie almost screamed.

'The police, social services, a solicitor – all three if you like,' Laura said, urging her back down the short drive to the pavement. But as they moved towards the car she glanced back at the house and looked up to a bedroom window where a slight movement had caught her eye. There she saw a small pale face staring at them. Anna, Laura thought, did not seem to want to attract her mother's attention, either to welcome or reject her. Whatever she was thinking, she certainly was not waving for help or crying out to be rescued, but there was little doubt that she was scared. Julie was leaning against the car with her back to her daughter and Laura quickly helped her into the passenger seat, without mentioning the child above.

'Where now?' Laura asked, knowing that she could not leave Julie on her own in her distraught state. The other woman shrugged and glanced at her watch.

'I'll have to get a solicitor, I suppose, though it's a bit late now for that.'

'If you were prepared to complain to the police about your husband's violent behaviour you might have a better chance of getting Anna back in the short-term,' Laura said as she pulled away from the kerb and began to weave her way back from the tree-lined streets to the bustling centre of Bradfield. Julie said nothing until, as they approached the town centre through the thickening rush-hour traffic, she grabbed Laura's arm convulsively, almost causing her to swerve into the kerb.

'Take me to the police station, then,' she said. 'You're right. I've got to stop him. I can't leave Anna with that maniac, even for a single night. I'll get him arrested for assault.'

DS Janet Richardson had reluctantly allowed Laura Ackroyd to remain with Julie Holden while she interviewed her.

'You're here strictly as a friend, not a

reporter,' Janet had said to Laura when Julie begged to keep Laura at her side. Laura knew she was being used by Julie as a lifeline and agreed to Janet's terms readily enough. What she heard in the police station would not add greatly to what Julie had already told her outside and she wanted to see the case against Bruce Holden progress just as much as Julie herself evidently did now a crisis had been provoked over Anna's safety. Whatever Anna had decided to do for herself, Laura knew that the wan face she had seen at the bedroom window was the face of a desperately unhappy child.

'So you're quite sure you want to make a complaint of assault against your husband, Mrs Holden?' Janet asked. And when Julie nodded, she persisted.

'You know the implications of that? It could lead to a prosecution and you would be expected to give evidence against your husband. You would have to describe in detail what injuries you sustained and how they were inflicted. We might also need to talk to your daughter, and other witnesses, in seeking corroboration of what you are saying. You would be cross-examined on it, not necessarily believed. It's not a pleasant business, Mrs Holden, and I want to be sure that you know exactly what it entails before I take your statement.'

'I want to go ahead,' Julie said, her voice

no more than a whisper. 'I have to go ahead. He's taken my daughter and I'm afraid for her safety.'

Laura listened impassively as Julie went through the same details that she had recounted to her the first time they had talked at the women's refuge. Julie was willing now, impelled by her fear for Anna, to go into more graphic detail: a catalogue of intimidation and physical violence dating back many months before she had finally cracked and decided to leave.

'Have you had medical treatment for any of your injuries?' Janet asked eventually, but Julie shook her head.

'I didn't dare go to the doctor.'

'So is there anyone who can provide evidence of what you went through? A friend you confided in, perhaps. Someone who has seen your injuries soon after they were inflicted?'

'I tried to keep my bruises covered when I went out,' Julie whispered, and Laura wondered angrily how anyone could be so ashamed of being a victim that she had refused to seek help for so long.

'You told Vicky,' she said gently. 'That's Vicky Mendelson,' she added for Janet Richardson's benefit.

'Yes, I told her some of it,' Julie admitted. 'Bruce had trodden on my hand during one of our rows. It was bruised. I thought maybe he'd broken it but it seemed to settle down... Anyway, Vicky noticed it when we were chatting outside the school one day and I was feeling so distraught that I told her some of it. Not everything.'

'So we could talk to Vicky Mendelson,' Janet said, making a note.

'I suppose,' Julie said.

'Vicky is David Mendelson's wife, the CPS lawyer,' Laura offered. Then a thought struck her.

'I wonder...' She hesitated, but Janet Richardson was not going to leave it at that.

'You wonder?'

'Well, there was an intruder at Vicky's house the other night. They called the police. It just struck me it could have been Bruce looking for Julie and Anna. He might have thought they were staying there. But I expect CID have thought of that.'

'I expect they have,' Janet said. 'But I'll pass it on, just in case. It might be useful if we're looking for a reason to bring Bruce in.'

She glanced back at Julie who seemed astonished by the implications of what she had set in train.

'You'll arrest Bruce? Then that would mean I could take charge of Anna again?'

'It could do, but I need to talk to some people first. Do you have any family in Bradfield? Anyone else who might have guessed

142

what was going on even if you didn't tell them?'

'Not my own family,' Julie said. 'They're all in Blackpool. There's my mother-in-law but I'm never sure whose side she's on. Bruce is an only child.'

'D'you think she suspects what's been going on?' Janet persisted.

'She adores Anna. It's possible Anna's let something slip... I never told her anything myself, not about the violence anyway.'

'And she hasn't mentioned it to you?'

Julie shook her head.

'Never,' she said.

'She does know,' Laura broke in. 'She's known for some time. I interviewed her for the article I'm writing on domestic violence and she said that she knew Bruce was being violent at home. And then when he moved in with her, he behaved the same way there. But like everyone else, she seemed to want to protect him...' She broke off, guessing that this was not helping Julie, who was looking distraught.

'But now you don't want to protect him any more, Mrs Holden. Right?' Janet said.

Julie nodded faintly.

'So I'd like you to make a formal statement detailing your complaint against your husband. Then I'll initiate some inquiries and hopefully, if I can get some corroboration from your friend Vicky, and your mother-in-law, and we'll have something to tackle him with by the end of the day. Is that OK with you?'

'Can Julie get Anna back immediately, then?' Laura asked.

'I'll let you know when I intend to go and visit him and if I invite him down to the station for questioning,' Janet said. 'At that stage I need to be sure Anna is in safe hands, and where could be safer than with her mother?' She gave Julie a warm smile.

'Come on, cheer up,' she said. 'If you're tough enough, and I'm sure you are, we can deal with men like this. You just have to be strong.'

'Fine,' Julie said, but as they left the police station after she had signed her statement, Laura still wondered if she would turn out to be strong enough to carry this through to the witness box.

Thackeray was late home that evening and when he finally came in, to find Laura sitting in front of the television news with a vodka and tonic in her hand, he hesitated at first to tell her the news that he knew she would not welcome.

'Good day?' he asked as he hung up his rain-soaked mac.

'So-so,' Laura said, zapping the TV news off and ready to fill him in on the latest details of Julie Holden's problems. But noticing his sombre expression, she hesitated.

'Can I get you a drink? You look as if you've had a bad day.' He shook his head, and to her surprise pre-empted the very subject that was at the forefront of her mind.

'I hear you came in with Mrs Holden,' he said. 'Janet Richardson filled me in.'

'She finally agreed to make a complaint,' Laura said enthusiastically. 'Have they tackled her husband yet?'

'Well, they would have done if they'd been able to find him,' Thackeray said. 'Janet had it all set up. But when she finally went up there to ask him to come to the station for questioning she found he'd gone. The house was empty and the garage door wide open. A neighbour said she'd seen him drive off with the child at about five and they hadn't been back since to her knowledge. I'm very afraid the bird's flown.'

'Oh, no,' Laura said. 'I knew it wasn't a good idea to go up there. I should have stopped her but she was so insistent.'

'Not the best idea in the circumstances,' Thackeray said dryly. 'If you want someone arrested, don't forewarn them you're coming if you can help it. I'd have told you that if you'd bothered to ask.'

'She wouldn't be persuaded,' Laura said. 'She needed to know where Anna was, that she was safe, that she hadn't been abducted by a stranger. *You* know. She was desperate.'

'I know,' Thackeray said. 'But it was still the wrong thing to do. He must have guessed she'd go to the police, or a solicitor, take some action against him. She had no choice. It could take months to track him down now. Tracing violent husbands is not exactly a high priority these days.'

'I don't suppose it is,' Laura said sadly. 'Does Julie know what's happened?'

'Janet's kept her informed,' Thackeray said. 'Apparently she's seeing a solicitor to-morrow morning. She's staying with Vicky and David tonight.'

Laura reached up to where Thackeray was standing and pulled his head down to kiss his cheek.

'Thanks for taking an interest,' she said. 'I know I shouldn't get so involved in these things but it's hard not to when you hear the unexpurgated version of what goes on. The man's a brute.'

'I did ask Mower to have another word with the older Mrs Holden, you know, after you spoke to her. But she's still insisting she doesn't remember what happened, whatever she's saying to you and her daughter-in-law. There's not much we can do. Janet's going to have a chat with her to see if she can persuade her to tell us what really happened. She may be more willing to talk to us now she knows that he's run off with Anna. Apparently she adores her granddaughter and won't want to lose contact with her any more than Julie does. She may also have some idea where Bruce might hole up with the child.'

'Ha! I said to Ted Grant that I'd deal with battered grannies too,' Laura said. 'He was a bit worried that battered wives were too right-on for his delicate sensibilities. I didn't realise we might find all this going on across the generations in one family.'

'Be careful, Laura. If you publish too many details of Julie's case you might prejudice a prosecution.'

Laura pulled a face at him.

'I'll tread on tippy-toes,' she said. 'We can always use assumed names if there's really a possibility of him being charged. But there's fat chance of that if you can't find him, isn't there? How are you going to get Anna back without publicity? Pictures in the *Gazette*, on TV, all the rest of it?'

'I don't know,' Thackeray said sombrely. 'I wouldn't bank on Julie getting Anna back at all.'

CHAPTER EIGHT

Amos Atherton, in greens and plastic apron, gazed at the distended mass of flesh, barely identifiable as the remains of a human being, that lay on his stainless steel table and shrugged faintly towards the unfamiliar police presence there to attend the post-mortem.

'It's been in the water some time,' he said. 'It's female. And that's about all you can tell at first glance.' The detective inspector from the east of the county who had been detailed to follow the body to Bradfield's pathology department was looking pale and Atherton doubted that his stomach would be strong enough to cope with the unpleasant task ahead.

'If you're going to throw up on me, perhaps you'd better watch from outside,' he said. 'It stinks now and is only going to get worse when I open her up.'

The hapless officer swallowed hard and retreated to a vantage point closer to the door.

'Chances are you'll get nothing out of this,' Atherton said grumpily. 'If she's drowned, I'll not be able to tell you whether it was an accident or suicide or murder. Where did you say she was found?'

'Ingleby, a village on the Maze down Selby way. The body was trapped under a bridge by a lot of debris after the floods. It could have gone in anywhere and been carried down the river while it was in spate. Could have ended up in the sea, for that matter, if it had drifted a few miles further and gone into the Ouse.'

'The obvious injuries are no more than you'd expect from the battering she must have taken in a flooded river – scratches, abrasions, cuts and so on,' Atherton said. 'Her clothes are in shreds, as you can see. But onward and inward as they say. Let's have a closer look.' And he began to dictate his description of the external state of the corpse. When he eventually picked up his scalpel to cut into the distended flesh and release the bloating gases, the DI hovering on the far side of the room turned even paler, muttered his excuses with his hand over his mouth, and rapidly left.

'Where do they get them from these days?' Atherton abstractedly asked his technician as he peered into the liquefying cavity he had created. The younger man grinned.

'Not everyone shares our tastes,' he said. 'Your mate DCI Thackeray always looks pretty sick when he has to be here.'

'Aye, he's a delicate flower underneath

that iron mask of his,' Atherton said, with a grin. 'I wonder if they're going to tell him about this lass.'

'Why should they?' the technician asked, taking the mass of almost unidentifiable flesh that Atherton handed him in gloved hands and weighing it carefully, before slicing a specimen and placing it is a bag for analysis. 'I thought this was an East Yorkshire job.'

'Well, she's obviously Asian, isn't she?' Atherton asked, running a gentle finger across the long dark hair that still surrounded the unrecognisable features of the girl on the table. 'And she was in the Maze. She might well be one of ours.'

It was an idea that lodged in his mind as he completed his examination of the corpse a couple of hours later and, even as he oversaw the replacement of the now plastic-wrapped organs, minus the samples for analysis, inside the decaying body, and began to think longingly of lunch. The thought eventually propelled him towards the phone in his office and a call to police HQ.

'Fancy a quick bite, Michael?' he asked DCI Thackeray when he eventually got through. 'Got something here that may be of interest, strictly off the record, mind.' Thackeray, bogged down in crime management statistics, agreed readily enough and the two men met an hour or so later in the bar of the Clarendon hotel, where the widely spaced tables ensured a level of privacy they would not get in a pub. When they had ordered drinks and sandwiches, Atherton leant back in his leather armchair and let out a sigh of contentment.

'Glad to get out this morning,' he said. 'Folk reckon we don't feel anything because we only deal with bodies. No empathy, all that bollocks. But it's not true, any more than it is with you lot. You build a shell. Have to. Enjoy the humour of it all when you can. Then try to forget it.'

Thackeray nodded, knowing that everyone had their own ways of dealing with the stresses of the job and that his own had been less than successful more than once during a career that had seen him progress much less far up the ladder than had once been predicted. He and Atherton were not friends in any real sense of the word. They seldom met outside the confines of Atherton's department in the bowels of the infirmary. But the pathologist was one of the few people Thackeray had already known when he had arrived in Bradfield as DCI and one to whom he was indissolubly linked by his own inglorious history. He would always be grateful to the man who had conducted the post-mortem on his baby son and who, when faced with a young copper distraught and at his lowest ebb, had offered consolation rather than the condemnation with which Thackeray had been assailed from all other directions. Gratitude had turned to trust as the two men renewed their acquaintance when Thackeray eventually came to work in Bradfield, just across the town hall square from the infirmary and Atherton's gloomy caverns in the basement. If Atherton uncharacteristically invited him out to lunch he knew there would be good reason.

'So what's rattled your cage then?' he asked as the roast beef sandwiches arrived and Atherton helped himself hungrily, before ordering another half pint of bitter for himself and an orange juice for Thackeray.

'A messy job I had this morning,' Atherton said through a mouthful of food. 'Woman found in the River Maze close to where it joins the Ouse. Only got asked to do it because of staff shortage down there, apparently. Not on your patch, I know, and I dare say East Yorkshire will think on to tell you eventually, but I reckoned you might like to know straight away.'

Thackeray nodded non-committally, knowing immediately what Atherton was implying.

'You mean she may have gone in much higher up the river?'

'She'd been in the water some time, that was obvious from the state of her. She was found wedged in amongst debris under a bridge down there, invisible till the water level dropped, and then a dog spotted her. She's not identifiable, I can tell you that for nothing. I've sent off a DNA sample, of course. I just thought you might like to check your missing persons. If you've seen the state of the river recently you'll know what I'm on about. I reckon she could have gone in anywhere from Arnedale down. It was still in spate the other day when I went over the bridge in Milford. We're lucky she didn't end up in the sea after all that rain and the flooding.'

'You say she's not identifiable,' Thackeray said, aware how quickly immersion in water could destroy the human body. 'But what about clothing? Nothing significant there? A watch? Jewellery? Teeth?'

'Clothing's largely gone. What's left is in shreds. You could look for dental records if you need to. Most of the teeth are still in the jaw. But the reason I thought you should know is that I think she's Asian. What the water hasn't got to is the hair, long and thick and very dark.'

Thackeray nodded slowly, his stomach clenching for a moment as he took in the implications of what Atherton was telling him for DC Mohammed Sharif. He knew with grim certainly and not a little foreboding that he needed this body identified as soon as humanly possible.

'Can you prioritise the DNA?' he asked.

'You've got someone missing?' Atherton asked.

'Maybe,' Thackeray said. 'Any indication that it was other than a drowning?'

'Nothing I could see. No convenient bullet in the inner recesses, skull and skeleton intact. No sign of a knife wound, although quite honestly that would be difficult to rule out, the state she was in. I can't give you my report directly, but I'm sure you can get hold of it through official channels. I'll be working on it this afternoon.'

'We do have a young Asian woman gone missing over the last few weeks,' Thackeray said. 'It could be her. I'm grateful for the warning, Amos. I'll get my colleagues down there to cut me in on your report as soon as it's available. They're supposed to circulate these things but in my experience it's a slow process. There's no chance of a visual identification then?'

'I wouldn't ask my worst enemy to look at her,' Atherton said, finishing his beer greedily. 'There's no face left to speak of. Turned the young DI who came over to the PM quite green, she did.'

'It'll be DNA then,' Thackeray said. 'That shouldn't be a problem. Let's hope it rules our missing person out. She's a relative of a bright young DC on my team and I'd hate to have to break it to him that she's dead.'

'At least that's one shitty job I don't have to share,' Atherton said as he lumbered to his feet. 'There's no bad news to break to my clients, is there? Thank God.'

DC Mohammed Sharif faced his uncle, his jaw clenched. He felt deeply sorry for him but Faisel Sharif was not a man to show his emotions or make any attempt to ease the younger man's own deep discomfort. He gazed at his nephew, mouth a thin line of distaste above the greying beard, his eyes opaque, as if he was being asked to compromise his deepest beliefs.

'It may not be Faria, God willing,' Sharif said. 'But unless they are able to do a DNA comparison we'll never know. Imran Aziz is still not at his house, so I can't ask him. There has to be something here of Faria's, or something of my aunt's or the other girls' which she's handled recently. That would be enough for a match. Believe me, it's much better to cooperate. They will get a sample one way or another if they think there's foul play involved, which we hope there wasn't. But we all need to know, one way or another.'

'This DNA is on her clothes?' Faisel asked sceptically.

'It's on everything you touch,' Sharif said flatly. 'It's becoming so sophisticated that you only have to breathe in a room or glance against someone for the forensic people to know you were there. But we're not trying to find suspects. We're trying to identify this poor woman who's not going to be identified any other way. It is possible to make an identification from a family member's DNA if it's necessary. Mine, for instance. But they'll want to try for hers first. And if it is Faria, we need to know, Uncle. This is my cousin, your daughter we're talking about. God willing, the body isn't hers, but we need to know.'

'You told your officers all about our family problems, then?' Faisel Sharif's face was closed tight, his eyes angry.

'I told you I had to tell them about Imran Aziz's strange behaviour. I had no choice,' Sharif said quietly. 'Inevitably, I had to mention Faria's absence as well. Now we have an unidentifiable body pulled from the river that runs no more than half a mile from her house.'

Mohammed Sharif stared at his uncle, baffled and angry at his attitude.

'There is no hiding this,' he said at length when his uncle did not reply. 'However painful it is for the family, there will be an investigation and you will have to answer questions. The best course is to help identify the body as quickly as possible. It may not even be Faria. God willing, it's not. But if you hinder the inquiry now it will only cast suspicion on the family if it turns out that it is. You have to assist the police with their inquiries. You know that.'

'It cannot be Faria,' Faisel said. 'She must be in Pakistan. Let me speak to your grandfather and discover the facts of the matter. I'll do that, I promise you.'

'It's too late for that now,' his nephew shot back. 'They want a DNA sample. If necessary they will break down Imran's door to get one, whether he's there or not. This could be a case of murder.'

He knew he had to be brutal as his mind shot back to the traumatic interview he had just had with a grim-faced Michael Thackeray when the DCI had broken the news that the unidentified, and almost unidentifiable, body of a possibly Asian woman had been found. He hoped that his boss had not noticed the uncontrollable shaking of the knees that he had tried to conceal by sinking uninvited into a chair in Thackeray's office and burying his face briefly in his hands.

'My family will want to know quickly whether or not it is Faria,' he had said, raising his head only when he thought he could control his voice adequately, and knowing that what he said was not necessarily true. The breath of scandal, especially if it impinged on the honour of a woman, was not something his family would welcome in any guise. But equally he knew that in this other world in which he worked, delay was not a possibility, and could only fuel the worst sort of suspicion.

'Let me try to locate something of Faria's from her parents' home if her husband is still away,' he offered Thackeray. 'If not, you can use my DNA. Would that be a close enough match?'

'A first cousin?' Thackeray had said. 'I'm not sure. But I can't wait long. The full PM report will be here tomorrow morning, the samples have already gone to the lab. There's no one on the official missing persons' register who immediately fits what limited description we have of this woman. We need to rule your cousin in or out quickly, Mohammed. I'm sorry. You can have until tomorrow morning to come up with something. Otherwise we'll have to make it more official.'

Sharif had driven round to his uncle's house immediately he finished his shift and to his relief found him at home alone. His wife and daughters, he said, were visiting friends. Now Sharif watched his uncle pace up and down the cramped living room before finally turning through the door and up the stairs, where he could hear him moving around in one of the bedrooms. Eventually, he returned holding a multi-coloured bundle of clothing in one hand with an expression of distaste on his face.

'These are hers,' he said. 'She left them for her sisters when she got married but I don't think Jamilla or Saira have ever worn them. They are still in a cupboard Faria used to use.'

Sharif took the clothes and shook out a couple of *shalwar kameez* in the bright colours he knew Faria liked to wear and shuddered slightly.

'Do you have a bag I could put them in?' he asked, and his uncle disappeared again and came back with a plastic supermarket carrier bag which he handed to his nephew without a word.

'How long will it take?' he asked.

'If they make it a priority, a couple of days,' Mohammed said, his mouth dry. 'Nothing much will happen until they've got an ID. You can't start an investigation when you don't know who the victim is. And apparently there's no possibility of recognising a likeness from what's left of the body.'

He walked slowly to the door, having obviously succeeded in shocking his uncle even more thoroughly than he expected. His face had turned to the colour of putty.

'Believe me, I hope there's no DNA match as much as you do,' Sharif said. 'I want Faria back with us, alive and well. But if the worst has happened, we need to know. Don't we?'

But there was no answering warmth in the

look his uncle gave him as he opened the door, more a blank dislike that he had never seen there before. He walked back to his car wondering slightly desperately whether Faisel knew more about Faria's fate than he was saying. Was there a family scandal here that he was not being told about because of his job? If so, he did not dare to think what it was or what would happen next.

Laura was shocked at Julie Holden's appearance when she called at Vicky Mendelson's home to collect her late that afternoon. She slid into the passenger seat without a word, looking pale and haggard, the dark circles under her eyes suggesting that in spite of Vicky and David's best efforts, she had barely slept.

'How are you?' Laura asked, but Julie simply shrugged and turned away.

'Have you seen a solicitor?' Laura persisted.

'David pulled a few strings to get me an appointment with someone this morning,' Julie mumbled. 'But it was a waste of time, really. If we can't find Bruce there's nothing much the law can do. If I want to initiate divorce proceedings and make a claim for custody of Anna, we still have to find him. If he's charged with assault I might get her back temporarily, but again, the police have to find him and charge him.'

'Have you no idea where he might be able to hole up? If he's not working he won't have access to much money, will he?'

'There's next to nothing in our joint account, but he does have a small savings account in his own name. We both do. I'm sure he'll use it if he needs to. He'll be all right for a while. But the mortgage and the household expenses were already getting to be a problem without Bruce's salary. I expect we'll lose the house, on top of everything else. I'd been supply teaching, when I wasn't black and blue, but I can't keep that up now. And what I can earn wouldn't cover the mortgage anyway.'

'D'you think your mother-in-law will know anything useful?' Laura asked, appalled at the disintegration of what must have seemed only a few months ago to be a comfortable middle-class lifestyle.

'I really don't know,' Julie said, obviously on the verge of tears. 'I really don't know what to think any more.'

Laura drove Julie to her mother-in-law's house in silence and when Vanessa opened the door the two women embraced, both on the edge of tears. Vanessa waved them into the sitting room, where the curtains where still drawn, just as they had been the last time Laura had visited Vanessa, and again she turned on the lights rather than opening the heavy drapes. Laura could see that her cheek was still an angry red surrounded by purple and yellow bruising that was only just beginning to fade. She had difficulty restraining her own anger at what was happening to this family.

'I'm sure you want to talk,' she said quietly. 'Would you like me to make some coffee or tea?' Vanessa glanced up at her gratefully from where she had sunk down beside Julie on the sofa, clutching her daughter-in-law's hand.

'That would be very kind,' she said. 'I'm still feeling quite groggy after my ... accident.'

'I know what happened,' Julie said. 'Laura told me. And now I've been to the police, you must too. This has got to stop.'

Laura left them to find her own way around Vanessa's untidy kitchen to rustle up a tray of tea and biscuits for the three of them. When she went back into the sitting room it was to find Vanessa crying quietly against Julie's shoulder. The older woman glanced up as Laura put the tray down.

'You're very kind. I don't deserve it,' she said, wiping her eyes with a crumpled tissue.

'Nonsense,' Laura replied. 'You can't blame yourself for what your son has done.'

'Oh, but I can. I think it's my fault.'

'How can that be, Vanessa?' Julie objected. 'He's an intelligent man, responsible for his own behaviour. It's nothing to do with you.'

'Perhaps I should have seen the warning

signs,' Vanessa said quietly. 'I think they were there, even before he went away to college. He was unpredictable, moody, given to outbursts that I don't think were normal even then. He used to fly into rages sometimes when he was here on vacation, not just slammed doors – more than that, worse than that, throwing things around in his room, destructive rages. I should have warned you before you married him.'

'I knew he had a temper,' Julie said. 'But it never appeared to be as bad as that when we first met. It was nothing I found particularly worrying.' She sighed. 'It was after we came to Bradfield that the whole thing began to escalate. He seemed less and less able to cope with the fact that there were three of us and I had to give a lot of time to Anna. I wonder now if he lost his job because of his unpredictable behaviour. Perhaps it's not just at home he goes a bit mad. I just don't know.'

'I should have warned you,' Vanessa said again. 'But it all happened so quickly, and once my husband got sick so soon after he retired...' She shrugged. 'It was a full-time job caring for him. I thought Bruce was settled and you were happy.'

'Listen,' Laura said gently to Vanessa, trying to hide her impatience with this breast-beating. 'All that's water under the bridge now. What we really need to think about is where Bruce might have gone with Anna. Can you think of anywhere he might have run to, given that he's not got much money, according to Julie?'

The two women looked at each other blankly for a moment, and then both seemed to come to the same conclusion at the same instant.

'Blackpool,' Julie said. 'He's not an adventurous man and he'll go somewhere he knows. And at this time of the year you can get accommodation very easily, at least until the summer season starts. The place is full of DSS claimants living in cheap boarding houses in the winter. It's obvious when you think about it.'

'He was talking about Blackpool last weekend,' Vanessa said. 'He wondered whether *you* might have taken Anna there.'

'It did cross my mind,' Julie said. 'I've still got my family there. But I thought it was too obvious, guessed he might work it out and come roaring over the M62 to harass my parents.'

'If you tell the police that Blackpool is a likely place to look for him, I'm sure they'll pass the message on to the Lancashire force. They do want to interview him, after all.' Laura offered the comment without huge confidence that the local police would do much about such a request, but it would be a first step, at least.

Julie nodded and turned back to her mother-in-law.

'Will you talk to the police as well?' she asked. 'It's really important. If they know he's assaulted you as well it might just stiffen their resolve to find him. With Laura planning to write something in the *Gazette*, they won't want it to look as if they're neglecting battered wives and mothers, will they?'

Laura smiled faintly.

'I don't think my partner would like to think you were trying to manipulate CID's priorities,' she said. 'But it's a good idea. Vanessa, the person you need to talk to is Janet Richardson in the domestic violence unit.'

'A young officer came to see me in the hospital and I told him lies, said I couldn't remember how I'd come to be attacked,' Vanessa said. 'I can't go back to them and tell them something different now.'

'Of course you can,' Laura said firmly. 'Just tell them you've recalled exactly what happened now. Lots of people cover these things up at first. They'll know all about that.'

'Do it, Vanessa, please,' Julie said and eventually her mother-in-law nodded.

'If it will help find Anna,' she said.

'I'm sure it will,' Laura tried to reassure her.

Back in the car, she glanced at Julie.

'Where now?' she said. 'Are you going to stay on with Vicky and David or go back to the refuge?'

'I'm going to Blackpool to look for them,' Julie said. Laura grinned, knowing that she would do exactly that even if Julie had not come to the same conclusion. She felt no inclination to let Bruce Holden off the hook if there was anything she could do about it. Julie might be distraught but her own more dispassionate assessment of the situation simply made her angry.

'I thought you might have that idea,' she said.

'Well, what would you do in my situation?' Julie said, suddenly looking more determined herself.

'Go to Blackpool and track the bastard down,' Laura agreed. 'But look, let's do this properly. Let me talk to my boss in the morning and tell him that I will be out for the day following up this story. Then I'll drive you over there and we'll see what we can see. Agreed?'

'Agreed,' Julie said.

By mid-morning the next day, Laura was driving slowly along the almost deserted promenade at the Lancashire resort, with only a broad expanse of walkway and the electric tram-track between the car and the buffeting gale-driven Irish Sea that swept

166

rain and spray across the steep sea-wall. Each wave seemed to toss itself more furiously against what, from this distance, seemed to be puny defenses, creating huge rippling lakes where in the summer thousands of holidaymakers strolled or sat in the northern sun. No one at all seemed brave enough this morning to be taking a walk, or even venturing as far as the sturdy shelters that dotted the promenade at intervals, allowing less intrepid visitors to look out over the coastline, relatively protected from whatever the elements threw at them. This morning the elements were drenching every corner with driving rain or churning seawater, and the famous sands, where in the summer thousands of families would play, were invisible beneath foaming rollers, and the piers, top-heavy with amusements of all kinds, looked in serious danger of being demolished by the fury of the tide, their entrance gates firmly closed, flags and bunting reduced to streaming rags in the wind.

'You mean people come here for fun?' Laura asked as she slowed to allow a swirl of sea water to subside across the carriageway in front of the car.

Julie Holden shrugged slightly.

'It can be a bit bleak at this time of the year,' she said, without much interest. Laura glanced to her right, where the Pleasure Beach funfair was almost obliterated by the driving rain and on past the tower, a mini-Eiffel with its head shrouded in cloud, and thought bleak, as a description, barely covered it. She drove on until eventually Julie instructed her to stop close to the North Pier, its entrance barricaded against anyone foolhardy enough to think of risking a walk along its sea and rain-soaked decks.

'I just can't remember how to get to Richard's place,' she said. 'I'll pop into the library just over there and see if I can get a look at a local map.'

Laura watched her cross the road and disappear into a building facing a small square that looked more modern than most of the buildings on the famous sea front, and for a second she wondered whether she had been foolish to indulge Julie's fierce determination to look for her husband and daughter in Blackpool. It turned out to be a bigger town than Laura had anticipated, never having visited the resort before, and finding anyone in the rain-lashed streets of boarding houses behind the famous Golden Mile of entertainments, or in the sprawling suburbs beyond, seemed now to be a more crazy enterprise even than Michael Thackeray had suggested when she had told him what she planned the night before.

'How can you possibly trace them if Holden doesn't want to be found?' Thackeray had asked, exasperated, but recognising the stubborn look in Laura's green eyes which he knew from bitter experience he would not shift an inch. She was on one of her crusades and his stomach clenched when he remembered how dangerous these had proved to be before.

'She says he has friends there that he may have turned to for help,' Laura said. 'She was brought up there, after all. They all lived there until Anna was five or six. She can't think of anywhere else Bruce might have gone to ground. She's planning to look for his former flatmate for a start. She thinks he's the one he'd turn to if he did go to Blackpool.'

'And what do you think you can do in the unlikely event you track him down?' Thackeray had asked. 'You know this man's violent. You can't tackle him on your own, much less try to snatch the child. If he's as volatile as his wife says he is, that would be madness. It could be dangerous, Laura, for everyone involved. Believe me.'

Laura had recognised the fear behind Thackeray's warning, but she had not been deterred, as he knew she would not be. Instead she had given him a lingering kiss and promised to be careful.

'Look, so long as Ted approves the trip it'll be a good addition to my feature. Julie doesn't imagine she's going to get Anna back just like that. I've told her the thing to do is go to the police for help if we do track him down. You do want to interview him, don't you? And the Lancashire police will know that, won't they?'

Thackeray shrugged.

'If anyone's bothered to take any notice of what we've circulated,' he said. 'Holden's not likely to be at the top of their most-wanted list, any more than he is of ours. It's not as if he's killed anyone.'

Laura glanced at Thackeray, slightly shocked at this too casual dismissal of the threat she believed Holden embodied.

'You know this could end up with murder,' she said quietly. 'You know how often it does.'

Thackeray put an arm round her.

'I'm sorry,' he said. 'I'm not unaware of the danger, you know that. It's just that in this case the wife has very sensibly left her husband and made a complaint against him. That's good. The fact that he's run off with his daughter is not so good, but we've absolutely no reason to fear he may hurt the child. On the other hand, there's an unidentified and well-nigh unrecognisable body of an Asian woman down in the mortuary, as we speak, that one of my detectives fears may be his cousin, whose marriage seems to have been 'arranged' against her will. Identifying her and discovering how she came to be in the River Maze is a bit more pressing just

170

now, that's all. That could really be domestic murder of a particularly unpleasant kind.'

'Ah,' Laura had said, understanding his lack of interest in Holden. 'That could be very nasty.'

'You have no idea just how difficult it could be,' Thackeray had said, his face bleak.

At that moment Julie flung herself back into the passenger seat of Laura's Golf, her waterproof jacket dripping copiously over the passenger compartment as she flung back the hood and tried to dry her face with a wad of paper tissues.

'God,' she said. 'I'd quite forgotten how grim winter can be on this coast. My home was in Lytham St Anne's, which is on the estuary and a bit more protected. That's one place we can be sure Bruce won't have gone. He wouldn't want to bump into my mother in the shopping precinct. Anyway, I've got the route to Richard's place. Stupid of me not to bring a map. He's not in the phone book, though, as far as I can see, so he may not even be there. I may have brought you on a complete wild goose chase.'

'Let's go,' Laura said, switching the wipers on to full speed to clear the streaming rain and sea spray that was obscuring her vision. 'Which way?'

'Straight on towards Cleveleys for a bit, and then I'll tell you where to turn.'

To Laura's surprise, Richard Churchward

was at home when they knocked on the door of his semi-detached house in Bispham, a 1930s suburb halfway between Blackpool proper and the less frenetic family resort of Cleveleys. He looked only slightly surprised when he recognised Julie, and Laura guessed that he had been half expecting her.

'That didn't take you long,' he said mildly after introductions had been made on the doorstep.

'Is he here?' Julie almost screamed, pushing sodden hair away from her face, and trying to peer around Churchward's paunchy figure into the hall behind him.

'No, no, of course not. He's not here,' Churchward exclaimed. 'You'd better come in.'

He let the two women dry off slightly in the kitchen and then directed them to the comfortable front room and brought them steaming mugs of coffee.

'I've had flu,' he said, by way of explanation for the clutter on the sofa and the mute TV showing twenty-four hour news in the corner. 'The wife's at work and the kids are at school. It was sheer chance that Bruce found me in. And you, too. I'd not have taken a call at work from either of you and they wouldn't have given out my mobile number. I really don't want to be involved in this.'

'You don't have a fixed phone?' Laura

asked, surprised.

'I'm out and about for work so much that we decided to rely on the mobiles.'

'So where's Bruce? You've obviously seen him,' Julie demanded, ignoring the coffee that Churchward had put on the low table in front of her. He shrugged.

'I don't know where he is now,' he said. 'Honestly, I don't. He turned up here yesterday with the little girl. Lovely kid by the way. I was feeling even worse then than I do now and I told him flat: we haven't got the space here to put him up, even if I'd wanted to. But he seemed to be completely manic. High as a kite. I certainly didn't want him around my kids. Anyway, I gave him the local paper and my mobile and let him get on with it. There's plenty of vacancies at this time of the year, bed sits, self-catering places, so long as you can pay a deposit up front, which he said he could. By teatime, when I woke up after having a bit of a rest upstairs, they'd gone.'

'No address?' Laura asked.

'I didn't want to know, to be honest. I knew someone would come looking. We used to be good mates in the old days, before you were married, but it was never quite the same after he had that spell in hospital. I thought he was over all that, but maybe that was only true while he kept taking the medication. Is all this because he's stopped taking the pills?'

'What pills?' Julie said faintly. Churchward really did look surprised this time, his heavy face sagging in disbelief.

'You didn't know? He didn't tell you? I mean, this happened before you got married. He was in hospital for about six months after a fight in a bar. I was there. He completely lost it. He was lucky not to end up in jail rather than the loony bin. But after that he really did seem to get better, much calmer, more even tempered. I don't think I ever saw him fly off the handle again while we lived together in that flat down Garstang Road. By the time he met you, the whole thing seemed like a bad episode that he'd got over, thankfully, but I must say I was always a bit edgy about him after that. But he seemed to be taking his medication regularly, so in the end I stopped worrying. I just assumed he would have told you all about it.'

'No,' Julie said dully. 'He never told me he'd been in a psychiatric hospital. He told me nothing about it at all.'

'But he's having bad episodes again? Flying into rages?' Churchward asked, his face full of anxiety.

'He's been beating me up,' Julie said. 'And beating up his mother.'

'He could have killed someone in that barroom brawl if I hadn't pulled him away. I was stronger than him, and got him out of the door in time. But it was a close run thing. He'd got a cut eye himself and I took him to A and E. He threw another wobbly there, attacked a nurse and after a lot of toing and froing with the police they put him on a section and kept him in the psychiatric ward. He was away six months, but his employers were very good, put him on sick leave so there was money to pay the rent. Eventually he came back to the flat and went back to work and seemed to be much better. All this was a year or so before he met you, I think. He'd moved out into that bed-sit in Squire's Gate by then and I wasn't seeing nearly so much of him. I just assumed...'

'Yes,' Julie said. 'Well, he didn't ever tell me anything about all this. Not a word.'

'Do you know what the diagnosis was?' Laura asked quietly. But Churchward shook his head.

'I've no idea. All I know is that the pills seemed to do the trick.'

'Well, judging by the way he's been behaving he didn't bother to get hold of any more of them after we moved to Bradfield. That's certainly when the trouble began,' Julie said. 'And now he's on the loose some-where with our daughter. That sounds to me like very bad news.'

CHAPTER NINE

DCI Michael Thackeray sat facing Superintendent Jack Longley in a silence so profound that he began to suspect that the senior officer had no answers to the dilemma that faced them. The file Thackeray had brought still lay still open on the super's desk but he stared into space over Thackeray's head, his normally alert expression dulled by a frown across the broad brow and a suspicion of perspiration on his bald, domed head. Eventually he seemed to shake himself back into the land of the living and met Thackeray's bleak expression with one just as grim.

'Nasty,' Longley said. 'Whichever way you look at it.'

Thackeray nodded. 'Especially for Sharif.'

'Keep him well away from this one,' Longley said. 'Send him on compassionate leave if you have to. Although that might give him too much time to poke his nose in where it's not wanted.'

'He got hold of her clothing from the family for the DNA match,' Thackeray said. 'He's as keen as anyone to get to the bottom of it.'

'He may not be when the reality of it hits him,' Longley said. 'Anyway, he can't be on the team. Not under any circumstances. He's too close to it, too emotionally involved. Send him up to see me if you have any problems getting that message across.'

'It could still be an accident, or suicide,' Thackeray said. 'There's no forensic evidence to indicate murder.'

'There's enough circumstantial evidence to launch a major inquiry,' Longley said flatly. 'You know that. A young married woman, pregnant, found dead in a river, and her husband missing from home. You know the usual formula we use when it's suicide: "no suspicious circumstances"? There's enough suspicious circumstances here for you to arrest the husband the moment you set hands on him. And if it throws a spotlight on the marriage practices of the Muslim community, that's just too bad. They'll have to live with it. I'll not have young women disposed of on my patch in the name of family honour or a husband's right to abuse his wife or anything else. And I'll not have community sensitivities interfering with a possible murder inquiry, and the community relations people will just have to live with that.'

'It's the spooks I'm more bothered about. They seem much more interested in why Imran Aziz was so desperate to get into Britain in the first place,' Thackeray said.

'They seem to think there's something going on in Milford that they should know about. Sharif himself came back from there a bit edgy about the new imam, and had the sense to fill me in.'

'I'll talk to those beggars,' Longley said. 'I don't want to get at cross-purposes with them if this turns out to be a murder investigation. I want Aziz found and questioned. And the rest of the family tackled about the marriage and the relationship between Aziz and – what's her name? – Faria? Did Amos find nothing to indicate foul play?'

'He didn't even spot that she was pregnant from the physical remains. It was the blood tests that showed it up. The family didn't seem to know she was expecting. Or at least they didn't mention it to us. I'll ask Amos to check his results again if you like. Even have another look at the body. She'll still be in the ice-box waiting for the identification. Now we've got it, the family will want her body back as soon as possible. You know how quickly Muslims require a burial.'

'That's up to the coroner where she was found, of course,' Longley said. 'If there are suspicions of foul play it won't be quick. They'll have to accept that. And I'll have to talk about liaison, but I think you can regard this as our case now we've got a name. Chances are she went into the river close to home. Where she finished up is neither here nor there.'

'I'll set the wheels in motion,' Thackeray said, with a sigh. 'First off, I'll have to talk to Mohammed Sharif.' Longley nodded gloomily, running a hand over his head as if to cement in place the few remaining hairs that straggled there.

'One way or another, I've got a feeling this is going to be a very messy one,' he said.

'I'm sure you're right,' Thackeray said.

'Keep me posted, Michael.'

'Of course, sir.'

DC 'Omar' Sharif took the news as badly as Thackeray expected he would when he summoned him to his office later that morning. He sat down abruptly as if his knees could no longer support him when the DCI told him that the body was undoubtedly his cousin Faria's, and gazed blindly out of the window behind Thackeray's desk as if an answer to the tragedy that had overwhelmed him was to be found in the grey clouds scudding ominously across the town centre from the looming grey Pennine hills beyond.

'There's no indication of how she died?'

'None so far,' Thackeray said quietly. 'It could have been an accident...'

'Or suicide, or even murder,' Sharif said angrily. 'You don't have to protect me, you know, sir.'

'Did you know she was expecting a baby?

You didn't mention it.'

Sharif glanced away, his face darkening.

'Her sister said she might be, but it wasn't definite. Her parents didn't seem to know. She hadn't told them. So it was true then?'

'According to Amos Atherton.' Thackeray hesitated for a moment.

'You can't be involved in this case, Mohammed,' he said at last. 'You're too close to it.'

Sharif gripped the arms of his chair until his knuckles stood out white against his brown skin.

'You need me,' he said. 'You need someone close to the community if you're ever to get to the bottom of this. She was my cousin. Almost as close as a sister. We grew up together, a couple of streets apart. I felt like the older brother she never had. Who could be better motivated to find out what happened to her?'

'No way,' Thackeray said. 'The closer you were to her the more you rule yourself off the team. We'll need a statement from you, for a start.'

'You mean I may be a suspect?' Sharif said, outraged.

Thackeray shook his head.

'You know I can't answer that in any sensible way,' he said. 'I don't even know if I'm looking for suspects yet. The first thing I need to do is build up a picture of what was going on in Faria's life before she died, and crucial to that is to find her husband. There's still no sign of him at the house. If we don't trace him today I'll get a warrant to break into the house. What I suggest for you is that you take some leave, be with your family at what's going to be an appalling time for them. Believe me, if Faria was murdered, I'll find out who did it. I promise you that.'

Sharif gazed out of the window again where the first splashes of icy rain were spattering against the glass, and Thackeray guessed he was far beyond the cloud-shrouded hills.

'Can I tell my uncle?' he asked at length.

'I'm sending Kevin Mower,' Thackeray said. 'You can go with him if you wish. Then take the rest of the week off, and we'll talk again after that.' And as Sharif opened his mouth to protest he said quietly: 'That's an order, Mohammed.'

Sharif struggled to his feet with some difficulty and left the DCI's office without another word. His head was swimming and he leant for a moment against the wall of the corridor before staggering to the men's room and leaning over a basin until the urge to vomit receded. Then he splashed his face with cold water and glanced at himself in the mirror as he dried himself on a paper towel. He met his own eyes just as the tears came and he retreated into a cubicle to bury his face in his hands for a long time. He had not seen his cousin's body but he had gathered from the grapevine that the unknown female pulled out of the river had been decomposed almost beyond recognition, and he knew that he would not see the beautiful young woman Faria had been ever again, even in death. Somehow that added an extra layer of horror to the turmoil of emotions he was experiencing and he knew his aunt and uncle and his younger cousins would feel the same. Their lovely, loving Faria had been reduced to a decaying chunk of meat and that was an outrage beyond bearing.

It was a long time before he could begin to compose himself and even then he replied only faintly to a voice he recognised calling his name apparently from outside. He smoothed his hair and wiped his face before unlocking the cubicle door and responding to DS Kevin Mower.

'God, you look rough,' Mower said, leaning against the door to the corridor to prevent anyone else interrupting them. 'The boss has just told me what's happened. Do you really want to come with me to break the news?'

'I must,' Sharif said. 'It's the best I can do. At least I can stay with them, make myself useful, do something for the family. The bastards here aren't going to let me anywhere near the inquiry.'

'No, I don't suppose they are, mate,' Mower said, putting a sympathetic hand on his shoulder. 'I don't suppose they are.'

Later that day, long after the final issues of the *Bradfield Gazette* had been bundled up into the company's yellow and blue vans and distributed around the town, the editor, Ted Grant, summoned Laura Ackroyd into his glass-walled office at the far end of the newsroom.

'What do you make of that?' he asked without preamble, handing her a brief print-out headed by the police logo. She read it quickly and shrugged.

'What are you thinking?' she asked. 'They're not ruling out suspicious circumstances, are they, which they usually do if they're sure it's suicide.' She glanced again at the brief details of the identification of a body that had been found in the River Maze some twenty miles downstream from Milford, where the dead woman had lived.

'Might be worth a look for this piece you're doing on wife battering,' Ted grunted. 'Have a word with your contacts, why don't you? See if they really think it's murder. See if you can get on the inside track. It'll be a news story if it is murder, of course, but it gives you a good peg to hang a discussion of this whole honour malarky with the Muslims.'

'You're jumping to conclusions, but I had thought of looking at the Asian angle anyway,' Laura said soberly. 'But you know how difficult it is to get a grip on. No one in the Asian community will talk about it openly, except a few women's groups.'

'Talk to them then,' Grant snapped. 'If they're not all raving lezzers.'

Laura smiled grimly.

'If they were, they really would stir the community leaders up. More than they do already. If there's one sin worse than adultery for Muslims, its homosexuality. I'll talk to some of the women I know, see what they've heard. But I do think you're jumping to conclusions. The poor woman may have fallen in the river by accident, for all we know.'

'And she might have jumped. But she might have been pushed,' Grant said. 'As far as I know, no one's reported her missing. We'd have heard. Use your nose, girl. That's what I pay you for. See what you can find out.' He tapped his own nose meaningfully.

'This one smells,' Grant said, in the tone his staff knew brooked no contradiction. 'From the sound of it, quite bloody literally.'

By the end of the afternoon Laura found herself being admitted to a terraced house on the very edge of Milford, ten miles or so outside Bradfield, and some distance from any of the mainly Asian areas of the two towns. The door was opened on a chain by a tall Asian woman in jeans and a loose sweatshirt, her hair long and loose, who glanced up and down the almost deserted street of identical houses before admitting Laura and closing and locking the door behind her. She ushered her into a cluttered office made gloomy by drawn blinds at the window in the main downstairs room of the house and again closed the door behind them.

'Thanks for making time, Ayesha,' Laura said. 'I know you're busy.'

Ayesha Farouk, organiser of Asian Women's Aid, a charity much condemned by some of the men of her own faith and others, but which struggled on regardless from one crisis to another, smiled faintly.

'You'd think with a long settled community like ours there'd be some change in traditional attitudes,' she said. 'Isn't that what's supposed to happen? Instead of which it's actually getting worse now. All these angry young men who've suddenly rediscovered religion are making life more difficult for women. They're like the Taliban. They'll be wanting us in burkas next.'

She sank onto a sagging sofa and Laura took the seat beside her, accepting a cup of thick black coffee from a pot which had been stewing on a corner shelf.

'Did you know a young Asian woman's

185

been found dead in the River Maze?' Laura asked. 'Faria Aziz, lived here in Milford, apparently, married but with no children. I just wondered if she was anyone you knew.'

'Faria's dead?' Ayesha asked, her eyes quickly filling with tears.

'You knew her?' Laura asked, surprised that she had struck gold so quickly.

'Yes, I knew her,' Ayesha said. 'I knew she was very unhappy, but I never thought she was so desperate that she would kill herself.'

Laura explained about the article she was writing and Ayesha looked at her uncertainly.

'I'm not sure I can break her confidence even now,' she said. 'She came here looking for help.'

'If you knew her at all, you'll have to talk to the police,' Laura said. 'I'm not sure that they've ruled out murder.'

Ayesha gasped slightly. 'Murder?' she whispered. 'God willing, not that.'

She sat for a moment in silence, gazing at the floor while Laura waited patiently until she seemed to come to a conclusion that gave her no pleasure.

'OK, it's not much,' Ayesha said. 'But I'll tell you, anyway. She only came here once, about six months ago, but it was obvious she was deeply unhappy in her marriage. She said her husband was much older than she was and though she never spelt it out I got the impression she had been persuaded into the marriage against her better judgment.'

'A forced marriage?'

'I'm not sure. Certainly arranged. She said she barely knew her husband when it happened. These things are not always easy to define. The men know how to bring pressure to bear in the name of family honour. You have no idea.'

'I'm beginning to learn,' Laura said grimly.

'Anyway, she came to ask advice about getting a divorce. I gave her the name of a sympathetic solicitor, but I've no idea whether or not she went to see him. You can be sure it would have been unpopular with her husband and the rest of the family. I never heard from her again.'

'Was she being abused?' Laura asked.

'She didn't say so,' Ayesha said. 'But it's not impossible. Her husband may have been worried about his immigration status if she divorced him. She is – was – British, of course. But that would certainly not give *him* a motive to get rid of her. Quite the reverse, in fact. He'd want her alive and married to him if he wanted to be sure of staying here.'

'You'll have to tell the police all this,' Laura said. 'What I can actually include in my article will depend very much on how their inquiry goes. Do you know where she lived or worked? I could maybe find out a bit more about her circumstances that way.'

'I'm heartbroken,' Ayesha said. 'I wish now I'd been able to do more for her.'

'I don't think you should blame yourself,' Laura said as Ayesha went to her desk and began to flick through her records, making brief notes that she gave to Laura.

'I suppose confidentiality doesn't really apply now she's dead,' she said. 'You might be able to do us some good by letting a little light into the murky areas my community doesn't want to talk about, particularly as they affect women. Let's hope so anyway.'

'And you'll talk to the police?'

'Of course,' Ayesha said. 'Someone's to blame for this and I want them punished.'

Laura drove thoughtfully back into the centre of Milford and eventually pulled up outside the address Ayesha had given her for Faria Aziz, but when she knocked on the door there was no answer. She looked up and down the street of terraced houses but apart from a couple of women deep in conversation at the very far end of the row of houses, it appeared deserted. It was probably not a good idea to approach Faria's husband, anyway, at the moment, she thought, even if she could track him down, as she turned the car round and drove back into the centre of the town. There, she quickly found the travel agent's office where Ayesha thought Faria had worked. She found a parking space and walked back to the shop and tentatively opened the door. Two assistants, one male and one female, looked up from their computers and offered her encouraging smiles as she approached the counter. Deliberately, Laura chose to take a seat opposite the plump young woman with dark hair, on the reasonable grounds that if Faria had confided in anyone here it would be a female rather than a male colleague. According to the neat notice at her work station, her name was Sandra Wright.

'I'm sorry,' Laura said with her most conciliatory smile. 'I'm not looking for a holiday booking, I'm afraid. I'm making inquiries about Faria Aziz. Someone told me she worked here.'

'Well, she does,' the woman said. 'But she's off sick at the moment. Her husband says she's got some virus. She hasn't been in for...' She glanced at her colleague. 'How long is it, Damien? A week or more?'

The young man at the other end of the counter gave the two women a harassed glance as his phone rang.

'Yeah, a week at least,' he said as he picked up the receiver and instantly retreated into a complicated conversation about tickets to Bahrain.

'Which means we're understaffed,' the young woman said. 'I hope to goodness she's back soon because I've got holiday booked for next week. And you are...?'

Laura froze, realising that Faria's colleagues had not yet been told what had happened to her and then berating herself silently for not foreseeing that this might be the case. Obviously the police had not yet traced where Faria worked. For once she was a jump ahead and very aware that this was not a comfortable place to be. She took a deep breath and introduced herself.

'I'm terribly sorry, Sandra,' she said. 'Obviously you haven't heard, and this is going to be a shock. But Faria has been found dead in the River Maze.' The woman looked at Laura, clearly stunned, her face turning a muddy shade of grey and her eyes staring.

'Oh my God,' she whispered. 'Oh my God.'

'It will be in the *Gazette* tomorrow, possibly on the local radio news tonight. It's not actually a secret.'

The woman had begun to cry quietly now, scrambling in her handbag for tissues, which she pressed to her eyes.

'Is there anywhere we can talk more privately?' Laura asked, glancing at Damien, who seemed to have taken in her message in spite of his telephone conversation, and was staring at her goggle-eyed. 'I didn't mean to shock you. I thought the police would have let you know by now.' She shrugged her shoulders helplessly.

'Come in the back,' Sandra said, wiping her eyes and getting to her feet. 'The manager's out this afternoon so we can use his office.'

'Were you good friends?' Laura asked when the woman had slumped into a chair in the cramped office behind the shop and she had handed her a plastic cup of water from the water-cooler in the corridor outside the door.

'Well, yes, I suppose so,' Sandra said. 'Office friends, you know? Nothing more than that. None of us were. I suppose I was sorry for her really. She never said a lot about her own home life but I could see she wasn't very happy. She was born here, you know, went to school here, in Bradfield, I think, though she wore traditional dress, you know? Trousers and the long loose tunic thing, and a scarf, though she didn't often have it over her head, just round her shoulders, in the office anyway. She once said her husband preferred it, the traditional dress, I mean, when I was chattering on about buying a new dress for a wedding and she looked a bit ... well ... jealous, I suppose. I can't believe this, you know.'

'I'm really sorry,' Laura said. 'I really thought you would have been told.'

'What happened? Did she kill herself? I never thought she was that unhappy. In fact...'

Sandra hesitated, and Laura wondered what was coming next.

'She told me in confidence,' Sandra said, echoing Ayesha's hesitation and then coming to the same conclusion, that it was too late now to be scrupulous in guarding Faria Aziz's secrets. 'Though I don't suppose that matters now. She told me a few weeks ago she was pregnant.'

'She must have been very happy about that,' Laura said automatically, knowing how happy she would be, and then realising that maybe Faria had not been happy at all if she had wanted a divorce from her husband.

'Well, I think so,' Sandra said. 'She seemed a bit nervous about it, actually. But maybe that's natural with a first baby. I've not been there myself... Can't afford it. My fiancé and me, we can hardly pay the mortgage some months...'

'So she was more scared than excited?'

'Yes, sort of. She never spoke much about her husband or family, you know? Not like me. I chatter on about my fiancé all the time. But she was more private. Maybe it was the different, what do you call it? Culture? A different culture. She was very nice, very good-tempered, not like me, I fly off all over the place when I'm stressed out. And she was good at the job. She dealt with all the Pak ... Asians ... who came in. Talked to them in their own languages sometimes. I can't believe she's dead.'

And Sandra burst into tears again, unrestrainedly this time, until her colleague put his head round the door wonderingly.

'There's a policeman outside wants to see the manager,' he said. 'I told him he's out. What on earth's going on?'

An hour later Laura found herself facing Michael Thackeray across his desk and was less than surprised to find him unhappy.

'I'm sorry, Michael,' she said. 'I wasn't trying to put myself a jump ahead. I just never thought there would be any mystery about where she worked. You know what I'm investigating. This looked like a perfect way into the domestic problems of Asian women.'

'And how did you discover so easily where she worked? We only managed to find out by contacting every travel agent in Milford.'

Laura could not resist a faint smile.

'I was lucky,' she said. 'I went to talk to the Asian women's advice centre in Milford and Faria had been there looking for help with a divorce. I asked Ayesha Farouk, who works there, to contact you. I hope she's done that.'

'I'll check,' Thackeray said. 'If not we'll chase her up.' He made a note on a pad on his desk and then leant back in his chair and sighed.

'It would have helped if you'd contacted me first,' he said, wondering how many more times their professional interests might clash before his bosses, if not hers, objected.

'Ted wouldn't like to think I was asking your permission to talk to people,' Laura said.

'No, I don't suppose he would. Anyway, you'd better give us a statement and tell Ted what's happened afterwards, as you've managed to get ahead of us on this one.'

'Fine,' Laura said. 'But tell me one thing. Where's Faria's husband?'

'I have no idea,' Thackeray said.

'Ah,' Laura breathed with sudden understanding. 'A very suspicious death then?'

Thackeray managed a smile then.

'You might think that, Ms Ackroyd. I couldn't possibly comment.'

CHAPTER TEN

By the middle of the next morning DC Mohammed Sharif was aware of just how isolated he had become. He had spent the previous evening with his family, most of whom had crowded into his uncle's house a couple of streets down from his own parents' home. The atmosphere was hysterical with grief and Sharif found himself comforting his young cousins, Jamilla and Saira, who had taken refuge in their bedroom upstairs to escape from the crush of adults bewailing Faria's fate in Punjabi below.

'She should never have married that man,' Jamilla had said in English in a fierce whisper when Sharif came in and closed the door carefully behind him. It was a sentiment Sharif shared but which he knew could not be spoken downstairs, where the rest of the family were giving vent to their grief and horror but without apparently ever touching on the subject of Imran Aziz and his unexplained absence from the home he had shared with Faria.

'I'm sure your father blames himself for insisting on it,' Sharif said. 'He regrets giving in to your grandfather.'

'Are they looking for Imran?' Jamilla asked. She seemed to be the calmest member of the family in the house although Sharif could see the pain in her eyes and knew that her self-control must be fragile.

'I think so,' Sharif had said, the policeman in him making him very cautious.

'Can you catch him?' Saira said. 'He must have driven her to this. She would never never have killed herself if she hadn't been driven to it. She used to be so happy here with us.' The younger girl collapsed on her bed in tears and her sister sat beside her, stroking her hair gently.

'Or did he kill her?' Jamilla asked, her own face beginning to crumple. 'Was she murdered?'

But Sharif could only shrug.

'I don't know,' he said. 'No one does. When you last spoke to her did she give you the feeling that she was depressed?'

'That she might kill herself, you mean? No, no, of course not. I told you. She said she might be pregnant and seemed – well, excited, I suppose. She would never kill herself. Not Faria. It must be Imran to blame. You'll catch him and find out, won't you? You won't let him get away with this?'

'They will find him,' Sharif said. 'Not me personally. They won't allow me to be involved, but my boss will catch him. Believe me. We'll find out what happened.

Did you tell your father about what she told you about a baby?'

'No, not yet,' Jamilla said. 'Do you think I should? It will only make him even more upset now, won't it?'

'Maybe,' Sharif said. 'I suppose there's no point. We don't even know if it's true.' He lied without a qualm, very aware that DS Mower had not mentioned this crucial piece of information to Faria's father when he had broken the news of her identification to him, and guessed that the DCI wanted to raise the issue with Faisel Sharif during the interviews that would inevitably follow. Perhaps Thackeray was right, he admitted to himself wearily. This was not a case he could be involved in.

Sharif had gone home to his own flat late, leaving a huddle of family members still distraught in his uncle's small living room, and found he could sleep only fitfully for the rest of the night. Rising early, and ignoring Thackeray's instruction to take some time off, he arrived in the CID office before eight-thirty and found it almost deserted. He tried to settle at his desk, dealing with some of the files he had abandoned in despair the previous day, but he could not concentrate and when some of his colleagues began to drift into the room, one or two giving him curious glances, he realised that there had been some sort of meeting from which he had been excluded. Getting to his feet he found himself face to face with DS Kevin Mower.

'What's going on?' he asked thickly.

'An early start,' Mower said. 'They've launched a major inquiry into your cousin's death, on the assumption it's probably murder. We've just had the first briefing. The DCI heard you were in and wants to see you straight away. He'll explain what's going on.'

Sharif found his fists clenched into balls at his side and he made a conscious effort to breathe normally and relax.

'Right,' he said. 'Thanks Sarge.' He did not hurry to the DCI's office, guessing he would get short shrift for disobeying an order to stay away, not relishing the dressing down that would provoke, and even more afraid of what Thackeray might tell him about his cousin's death. Something must have caused this morning's upgrade of the inquiry, and he knew that the grounds for it could only be bad news for him and his family.

Thackeray was on the phone when DC Sharif opened the door of his office but he gestured for him to come in and sit as he finished his call abruptly and slammed the receiver down.

'I told you to take time off,' he said, his tone harsh. 'That was for your own good, Mohammed. You look like death warmed up.'

'Sir,' Sharif mumbled, knowing from his own inspection of the dark circles beneath his eyes in his shaving mirror early that morning that the DCI's comment was more than justified.

'So why are you here?' Thackeray demanded, slightly more gently.

'I needed to know what was going on,' Sharif said. 'My family need to know what's going on.'

'They'll be informed,' Thackeray said. 'I've appointed a family liaison officer to keep them informed. You know how these things work and you know you can't be involved in any way.'

'You've upgraded the inquiry...' Sharif muttered. 'Is there a reason?'

'Two reasons, as it happens,' Thackeray said sharply. 'Firstly additional forensic information, which came in late yesterday. And secondly the sudden interest the security services have taken in Imran Aziz. Since you saw our friend McKinnon from Manchester the other day they say they have intelligence from Pakistan that makes them wonder why he was so desperate to get a visa to come to this country that he divorced one wife and married another.'

'You mean...'

'I don't know what they mean, Mohammed. Apparently he hadn't crossed their radar until now. I think what you told Mc-

Kinnon about Aziz and the new imam in Milford was genuinely news to them, but since then they've obviously been talking to their friends in Islamabad. You know how it is. Any hint of suspicion is enough.'

'I think the Muslim community's got that message, loud and clear,' Sharif said, his voice bitter. 'Break the door down, why don't you? Smash the place up. Shoot us by accident. We're all suspects now. Even me, I suppose.'

Thackeray looked at the younger man wearily.

'I'm sorry it seems that way,' he said. 'Believe me.'

'So what's this new forensic evidence?' Sharif asked.

'The toxicology report. They've found traces of narcotics,' Thackeray said. 'Have you any reason to believe that your cousin might have been taking drugs – legally or illegally?'

'No, of course not,' Sharif said. 'Are you saying she was an addict? I can't believe that for a moment. Absolutely not.'

'I've asked Amos Atherton to take another look at the body, in case there's anything he missed. Puncture marks for instance, in the unlikely event they might still be visible after she'd been in the water so long. Though Amos isn't given to careless mistakes, I have to say. But whatever the cause, it is possible that your cousin was in a disoriented state when she went into the river, whether it was by accident or design. It offers us another line of inquiry. Puts the whole thing in a more sinister light.'

'Wonderful,' Sharif said, his already haggard face taking on a slight sneer. 'I don't think I'll pass that suggestion on to my aunt and uncle.'

'I don't want you telling your uncle, or anyone else, anything you pick up here about this investigation,' Thackeray said sharply. 'Which is why I want you on leave until I tell you you can come back. I mean that, Mohammed. It's not in your interests to be here at all. Go home and see what you can do to help your family in what must be a terrible situation.'

'So do I have a career left when this is over, sir?' Sharif asked, getting to his feet slowly.

'Of course you do,' Thackeray said. 'This is unpleasant for you, but it will pass. You did the right thing bringing your initial suspicions to my attention. No one can fault you as a police officer in any way. But now you must take my advice. Go home, stay away, probably until this is resolved. That way your integrity remains intact. Believe me, it's for your own good. If it goes on too long I'll see if I can get you a temporary transfer to another division. But in the meantime, take a holiday.'

'Right, sir,' Sharif said, hoping Thackeray could not see how reluctantly the words were forced from him. 'I'm sure you're right.'

'I'm sorry,' Thackeray said as DC Sharif turned away. 'I really am.'

As soon as he was sure that DC Mohammed Sharif had obeyed his instructions and left police headquarters, DCI Michael Thackeray went upstairs and knocked on the door of Superintendent Jack Longley's office. As he expected, he found the super at his conference table with Doug McKinnon of the anti-terrorism unit in Manchester, flanked by two officers he did not know and Chief Inspector Bradley Smith, a young high flyer who had recently taken charge of the uniformed wing of the force in Bradfield. Introductions to McKinnon's colleagues made, Thackeray slipped into the vacant chair next to Longley as all eyes swivelled in his direction.

'I still have no absolutely firm evidence that Faria Aziz was murdered,' he said. 'But given the latest information, that she had either taken or been given some sort of narcotic before she went into the river and drowned – we're waiting for an identification on the drug – it looks increasingly likely. On top of that we have evidence that she was considering a divorce, even though she was pregnant. Murder's certainly a possibility we can no longer ignore, especially as the husband's nowhere to be found.'

'Any news on his whereabouts?' McKinnon asked.

'Nothing,' Thackeray said. 'No sightings. We've checked out his car and it's still parked in the street close to the house with a flat tyre. So wherever he's gone he's either gone by public transport or in someone else's vehicle.'

'Or he's dead,' Bradley Smith offered. 'Isn't that a classic scenario for a domestic? Murder followed by suicide? Maybe he's in the river too, and we simply haven't found his body yet. Isn't that what you're looking for?' He addressed his final question to McKinnon. 'A reason to search the house? Surely we're concerned for the man's well-being, aren't we? That's more than enough reason to go in without a lot of fuss. We don't need to mobilise armed officers and the full paraphernalia of a terror raid, just force the door and have a look round inside, in the interests of Imran Aziz's safety. For all we know, he may be lying dead or injured in there. It's much less upsetting for the neighbours if we do it softly softly. All the neighbours.' He glanced at Longley, who was nodding his head slowly, considering what Smith had said.

'There's no reason why you can't go in

with my officers,' he said to McKinnon.

'I need a full forensic search,' McKinnon said. 'The works.'

'It's quite possible we'll need one as well, dependent on what we find,' Longley said.

'Look, I know why you may want to pussyfoot about,' McKinnon said. 'Community relations and all that. But I've got inquiries launched in Pakistan about this man and his unusual determination to get into this country. And you've had one of your own officers raising doubts about the mosque in Milford. Where is he, by the way? What's his name? Sharif?'

Thackeray glanced at Longley, who nodded almost imperceptibly.

'I've sent him home,' the DCI said. 'The dead woman is his cousin and I can't have him involved in the investigation.'

'Right,' McKinnon said. 'Keep tabs on him, though. I may want to talk to him again.'

Thackeray nodded, trying to conceal a sudden surge of anger that he knew was irrational, but McKinnon neither noticed nor, Thackeray was sure, would have cared much if he had. He was single-minded in his pursuit of what he wanted in a way Thackeray doubted he would ever be, and that, he thought with a slight sense of shock, was his weakness as a policeman and why he would never go further. He worried too much about what he was doing and it's effect on the innocent. McKinnon, he realised with a start, was pressing on regardless, as he always would, no matter who got trampled underfoot.

'But as for Aziz's house, you know we can't take any chances in the current circumstances. You may be right. It may simply be a tragic domestic incident. But we have to be sure. We need to go in, straight away, no messing about. I want documents, computers, phone records, the lot. And a full forensic examination of the premises. Whether or not you use armed officers is up to you, how many uniforms you throw at it is your decision, but there's no way all that is going to happen without any of the neighbours noticing, is there? Let's be realistic. If there's a reaction, you'll have to live with it. Is it a heavily Muslim street?'

'Apparently not,' Thackeray said. 'All we'll be doing is confirming the white neighbours' worst suspicions.'

Longley nodded slowly.

'Right,' he said, glancing at Thackeray and at Bradley Smith for confirmation. 'Go ahead with a raid. Keep me fully informed, please. As far as we're concerned, this is probably a murder inquiry and CID will proceed on that basis until we hear that there is solid evidence of something worse. Thank you, gentlemen.'

By one o'clock that afternoon the news-room at the *Bradfield Gazette* was in a ferment and Laura Ackroyd felt besieged at her desk. She had spun her chair away from her computer screen the better to confront Ted Grant and the crime reporter Bob Baker, who were standing close to her desk, almost breathing down her neck.

'You must have got some inkling of this, surely,' Grant said, his face flushed with excitement. 'We were bloody lucky to hear anything at all about it in time for the final edition. It was only because one of the neighbours had the sense to call Bob that we knew anything was going down. The bloody Press Office didn't breathe a word. Said they were going to issue something later in the day when the operation was complete.' Grant, purple-faced, spluttered with such outrage that Laura feared for his health.

'But you got there in time?' Laura asked Baker.

'Oh yes, we've got some good pics of them breaking the door down, and forensic officers going in. We got damn all out of the inspector who seemed to be in charge, but judging by the stuff they were taking out this is a whole lot more than a murder inquiry. It looked to me as if special branch was involved, or whatever they call them-selves these days. It looked like a terror raid,

206

if a bit low key. And it was certainly annoying some of the bearded weirdies who came cruising down from the mosque and hung about outside. They didn't seem like happy bunnies, I can tell you.'

'So, what's your take on it, Laura?' Grant asked. 'Have you heard anything on the grapevine? You've been looking into this on your own account, the death of this man Aziz's wife, haven't you? Is it just a case of domestic problems gone too far? A domestic? Or is there more to it? You must have picked something up from your boyfriend, surely? Don't tell me you don't discuss what you're working on with him, because I don't believe you.'

'Well, I was going to tell you where I'd got on that when I'd finished this piece for tomorrow,' Laura said. 'But you know I was coming at it from a completely different angle, from the possibility she'd been forced into a marriage she didn't want and had been desperate afterwards, desperate enough maybe to kill herself. That possibility certainly stands up. I discovered she wanted a divorce from Imran Aziz. You can read my notes if you like. But I got no hint of any terror connection, if that's what you think's been going on in Milford. Not a breath of that. And as it happens, I did have to talk to Michael Thackeray about it because I actually got a step ahead of the police at one

207

stage yesterday. I discovered where Faria Aziz worked before he did.' She grinned slightly at the surprise that neither Grant nor Baker could hide.

'It was pure chance,' she said. 'I had to tell Michael, obviously. But he gave no hint that he thought Faria's death was any more of a mystery than we already supposed. He gave me the impression that he was beginning to think she might possibly have been murdered, rather than killing herself, but he didn't elaborate. I didn't ask him, either. We can't get into each other's pockets as far as work is concerned. You know that. Nothing's changed.'

'Right, well, Bob's doing a front page splash on the raid, so liaise with him, will you, as you've picked up some of the background,' said Ted, taking on the demeanour of a Second World War field-marshal rallying his troops. 'I'll get on to the police press office and squeeze some sort of comment out of them. They'll be a bit more co-operative if they know we're going ahead with a story anyway. I can't imagine why they think they can cover something like this up. Bloody stupid, if you ask me. You've got thirty minutes max to get this onto the front page, not a second more. Right?'

'Right,' Baker said, as Laura nodded her acquiescence. Grant, in full London tabloid mode, was unstoppable.

DCI Michael Thackeray decided that it was in everyone's interests for him personally to interview Faria Aziz's family at this stage of the investigation. When the anti-terrorist officers had concluded whatever they eventually concluded from their forensic examination of Imran Aziz's home, he guessed they would turn their attention to the rest of Faria's relatives, but, in the meantime, he still had a specific inquiry to conduct into her death, and he had no intention of waiting for McKinnon's permission to pursue it. He took DS Kevin Mower with him because the sergeant had made some effort when he transferred from London to Bradfield to learn Punjabi, the most common language used by the town's Asian community. They drove slowly through the narrow streets around Aysgarth Lane until they found the right address amongst the long terraced rows of stone houses with only the tiniest strip of garden between the front door and the street.

Faisel Sharif opened the door to the two officers himself. He was a tall man, dressed in a dark-coloured western suit, his neatly bearded, aquiline face haggard and his eyes red-rimmed. He nodded with little apparent interest at the officers' identification and held open the door to allow them to follow him into the cramped living room, where the curtains were drawn and his wife was sitting alone, slumped in an armchair, evidently finding it difficult to move. She glanced at the two visitors with heavy eyes, pulling her scarf around her to shield her grief-stricken face, then struggled to her feet and left the room. Sharif shrugged slightly and made no comment.

'Tell me, Chief Inspector, when I will be able to bury my daughter?' he asked.

'I'm sorry, Mr Sharif,' Thackeray said. 'I can't tell you that. There are still tests being conducted on her body to try to determine exactly how she died. The coroner will release the body as soon as he can but I have no idea when that will be. We're not yet able to treat this definitely as a murder inquiry, but I have to tell you that we are increasingly sure that is what we are dealing with. I'm very sorry.'

Faisel Sharif muttered something in Punjabi and Thackeray glanced at Mower for a translation but the sergeant shook his head slightly, not wanting to antagonise Sharif, who had merely bewailed the God-lessness of his adopted country. Thackeray pressed on.

'At this stage, I hoped you might be able to help me with some background detail about Faria and her husband Imran Aziz. Your nephew has explained to me the circum-stances of your daughter's marriage to Aziz,'

210

Thackeray said carefully. 'But I would like to be reassured that she was not persuaded to marry against her will. You know that is illegal in this country, and she could have had the marriage annulled under British law.'

Sharif's face flushed.

'She agreed to the marriage,' he said thickly. 'She was a willing party to it.'

'Are you quite sure about that?' Thackeray persisted.

'I am quite sure.'

'But the marriage did not turn out to be a very happy one, I'm told.'

'Did Mohammed tell you that also?' Sharif shot back. 'That boy knows nothing about family loyalty and honour. He is a disgrace.'

'Was the marriage happy, Mr Sharif?' Thackeray insisted.

'I don't know, Faria told me nothing about her marriage,' her father said. 'Perhaps she spoke to her mother or her sisters. Not to me.'

'Then I will have to speak to your wife and daughters in due course,' Thackeray said. 'If they were aware that she was depressed or seriously unhappy that may have a bearing on her death.'

Sharif took a deep breath and did not answer. His outrage at this invasion of his family space and the inevitable trampling over his traditions was evident in every inch of his rigid posture. 'You must do what you have to do, Chief Inspector,' he said at length. 'I cannot prevent you. But my daughter appeared quite normal the last time I saw her.'

'So you had no idea she might be unhappy with her husband? No idea that she had sought some advice about a divorce?'

'No,' Sharif said, outrage in every inch of him. 'Certainly not.'

'Did you know she was pregnant? The post-mortem results made that clear.'

'No, I didn't know that either. She did not tell me or my wife before she died. My daughter Jamilla told me last night that Faria had said she might be,' Sharif could not conceal the anguish that answer gave him and Thackeray paused before resuming his questions.

'Isn't it important for you to know what happened to your daughter?' Thackeray asked more quietly. 'As we're beginning to believe that this may be a case of murder, and your son-in-law is inexplicably absent from home, we have to suspect that he may be implicated in Faria's death. Do you have any idea where Imran Aziz may be?'

'I had very little contact with Imran after he and my daughter moved to Milford,' Sharif said. 'He kept his distance.'

'But he was what? A nephew of yours? Or a cousin? Did you know him well in Pakistan before the marriage?'

'No, not well,' Sharif said. 'He worked in Lahore and was seldom in my village when we visited my parents. His father, my great-uncle, I knew, but not Imran.'

'So Faria did not know him well either, when she married?'

'There were good family reasons for the marriage,' Sharif said sharply. 'Faria knew that and accepted it. She was not forced.'

'I have to accept your word on that, as we can't ask her,' Thackeray said dryly. 'But tell me more about Imran. If he was working in Lahore, what was he doing, and why did he suddenly decide that he wished to come to this country? Was it a sudden decision?'

'He was in business in Lahore, import and export. But the company ran into difficulties. I think he felt that a new start in a new country would be advantageous. He had been quite prosperous for a time, but things began to go wrong. I know no details about this. There were other reasons for the marriage within the family. It had been arranged many years ago. It was not unexpected. It had been planned.'

'While Faria was a child?' Thackeray asked. Kevin Mower drew a sharp breath, knowing how close to the edge the interview was straying.

'You do not understand our culture,' Sharif said with angry contempt. 'You know nothing.'

'I do find it difficult to understand some aspects of your culture, Mr Sharif,' Thackeray said. 'And I'm sorry if that upsets you, but I do know that you regard murder as a crime just as I do, and I hope that as her father you may be able to help me understand why Faria has been killed, if indeed she has been killed. If the motive has anything to do with aspects of your culture that I don't understand, then I would expect you to help me with those. All this is hypothetical, of course, but I think you should understand that if I were to suspect that you didn't want her killer identified, I would find that very difficult indeed to comprehend. In fact, it might lead me to conclude that you had some involvement in her death.'

Sharif's face flushed at that and he sat down as if his legs would no longer hold him up.

'Faria was the light of my life,' he said. 'She was my first born, my beautiful eldest daughter who, I hoped, God willing, would give me grandchildren and be a blessing in my old age.'

Thackeray sighed.

'I won't trouble you any more now, Mr Sharif,' he said. 'I hope to know very soon how your daughter died and whether we will be pursuing anyone else in relation to her death. But you do need to know that we have entered Imran Aziz's house this morning in the interests of his safety. He was not there.'

'Find him, Chief Inspector,' Sharif said thickly. 'If he is responsible for my daughter's death, find him, and keep him away from me because if I find him first I might kill him.'

'Whew,' DS Kevin Mower whistled as the two officers returned slowly to their car. 'You were quite hard on him, I thought.'

'You know as well as I do where concepts of family honour can lead,' Thackeray said. 'If I have evidence there's anything remotely like that involved, I'll be hard on her father and her mother and sisters as well, if need be. That's why DC Sharif needs to be kept well away from this case. It could get very unpleasant.'

'You don't think the spooks are on the right track, then?'

'I've no idea,' Thackeray said. 'My concern is Faria Aziz and why she and her unborn child ended up in the river. That's quite enough to be going on with.'

Laura Ackroyd and Bob Baker met their deadline and the details of the police search of Imran Aziz's house in Milford appeared on the front page of the *Gazette* that afternoon. Baker had been left fuming at the lack of cooperation he felt he had got from the press office at County Police HQ, and the story

215

appeared without any explanation from police sources as to why Aziz's neighbours had seen officers removing large quantities of material from the small terraced house or why officers in forensic protective suits then spent many hours inside the premises.

Laura was not surprised when Thackeray arrived home that evening to find herself the object of a somewhat frosty gaze as he took his coat off, kissed her cheek perfunctorily, and waved a copy of the *Gazette*, with her name prominently displayed on the front page.

'How did you get involved in Bob Baker's wilder speculations?' he asked.

'Is it speculation?' Laura said, stirring her risotto with more determination than it warranted. 'Do you want a salad with this?'

'Diversionary tactics won't work, madam,' Thackeray said with a faint smile. 'Your piece was not very welcome at a time when we still don't know for sure whether or not this young woman committed suicide.'

'So why go into the house with all guns blazing?' Laura asked. 'Someone somewhere obviously suspects that something's been going on there. Are they looking for terrorists, or what? If you don't tell the public what's happening there'll be all sorts of rumours flying around, and that could be dangerous.'

'You know I can't tell you anything about

it,' Thackeray said, turning away to get himself a drink of tonic water from the fridge. 'Do you want a drink?'

'V and T,' Laura said. She turned the gas down under her pan and followed Thackeray into the living room, where he was reading, obviously not for the first time, the results of her day's work, splashed under a headline, *Milford Terror Raid Shock*, that she had to admit was not entirely supported by the facts she and Bob Baker had been able to glean from the eyewitnesses who had seen the police go in.

'You know I don't write the headlines,' she said, by way of a peace offering. 'But you can't hide this sort of thing, especially when people are so jumpy. Someone's going to let us know what's going on. They ring in with all sorts of stuff. You know that.'

'Evidently,' Thackeray said, putting an arm round her and pulling her onto the sofa beside him, his face serious. 'You know, there are any number of reasons why people might think we're not a very compatible couple...' Laura made to protest, but he put a finger on her lips. 'Any number,' he said. 'And don't think I haven't rehearsed them all many times. But the only serious one, I think, is this.' And he tapped the front page. 'You know you really must be careful not to give the impression that you're privy to information that you shouldn't have. For both our sakes.'

'I know, I know,' Laura said. 'But it's difficult when Ted Grant seems to imagine that we spend every night going over your cases in fine detail before we go to sleep.'

'Just tell him we've got much better things to do before we go to sleep,' Thackeray said, pulling her towards him and kissing her in a way that drove any thoughts of incompatibility out of both their heads.

'The risotto will burn,' she murmured, making a not very convincing attempt to struggle free from his embrace.

'Sod the risotto,' he said. 'We can always get a pizza – if we're hungry.'

CHAPTER ELEVEN

Mohammed Sharif was at a loose end. He had attempted to stay in bed late, as going to work now seemed a prospect that was receding into the distant future, but his whirling mind soon put paid to that idea and he gave up the unequal battle with his tangled sheets and rolled out of bed. To his annoyance, Louise had refused to stay the night, pleading an early start the next day, though he had been left with the distinct impression that she was worried, and not necessarily totally sympathetic, about his new workless state.

He padded around his flat in his underwear for a while, picking at toast and fuelling his anguish with coffee, before flinging on his clothes and going out to his car. He sat for a moment drumming his fingers on the steering wheel before starting up and taking the valley road out of town towards Milford. It did not take a brilliant detective to work out that it was in the small mill town, now little more than a minor shopping centre and home to the massive concrete headquarters of one of Yorkshire's many building societies, that the key to his cousin's death lay. And he knew with absolute certainty that his colleagues' raid on Imran Aziz's house the previous day, which he had read about avidly in the Gazette, would have sparked some sort of reaction, for good or ill – and he suspected ill – in the local Asian community. People were hyper-sensitive about police bashing down front doors these days, deeply sceptical that the authorities had any more idea than the average man on the street where to target their attentions with any real justification. Sharif had slightly more faith in the intelligence that the security services worked on than that, but he had serious doubts about the conclusions that seemed to have been reached in this case, and a deep sense of frustration that he had been shut out of the loop so comprehensively.

Thinking back to the limited contact he had had with his cousin's husband, he recalled a quiet man, evidently unsure of his place in his new family and his new country, moderate enough in his views, as far as Sharif had had time to explore them, and regular but not over-enthusiastic in his observance of his religious duties. Sharif had found little difficulty in explaining to Imran, a man who had spent most of his adult life in the bustling city of Lahore, his own decision to lead a secular and essentially westernised life. Sharif had not felt uncomfortable with Imran Aziz, and he seriously doubted that he was a fanatic of any sort, although to his eyes this was exactly what the *Gazette* was suggesting in its not very subtle way.

He drove the short distance to Milford and parked discreetly close to his cousin's home and then walked cautiously down the modest street, only to find her house still cordoned off with blue and white police tape and forensic officers in their white plastic coveralls still visible at the windows. He walked past on the other side of the road but could glean nothing from his sidelong glances in their direction. He knew that he should not have come, that if anyone recognised him, DCI Thackeray would be justifiably furious. But he was driven by grief and rage at what had happened to Faria and felt that justification enough. He soon became aware of being watched, not by his colleagues but by several of Faria's neighbours in houses further along the street. And, as he passed a group of youths halfway back towards the main road, he picked up muttered abuse as he passed by. He gritted his teeth, not daring to respond in case he sparked a violent incident that would instantly get back to the DCI in Bradfield. There was no doubt that Milford was uneasy with the notoriety its 'terrorism raid' had brought, and it might take only the smallest spark to provoke trouble on the streets.

At the end of the road, he turned again towards the mosque. It was Friday and a crowd of men was emerging from the arched doorway of the old chapel. Most of them were in traditional dress and were joined by a handful of women, who had their faces fully veiled. It was, Sharif thought, a much more traditional looking crowd than he was used to in Bradfield, where most of the men, at least, wore western clothes, and the women a simple long scarf round hair and shoulders. He mingled with the crowd, attracting a few curious glances, seeking out the imam. Failing to spot him, he took off his shoes and entered the mosque, where he located his quarry deep in conversation with a young man whose beard was almost as luxuriant as the imam's own. Becoming aware of his presence the two men broke off their conversation and the younger man turned away and left the building while Abdel Abdullah himself waited for Sharif to approach.

'I am glad you came back,' he said in Punjabi. 'I was going to telephone you. I heard about your cousin's body being discovered. I was very sorry to hear how your search for her had ended. Please convey my condolences to your family.'

'Thank you,' Sharif said, aware that the imam was looking at him with unusual intensity.

'You didn't tell me that you were connected with the police yourself,' he said. 'A detective, I understand.' Sharif suddenly found the atmosphere in the old building inexplicably chilly and shivered.

'There was no need,' he said. 'My inquiries were personal. Who told you I was a police officer?'

'Your colleagues were here asking questions this morning about Imran Aziz. One of them told me the dead woman was related to a police detective in Bradfield. I realised then that I had already met this cousin.'

'I was making a personal inquiry,' Sharif repeated. 'Now it's become official, now we know she's dead. But I'm not part of the inquiry into her death, anyway. My superiors say I'm too close to it to be involved.'

'And they will not want an Asian on their inquiry, will they? We are all suspect now,' Abdullah suggested, his voice hardening.

'I have no reason to suspect that Imran Aziz was involved in anything to do with terrorism,' Sharif said carefully. 'Have you?'

'None at all, but as far as I can see it isn't necessary for there to be any evidence to be marked down as suspect in this country. To be Muslim is enough.'

Sharif hesitated, knowing that to agree with this assessment threw his whole career into doubt but tempted even so to nod.

'I don't think that's entirely true,' he

prevaricated. 'You can understand why the authorities feel justified in what they do. There is a real threat from a minority. I know that as well as anyone and I hope you do too, in your position. It's hard to feel that you have to prove your innocence all the time, every day, with no end in sight. But until these young idiots stop their plotting, there will be no end to it. Nothing that goes on abroad can justify bombing innocent people going about their daily lives. There is nothing in the holy Qu'ran to justify that.'

'I was surprised when I came here to discover how angry the young men are,' Abdullah said. 'Much more angry, I think, some of them, than most young men at home. But I never heard Imran Aziz discuss politics. He came to pray only rarely in my time here and did not stay to talk afterwards. He seemed to me to be a quiet man, not much given to anger or disputation.'

'That was my own impression of him,' Sharif said. 'The only question that seems to have been raised by his conduct is the fact that he divorced his first wife and married my cousin quite suddenly, possibly as a way to gain access to this country.'

'Like many, he wanted to share in the wealth of the west,' the imam said dryly. 'But he did not seem to be doing well here. He wasn't able to get a job that suited his qualifications, I was told.'

'That's true,' Sharif said. 'He had been a successful businessman in Lahore. Here he was working in a factory. It doesn't seem to have been a successful move. Which is no doubt why there is suspicion that he had an ulterior motive for his divorce and remarriage.'

'Perhaps it had more to do with the fact that his wife in Lahore had given him no children,' Abdullah said. 'I was told that also. If you look only for the worst interpretation you may be led astray.'

'Perhaps,' Sharif said. 'But now he's vanished and his new wife is dead. There is more than one possible interpretation and they must all be explored. God willing, it's not the worst one that turns out to be true. Will you contact me if you hear anything of interest?'

To Sharif's surprise, the imam nodded his assent.

'I will,' he said. 'It is best for all of us if Imran Aziz is found quickly. God willing, he will be found innocent of any crime.'

'God willing,' Sharif said automatically, without any hope that the imam's prayer would bear fruit. Faria's ghost told him otherwise.

As he walked back to his car he became aware of a presence behind him and, half turning, he found himself face to face with the bearded young man who had been talking to the imam when he had gone into the mosque.

'I hear you are a policeman, brother,' the man said.

'That's right,' Sharif said. 'But not on duty.'

'When is a policeman not on duty?' his companion asked, falling into step beside him. Sharif shrugged, knowing how difficult that question was to answer in the current climate. He knew that all officers were used to the sudden discomfort of almost everyone when they admitted to their profession and knew that for him it was worse, straddling, as he did, two communities whose mutual suspicion seemed to grow worse by the day.

'My cousin, Faria Aziz, is dead, possibly murdered,' he said. 'This is a family matter, not for me a police matter. If it is any of your concern.'

'The welfare of all Muslims is our concern at the mosque,' the young man said.

'So you will be concerned to discover whether or not Imran Aziz has harmed his wife,' Sharif said angrily.

'It does not seem that is the first priority of those who have knocked down his front door and are searching his house. They have other suspicions clearly.'

'And are they justified?' Sharif snapped back.

The young man shrugged and Sharif

turned on him angrily.

'Do you mean you don't know or you don't care?' he asked. 'Is it justified to look for a man who may have harmed his wife but not for one who may be planning mass murder? Just what are you complaining of here?'

'Abdel Abdullah, our imam, was not happy that you failed to tell him you were a policeman. He felt you were sent to spy on him.'

Sharif groaned quietly.

'He knows why I came,' he said. 'My cousin is dead.'

'You are in an impossible position here, brother,' the young man said. 'You can only be seen as a spy. You are no longer one of our community. You have become one of them.'

They had reached Sharif's car and he flicked open the doors.

'Do you think your community would be safe without the police?' he said bitterly. 'Do you think the BNP and the rest would not be harassing you day and night if it wasn't for us? Do you think you and your wives and children could go about their lives safely without us? Think about it. Think about what some of our so-called brothers did in London, and Madrid and New York, and then ask yourself how peacefully you are able to live your life and thank Allah for the police who make it possible. Stop talking like a fool, brother, and thank Allah that I exist.'

And Sharif got into his car and drove away quickly, his heart thumping at the unfairness of it all.

Laura Ackroyd picked up her phone and felt slightly guilty as she recognised Julie Holden's voice. She had been distracted from Julie's plight by the *Gazette*'s intense interest in Faria Aziz's death and her husband's disappearance, and she had as yet done nothing to follow up her inquiries after their visit to Blackpool, except give Thackeray a brief account of what they had uncovered.

'Why don't we meet at lunchtime and I'll see what I can find out for you,' she said.

'I've already talked to the hospital in Blackpool,' Julie said. 'I managed to get through to the psychiatric consultant who treated him. They didn't want to put me through but in the end when I said I was his wife and shouted and screamed and said I was afraid for my life, they connected me. He didn't want to talk to me either, but in the end he confirmed more or less what Richard told us. He'd been an in-patient there for several months before I met him, but his condition had been brought under control with drugs and as far as they were concerned he should have been fine so long as he continued to take his medication.'

'Which obviously he hasn't been doing,' Laura said.

'I never knew he was on medication, so I've no idea when he stopped.' Julie's voice teetered on the edge of hysteria and there was a long silence before she seemed to calm down enough to continue. 'The doctor said that if he was experiencing these violent outbursts he must have stopped taking it. I spoke to his former boss in Blackpool as well. And he said that after his spell in hospital Bruce seemed OK, and they were all very pleased that he settled down again and eventually got married. There was no particular reason on their side why he should have left the company. He wasn't sacked or anything. The job in Bradfield, as they understood it, was a promotion. But that was a discrepancy, because Bruce persuaded me to move to Bradfield by telling me that he wanted to be nearer his mother once she was on her own. He was very insistent on that and I didn't mind too much. My parents were fine where they were. And my sister was in Blackpool so they didn't need me to be close by. It seemed to make perfect sense at the time.'

'But he's probably not had any treatment since you moved?'

'I don't think so,' Julie said. 'Even his mother seemed to know nothing about this illness. He was obviously very good at hiding his tracks. We had no idea. Nor apparently had our doctor in Bradfield. I couldn't even remember the last time Bruce consulted him, and of course he went on about patient confidentiality and all that as well, but when I asked him straight if he'd treated Bruce for any mental illness, he just said no. So unless he's been to some other doctor privately, he's been off his pills for a long time. And getting more erratic for a long time, I realise now. It all makes sense. And to think I was blaming myself for the marriage going wrong.'

'Let's meet at lunchtime anyway and try to work out a way to track him down,' Laura said. 'Maybe you need a private detective in Blackpool, if that's where he's holed up. There must be some way of tracing him.' She suggested a time and a place and when she had finished her morning's work she made her way across town to a wine bar in the bowels of the old gothic wool exchange, where she found Julie Holden already waiting for her at a table in a shadowy corner, a half-finished glass of wine in front of her. She glanced up at Laura with an expression of fear in her eyes. She looked pale and haggard and her hand trembled slightly as she toyed with her glass.

'This isn't getting any better, is it?' she said. 'We're still in the same dead end we were in when we came back from Blackpool.'

'I've been thinking about this, Julie,' Laura said when she had got herself a glass of wine and ordered some sandwiches for the two of them. 'I think the best thing to do is to fill the police in on what we've discovered. They said they'd let the Lancashire police know Bruce might have gone over there, but now we're sure he's in Blackpool we should let them know that too. It would be cheaper to let the police track him down than to do it through a detective agency. You have to give them a chance.'

'I suppose so,' Julie said dully.

'Did your mother-in-law make a complaint?'

'Yes, I think the woman we went to see came out to interview her.'

'Janet Richardson? Right, well let's see if we can go and have a chat with her as well.' Laura pulled out her mobile and evidently got a positive response.

'Come on,' she said cheerfully as a waitress brought their sandwiches. 'You don't look as if you've eaten anything for a month. Eat up, and then we can go to see Janet straight away. She's in her office and is expecting us.'

The detective sergeant, when she came to meet her two visitors in a bland interview room at police headquarters, looked tired as well and Laura began to wonder how many people were being slowly ground down by the cycle of violence that seemed to afflict so many families. There were dark circles under the sergeant's eyes, and Laura got the feeling she was only half listening as Julie explained how her husband had deceived her about his previous history and had begun to behave more and more erratically as time had gone by.

'We know he's gone back to Blackpool,' she said. 'Or that area, anyway. There's lots of accommodation there in the winter, when there are no visitors. It's an ideal place for him to hide. Can you get the police over there to find him? Please?'

'I'll pass on the details,' Janet said. 'A man with a small girl in tow should be more noticeable that a man on his own. But I can't guarantee they'll give it a high priority. It'll be a bit like looking for the proverbial needle.'

'He's not safe to be in charge of Anna,' Julie said, her voice shrill, but Janet shrugged.

'You may think that but he's her father and you say he's never harmed her. You'll have to settle the custody dispute in court if you can't come to an agreement yourselves. But so far all the violence has been aimed at you, not Anna. We can't treat it as an abduction and we have no evidence Anna's in danger. All we can do is look for him in connection with your complaint of assault. Not taking your medication if you're sick

232

isn't a crime, you know.'

Laura had not intervened in the conversation until then but she suddenly felt angry herself at the DS's attitude.

'Two complaints of assault,' she said. 'You're forgetting his mother. Surely that's enough for you to regard him as dangerously violent and arrest him. Or is that just 'domestic' too and not worth the effort? I thought the police were treating this sort of thing more seriously now. I thought that was your job.'

Janet flushed slightly.

'It is and we do,' she said quietly. 'We treat it very seriously. But that doesn't mean there are enough resources to make our efforts effective if we can't easily get our hands on a perpetrator. I'll talk to my opposite number in Blackpool and see what I can do, I promise. But I'm trying to be realistic here. I don't want to raise your hopes when it seems such a long shot that we'll track him down.'

And with that they had to be satisfied. But when Thackeray came home that evening Laura did not hesitate to express her own frustration with Julie's situation.

'Janet Richardson really didn't seem to be taking it very seriously at all,' she complained after they had eaten.

'Janet Richardson handles dozens of these cases every week,' Thackeray said sharply. 'It's her job and she's very good at it. Her top priority is always to prevent more violence, by arresting people if necessary. But in this case, with Holden well away from his wife and his mother, there doesn't seem much risk of that, and I'm sure that's what the Blackpool police will say. He'll come well down the list. Nothing in what you've told me says he's going to hurt his daughter.'

'He's mentally ill,' Laura said.

'Well, he may be, though we've no real evidence for that. He was mentally ill years ago. That's not evidence he is now. And being mentally ill isn't a crime, either. If we catch up with him he'll probably just claim he took the child away for a few days to the seaside without asking her mother first.'

'I hope she doesn't get hurt,' Laura said. 'I hope no one gets hurt.'

Thackeray looked at Laura across the table and sighed.

'You're letting your heart rule your head again,' he said.

'Maybe,' Laura said wearily. 'But has it crossed your mind that Bruce Holden might have been Vicky's mysterious intruder? I did mention it to Janet. He might have been skulking around up there looking for his wife. So just what would have happened if he'd found her? And to Vicky, too?'

'I think Janet's passed that thought on to the lads who are investigating that incident. But I'll check tomorrow.'

'Julie says he's like an unexploded bomb,' Laura said quietly. 'And the slightest thing might set him off again.' She realised now, if she had not before, that no one was going to take Julie's fears seriously. If Julie wanted Bruce found she would have to find him herself, and if no one else would help her, Laura would have to join in the hunt. She got up from the table and kissed Thackeray lightly on the cheek.

'I'll clear away now and then I think I'll have an early night. I've got a busy day tomorrow.'

CHAPTER TWELVE

Mohammed Sharif felt in need of some rest and recreation that evening. He had called Louise Bentley earlier and they met in a smart bar in the centre of Leeds, a safe ten miles from Bradfield and the censorious eyes that Sharif knew would follow his every move if anyone he knew, and perhaps some he didn't know, spotted him with a woman who was obviously not a Muslim. He bought the first drinks, still not entirely comfortable with Louise's insistence on paying her own way. In the cosmopolitan crowd of young people who surrounded them they were in no way unusual. Life here, he thought as he glanced around, had thankfully moved on from the clannish insularity of so many on both sides of the racial divide in Bradfield. Here, he thought, they could breathe easily.

But although he had gone home to shower and change he still had not been able to lift the anxiety that had enveloped him ever since he had learnt of Faria's death, insistent fingers of suspicion pointing first this way and then that, and Louise was soon demanding an explanation. When he had finished telling her all that had happened, she put a hand on his.

'I'm sorry about your cousin,' she said. 'Were you very close?'

'I'm much older than she was,' he said. 'But yes, I thought of her as another sister pretty much. We lived a few streets away. She and her younger sisters were part of my family too. I used to help them with their homework.' He stopped suddenly, half choked with emotion, and took a deep breath to fight back the tears that threatened to overwhelm him for the first time. 'I feel as if I should have been able to protect her,' he said. 'She had no brothers of her own.'

'Do you really think her husband has killed her?' Louise asked.

'It's beginning to look that way,' he said. 'At first I hoped it was an accident. Then I hoped it was suicide. Now it looks as if she was deliberately killed. It couldn't be any worse.'

'But you said she was pregnant. Would her husband really kill her when they were expecting a baby?'

Sharif hesitated. He knew that there were circumstances in which a Muslim husband might conceivably kill his wife *because* she was expecting a baby, if he suspected it was not his child. But he did not want to elaborate. He avoided the subject of religion with Louise, beyond saying that he no longer attended the mosque, and he was even more reluctant to discuss some of the traditions that lingered on in the community, particularly in relation to marriage, which he knew he would find difficult to justify and she would find difficult to understand. His ambition, as far as Louise was concerned, just as it was at work, was to be regarded as a thoroughly modern man. So he merely shrugged in response to her question.

'It's difficult to know what goes on in a marriage, isn't it?' he said. 'I don't know my cousin's husband very well. It's all a complete mystery to me.'

'I'm so sorry,' Louise said. 'And it must be even worse if they're not letting you help with the investigation. That must be very hard.'

'My DCI is right,' Sharif said. 'Though I wish he weren't. I'm too involved to go anywhere near it.'

He sipped his lager thoughtfully. Alcohol was one of the prohibitions of his religion he chose to ignore although he was an abstemious drinker, a late starter who found no pleasure in excess and with a tendency in a crowd to stick to the orange juice his colleagues half expected. There was no way he had ever felt able to compete in the alcoholic league most of them, men and women alike, played in.

'Do you feel like going away this weekend?' he asked suddenly. 'Maybe we could go down to London and stop over Saturday night? I really feel like getting away for a bit.'

'That would be good,' Louise said.

'Let's go back to mine and see what we can find on the internet,' he said. 'It's the best place for last minute hotels.' Louise smiled encouragingly.

'I'll pick up a few things from my place,' she suggested. 'I don't have any marking to do, for once, so we can make a weekend of it. You look as if you need a break.' She smiled again and Sharif saw the promise there. He linked his fingers into hers across the table.

'I think you're good for me,' he said quietly. She was not the first white girl he had taken out but she was the first whom he felt was not just leading him on out of curiosity, looking for a taste of the exotic to discuss with friends on the next girls' night out. Louise was different, not easy in any sense, making him wait before agreeing to share his bed and in one sense making him uneasy. If, as he thought she might, she had marriage in mind, there would be a mountain to climb with his family, and in present circumstances it was a mountain he could only shove away to a distant horizon. Faria's death had thrown everything into grief and confusion and he and Louise would have to live for the moment. Nothing else was remotely possible.

Sharif woke on Monday morning and lay in bed for a moment feeling relaxed and happy for the first time in days. It had been a good weekend, a companionable trip south by train, a comfortable enough tourist hotel near Kings Cross and some gentle sight-seeing from Tate Modern (her choice) to Westminster (his). They had made love that night and lain in bed late on Sunday morning before meandering back to the station and taking the train back to Leeds, from where they made their separate ways home. They had not discussed the future, Sharif because it was simply too difficult to think about and Louise, he suspected, because she too could see the obstacles they would have to overcome if they were to stay together, but they had been very happy for a brief time and both seemed able to accept that this was enough for now.

As he lay there in the warm afterglow of the weekend, Sharif tried to thrust away unwelcome thoughts of what was happening in the rest of his life, but in the end he tossed the duvet off irritably and got out of bed as the harsh reality of Faria's death and his own equivocal situation returned to overwhelm him again. He dressed and shaved, but found he could only pick at toast and coffee, before giving in to the urge to phone police HQ and ask for Kevin Mower.

The sergeant answered his call with obvious caution.

'Have there been any developments?' Sharif asked, his voice tight with tension. 'I've been away for a couple of days...'

'Omar, you know you're supposed to be keeping out of this,' Mower said. 'But no, there's nothing new. No sightings of Imran Aziz, nothing yet from pathology. Maybe there's nothing more for forensics to find. But seriously – don't call me again, mate. I really can't help you on this. You know how it is.'

Sharif hung up with a feeling of despair. There was nothing to keep him in the empty flat and he grabbed his coat and went downstairs quickly and out of the front door, heading round the back of the building to where his car was parked. He could do worse, he thought, than talk to his father and try to tease out any slight thread of information that might indicate why his cousin had been killed. He was bound to have more success at that than his colleagues, who knew little and sympathised less with a family like his. The morning was dark and gloomy, with rain in the air, and as Sharif reached for the car door he half-turned, hearing a slight sound behind him, and then a shout of pure hate. But that was all he heard before a blow to the head pole-axed him to the concrete floor, and he felt

241

more blows rain down on his head and body, before darkness took him and he lay abandoned and senseless in a widening pool of blood.

DCI Michael Thackeray and DS Kevin Mower gazed through the glass panel at the bed in A and E where Mohammed Sharif lay hooked up to a plethora of monitoring devices, profoundly unconscious. Both officers looked grim but Thackeray was finding it difficult to control the anger that had overtaken him ever since the first reports had come in of his DC's condition, after he had been found close to his home, appearing to the ambulance crew who attended to him to be more dead than alive. The two officers had hurried to the infirmary across the town hall square and had arrived even before the medics had come to any conclusion about the extent of Sharif's injuries. Their wait had been silent and anxious. Mower hardly daring to look at the DCI, whose jaw seemed to have set like stone as soon as the initial message had been received. For fifteen minutes or more Thackeray had paced up and down outside the room where Sharif was being treated until at last a young doctor came out of the room and turned to Thackeray with a slight shrug.

'There's no skull fracture, which is something to be thankful for,' he said. 'But he has four cracked ribs, a smashed hand, which looks as though it has been stamped on, and he's lost a hell of a lot of blood. He's not regained consciousness yet, so we're taking him up to intensive care.'

'Is it life-threatening?' Thackeray asked, his mouth dry.

'It shouldn't be at his age. He's young and fit. But he's taken a hell of a beating, boots *and* fists, I'd say, and the blow to the head looks as if it was from something like a baseball bat or a pickaxe handle. Somebody really, really didn't like him. If he'd been brought in at chucking out time on a Friday night I wouldn't have been surprised, but at this time of the morning... Very odd.'

'Has his family been informed?' Thackeray asked Mower, and the sergeant nodded.

'They're on their way,' he said. 'I called them myself.'

'Right, we'll get back and see if we can find any witnesses to this.'

'Uniform are already up there, going door-to-door,' Mower said.

'I want CID up there too,' Thackeray almost snarled. 'If this is a racist attack I want someone hung out to dry.'

'There's no evidence of any motive yet,' Mower said. 'He had his wallet on him and it wasn't touched. Nor his car keys and phone. He was found right beside his car, as if he was going somewhere. He'd only just called me and I think he was at home then. He must have gone straight out to the car. But it obviously wasn't a robbery, unless they were disturbed before they could grab his stuff.'

'That level of violence isn't a mugging,' Thackeray said flatly. 'There's no need for it. This was targeted, either because he's Asian or because he's a copper.'

'Or for some reason we don't even know about,' Mower said. 'He walks a thin line, does Omar. Maybe he overstepped it.'

As they left the main hospital entrance Thackeray recognised the Asian man and woman approaching from the street and moved over quickly to greet them, holding out his hand, which Sharif's father took without enthusiasm.

'Mr Sharif, I'm incredibly sorry about this. Especially at a time when you've just lost your niece. We'll find out who's done this, I promise you. It will be a priority for all of us.'

Sharif nodded dully, and his wife gazed at the ground, not meeting the eyes of Thackeray or Mower.

'Mohammed is an excellent young officer,' Thackeray said. 'Believe me, this won't go unpunished.'

Sharif pushed past the DCI without a word and his wife followed close behind, her eyes full of tears. Mower glanced warily at his boss and away again. He had felt the full force of his superior's anger once or twice during his own somewhat chequered career and did not envy Sharif's assailants if they ever came face to face with it themselves.

'I'll roust out the usual suspects,' he said. 'The raving right. They've been pretty quiet recently, but this has to be racist. What else could it be?'

'Something to do with his cousin's death, maybe,' Thackeray suggested quietly. 'Something we don't know about, maybe, and may never know about? I thought I'd done the best thing taking him off the case, away from it all, but maybe he's the man I should have been talking to. He's our best link to that community and I've let him go. And now where are we? One member of the family dead, and another half-dead, and no lead in sight.'

It was on the tip of Mower's tongue to advise Thackeray not to blame himself but he checked himself in time. He knew he would be wasting his breath.

Mohammed Sharif regained consciousness that afternoon, struggling up through swirls of mist into a world of confusion and pain that made him crave the oblivion that had cradled him safely in its arms for most of the day. He opened his eyes tentatively, knowing instantly that he was in hospital and guessing that he was lucky to be alive. There was no one close to his bed but further down the small ward he could see nurses clustered around another bed where someone else was hooked up to the same monitoring devices that he became aware surrounded him too. He groaned slightly as he tried to move and a pain stabbed viciously through his chest. His head throbbed unbearably beneath what seemed to be a helmet of dressings and he could feel an oxygen feed strapped to his nose. He took a deep breath and felt slightly more alert as the life-giving gas did its job. But he closed his eyes again.

He was slightly surprised that there was no uniformed figure at his bedside, keeping watch and waiting to question him about what had happened. For a moment he felt an urge to weep, and fought hard to contain the tears that welled up behind his eyelids. Perhaps his worst nightmares were true, he thought, and he, the outsider, was expendable, his fate of no concern to his colleagues or superiors, prey to any mad racist who took a dislike to the colour of his skin. Where were his brother officers when he needed them? Or even a sister, one of the women he had made a special effort to accept as his equal, or even sometimes his superior, after a lifetime of tacitly denying that possibility. Had they made a similar effort to accept him? he wondered bitterly.

He shook his head slightly, a mistake as it

intensified the throbbing, but the action at least forced him to open his eyes again and banish the incipient paranoia that threatened to overwhelm him, and suddenly he was no longer alone as a nurse and DS Kevin Mower approached his bed, both of them smiling some sort of a welcome as he struggled to offer a grimace of recognition in return.

'You're awake then,' Mower said cheerfully. 'Thank God for that.'

The nurse began to check the monitors that surrounded Sharif's bed and then nodded.

'You seem to be fine,' she said. 'I'll get the doctor to come and check you out but I should think we'll be able to move you down to a normal ward later on. They'll want to keep you in overnight, maybe longer.'

'Your parents were here,' Mower said. 'They just went home to get something to eat.'

Sharif tried to say something but his voice seemed to be reduced to a mumble. Mower took the chair alongside the bed.

'What's the damage?' Sharif whispered.

'A nasty gash on the head,' Mower said. 'That's what the doctors were really worried about. A few cracked ribs. And your hand – some bones broken. You were lucky, by all accounts. Can you remember what happened?'

Sharif glanced at the bandages on his left

hand and winced as he tried to flex the fingers. 'Not really,' he said. 'They came up behind me as I was opening the car door.'

'More than one of them, then?'

'I think so, yes.'

'But you didn't get a sight of them?'

'No,' Sharif said. 'No, I didn't.' He closed his eyes again, the effort of speaking redoubling the pain in his head. 'Can you get the nurse,' he said. 'I think my head's going to explode.'

'We'll talk later, mate,' Mower said getting to his feet. 'I'll get back and tell them you're back in the land of the living. Everyone will be pleased.'

And after his pain-killing injection, Sharif was grateful to close his eyes and allow himself to drift back into sleep. But as he did so he could hear an insistent cry somewhere in the farthest recesses of his fuddled brain. '*Allahu Akbar,*' it came repeatedly. 'God is great.' And the more he tried to drive it from his mind the more insistent it became and he knew he had heard it quite clearly before the first blow that had beaten him to the ground. He knew he had not been attacked by white racists, as his colleagues had no doubt instantly assumed. He had been attacked by members of his own community. And that filled him with overwhelming dread.

Laura Ackroyd was surprised at how soon her freelance efforts to track down Bruce Holden bore fruit, though it was not exactly the fruit she had anticipated. On Saturday she had called the offices of the local evening paper in Blackpool and spoken to the newsdesk, and then to a reporter, who listened sympathetically and then promised to write a short item about Holden's disappearance from Bradfield with his daughter. She had given him Julie's mobile number and emailed a photograph of Holden to the Lancashire paper, in the hope that the newspaper might flush him out where the police had proved so reluctant to do so.

By lunchtime on Monday, Julie had phoned her, almost incoherent at the other end, to say that Bruce had already been in touch, incandescent with rage himself, and threatening to kill himself and Anna if she did not leave them alone, promising to jump off the end of the pier with the child if his cover was blown.

'He's mad enough to do it,' Julie sobbed. 'Believe me. He's crazy. And Anna can't swim.'

'This is all because the paper published his picture, presumably?' Laura asked.

'That's what he said. He said he'd have to get out of Blackpool now, before someone recognised him. He said a lot more, about what he'll do to me when he catches up with me. It sounded as if he was heading back here...' Julie broke off and Laura waited patiently until she began to sound coherent again.

'You'd better talk to Janet Richardson at police HQ,' she said. 'Will you do that now? Straight away? He's threatening Anna now and she needs to know that.'

'Yes, yes,' Julie said. 'Straight away.'

'Where are you staying?' Laura asked.

'At home. I moved back into the house.'

'Well, I should move out again if I were you,' Laura said. 'It's far too easy for him to find you there. Let me know where you go.'

When she had rung off, Laura gazed across the busy newsroom without taking in any part of her colleagues' intense concentration as they came up to their deadline for the day's paper. Then she picked up the phone again and punched in Michael Thackeray's direct line. Unusually she got an instant response.

'Michael,' she said. 'You're not going to like this.' And she told him what she had done and Holden's response. There was a long silence at the other end of the line and Laura guessed that Thackeray was torn between an angry personal reaction to her initiative and a professional one to the threat to the child.

'Right,' he said at length, his voice as chilly as she knew his expression would be. 'I'll talk to Janet Richardson and see what her assessment of the threat is. At first glance it's serious and we'll very likely put out a call for the two of them, starting in Blackpool, of course. Is Julie Holden back at her own house?'

'At the moment,' Laura said. 'I suggested she move out again.'

'Well, that's one sensible thing you've done. I just hope she's taken your advice,' Thackeray said flatly. 'But we'll talk later. Right now I need to set things in motion here.' And he hung up without saying good-bye.

CHAPTER THIRTEEN

The next morning, Faisal Sharif sat uncomfortably, his beard resting on his clenched fist, across an interview room table from DCI Michael Thackeray, who had deliberately chosen to conduct this interview himself, with Kevin Mower at his side, rather than leave sensitive questions to less experienced officers.

'I have to ask you this, Mr Sharif,' Thackeray said. 'Do you know any reason why Imran Aziz might feel justified in killing his wife? A reason of honour in your culture, maybe?'

Sharif winced, as if the very question was insulting, and shook his head heavily.

'I know nothing of that sort,' he said. 'No reason.'

'So tell me, how traditional a Muslim is Aziz? Are his expectations stricter than your own, for instance, coming as he did more recently from Pakistan?'

'He too is a member of my family,' Sharif said. 'He and Faria are cousins. We are not fanatics, Mr Thackeray, and Imran certainly was not. But we do wish to maintain our traditions in a culture where I understand very well that they are not usual. I see it for myself all around me. I do not want my daughters staggering around the town on a Friday night half naked and under the influence of alcohol. I do not want them being tempted by young men of loose morals. That is not our way.'

'So you have brought up your daughters traditionally and Faria accepted an arranged marriage? You chose her husband for her?' Thackeray asked, his voice even, giving nothing away.

'Her grandfather and I suggested a match,' Sharif said coldly. 'Faria accepted our suggestion. It is not permissible to force a young woman into marriage in Islam. Families can suggest, young women decide.'

'But Imran Aziz was older than she was, and had been married before?'

'He was divorced. There had been no children of that marriage. Divorce is not difficult in Pakistan, for a man.'

Thackeray checked himself from putting the obvious question in response to that. 'Wasn't it rather that Imran divorced his wife so he could marry a British citizen and gain entry to the UK that way?' he asked sharply instead.

'Not at all,' Sharif insisted. 'His first marriage had not been successful. His business dealings were not going well. He wanted to make a new start in a new country with a new wife. There is nothing sinister in that.'

'Did you discuss politics with your son-in-law?'

'Imran was in business in Lahore. He was a very busy man. I am not aware that he took any great interest in politics.'

'You realise that his disappearance is bound to attract the notice of other sections of the police force, times being what they are?'

'If you knew Imran Aziz as I do you would know that he would be a very unlikely terrorist,' Sharif said, his lips tightening with distaste. 'His interest in coming to this country was to restore his fortunes, not blow people up. He had been successful at home, but ran into difficulties. He thought there would be more opportunities here.'

'And have there been? More opportunities? Was he making a success of life here?'

Sharif hesitated for a moment and then shrugged.

'It's not as easy as it used to be,' he said. 'I think he found it hard. I think perhaps that is why he did not keep in touch and seemed to be trying to keep Faria apart from her mother... He was not doing as well as he had hoped, not making enough money. He felt shamed by that. It was a difficult time for us all.'

'But if he wanted children then this should have been a good time for Imran and Faria, surely? She was pregnant after – what? Two years of marriage? Wasn't Imran delighted?'

'I haven't spoken to my son-in-law about this,' Sharif said, glancing away as he spoke. 'He had not told me that Faria was expecting a baby. Neither of them had told me. She only told her sisters. I only learnt of it after her death. But yes, I would expect him to be pleased. Are we not always pleased when children come?' Faisel Sharif's face looked gaunt in the harsh light of the interview room.

'Generally people are pleased,' Thackeray said quietly, aware of the gulf between a traditional paternalist and a society where sex was often casual and its consequences often unwelcome. 'But not always,' he added, uneasy at the turn the conversation was taking.

He took a deep breath. He knew he was getting nowhere with this bearded patriarch whose values were so different from the norm, though not that different from those of his own father, who had followed a religious path nearly as uncompromising and puritanical as Sharif's. Neither, he thought wryly, would have welcomed the comparison, though it was a fair one.

'Mr Sharif,' he said. 'You must understand that we need to find your son-in-law urgently. Do you have any idea where he might be?'

Sharif looked at the DCI silently for a

moment, his eyes unfathomably dark, and then shook his head impatiently.

'Do you think, if he is the one who has killed my daughter, I would not wish him found and brought to justice? I have no idea where he is. But I pray to Allah that you find him soon.'

When Sharif had departed Thackeray turned to Mower in exasperation.

'Can he really have known so little about what was going on with this couple?' he asked. 'It sounds like wilful ignorance, as if there were things he actually didn't want to know about.'

'It doesn't make sense, guv,' Mower said. 'If Aziz divorced his first wife because there were no children, why would he kill Faria just when she had fallen pregnant? Someone's lying. But who?'

'We need to talk to Faria's mother and sisters as well, but perhaps we'd better do that in their own home. Arrange to talk to them yourself, Kevin, will you, and take that young Asian PC with you. What's she called, Nasreem something? We don't want to upset the community too much at this stage, although I'll arrest the whole family if I can't get any sense out of them any other way.'

'This is where we'll miss Omar,' Mower said, but his remark met only a stony stare from Thackeray. The DCI followed the sergeant downstairs but then hesitated in the doorway to his own office.

'The terrorist officers are working on all the stuff they took out of Aziz's house. I'll talk to Doug McKinnon later and see if I can get any indication of how that's going so we know where we stand. If this is anything more than a simple murder case, we need to know as soon as possible. In the meantime, chase up any sightings there may have been of Aziz. One thing I'll ask McKinnon is whether he has any objection to us issuing a photograph of him if they've found one. There'll be much more chance of finding him if we can get his face onto the front page of the *Gazette* and onto local TV.'

'Guv,' Mower said.

But within ten minutes he was back, knocking on Thackeray's door and poking his head round tentatively.

'I thought you'd want to know that there've been some developments in the Bruce Holden case, the bloke who's run off with his daughter...'

Thackeray hesitated for a beat.

'I know he's been threatening his wife by phone, threatening the child,' he said reluctantly.

'Janet Richardson's been following up,' Mower said. 'Two developments. Blackpool police had a call from a landlord who let Holden a flat. Recognised his picture in the

257

local paper, apparently. I don't know who...' he stopped, suddenly realising who might have used the local press to such good effect. 'Anyway, they've done a flit, as they used to say. Packed their bags and moved on, according to the landlord. Blackpool say they'll keep an eye out but they don't sound too optimistic.'

'And the other development?' Thackeray asked quickly.

'Fingerprints from the Mendelsons' place, on the back door. They match Holden's, which turned up on file. Some road rage fracas a year or so back in Milford. He was arrested but the charges weren't proceeded with. CPS decided it was six of one and half a dozen of the other after a minor collision. Did nothing about it in the end.'

'Did you tell Blackpool that?'

'Yes, told them we had reason to hold him on suspicion of breaking and entering as well as the assaults. Not to hesitate if they locate him, he could be violent.'

'They should have a record of him. Apparently he was sectioned after some violent incident with the police over there. That's twice he's been let off when perhaps he should have been charged.'

'They didn't mention it. Anyway, we've circulated the registration number of his four-by-four. Someone somewhere will pick him up in the car in the end.'

'Good, let's hope so,' Thackeray said. 'If he's threatening the child we need to get hold of him quickly. We've already got every reason to arrest him. We should have done it by now.'

'Did you get anything out of Doug McKinnon on the Aziz case?' Mower asked.

'Not a lot. They've done a quick trawl through Aziz's phone records but not come up with anything suspicious so far. His computer will take much longer. They've not found any mobiles in the house but there is a charger so at least one of them had a handset, but of course they might have been carrying it when they left. No sign of bills from a mobile company apparently, but they could be using pay-as-you-go. You can ask Faria's sisters if she used a mobile. They'll certainly know.'

'A lot of Asian girls have mobiles their parents don't know about. Perhaps it goes for wives too. So do we publish Aziz's picture?'

'Not yet,' Thackeray said, not bothering to hide his frustration. 'McKinnon says it will compromise his investigation.'

'If Aziz has contacts he shouldn't have, they'll know all about his disappearance by now,' Mower said. 'They'll probably have organised it. What do our own terrorism people at county say?'

'Not on their radar,' Thackeray said.

'But that means nothing?'

'Nothing at all,' Thackeray agreed gloomily. 'The ones not on the radar are the ones we need to worry about.'

'And what about the assault on Omar? Any progress?'

'Nothing so far, guv. He's still very confused and says he didn't see anyone. We're looking for witnesses but nothing's turned up so far.'

'Right. Don't let it slip. I want those bastards caught.'

Mohammed Sharif was let out of hospital that afternoon, his ribs strapped, his head and hand bandaged and a large bottle of pain-killers in his pocket. He was no longer regarded as in danger and his bed was needed. He took a taxi back to his flat and, exhausted by the effort of getting home, he lay down on his bed with the blinds down, half sleeping, half waking, as the winter evening closed in, and he eventually found himself in the near-dark wincing with pain as the effect of the painkillers wore off. Groaning, he slid off the bed and gingerly made his way to his tiny kitchen, where he swallowed another handful of pills with a glass of water and then lowered himself gingerly into an armchair in the living room and looked for messages on his mobile. There were none. No one – family, friends or colleagues – had tried to contact him since the assault. Not even Louise, who was unlikely to know about the assault, had so much as sent him a text.

It was as if he had dropped out of existence, he thought, and not for the first time he wondered whether the path he had chosen, semi-estranged from his own community and not really accepted by the rest, was sustainable. People talked about integration but there were times when it felt more like exile to him. And now he seemed to have angered Muslims who were prepared to use violence against him, and he did not know who they were or why they had attacked him so ferociously – whether it was his police work or his girlfriend they had taken exception to – and he wondered whether he could bring himself to report what he suspected.

He called Louise to explain what had happened to him, but only got her voicemail and then remembered that she would still be at work, rehearsing the school play. His depression deepened as he tried to persuade his mind to clear the miasma that infected it after twenty four hours of pain and drugs, but failed, and the next thing he knew he was awake again but in darkness, the blinds he did not recall pulling down keeping out the orange glow of the street lights outside, and not even an electronic standby light providing any orientation in a space that suddenly seemed completely alien. With a groan he hauled himself to his feet and stumbled to the light switch by the door and found himself almost blinded by the glare. But as the lights came on and his brain kicked back into gear, in spite of the jabbing pain in his side and his thumping head, he suddenly knew what he had to do.

He moved slowly to his computer on the other side of the room and logged on to a travel site he had used before. Thackeray's ban on his involvement in the investigation into his cousin's death was even less likely to be lifted now he was injured, he thought. But there was one other course open to him. Given a little time for his ribs and other injuries to mend, he would go to Pakistan and see what he could uncover about his cousin's marriage and her husband's previous life in Lahore. In fact the more he thought about it, the more he felt convinced that the answer to her death lay there. With a faint feeling of excitement mitigating his gloom, he booked a seat on a flight to Lahore in two days' time.

Bruce Holden took the back roads across the Pennine hills, reasoning that a muddy four-by-four would be less noticeable there and would avoid the cameras that increasingly infested the motorways. He felt calm now, the rage that had infused his last convers-ation with Julie dissipated into a manic clarity as he formulated a plan. He had bundled up the few possessions the two of them had taken with them to Blackpool and roused his daughter at three that morning, bundling her in a blanket and strapping her into the front seat. She had barely protested and had fallen asleep again before he had reached the outskirts of the town. He had headed north then, weaving through the old mill towns, almost deserted at that time in the morning, and reaching the bare summit of the hills above Colne before the eastern sky showed the faintest streak of dawn.

By five-thirty he had pulled up in a narrow gap between other parked cars outside his mother's house and, leaving Anna still asleep in the front seat, let himself in with the key she had given him when he had stayed there. He took the stairs two at a time and opened his mother's bedroom door. She was asleep, the duvet pulled tightly up to her ears but she woke at once, plainly terrified, when he shook her shoulder roughly.

'Get some clothes on,' he said. 'I've got a little job for you.' He glanced at the bedside table for a second before unplugging the phone and carrying it with him out of the room.

'Be quick,' he said over his shoulder. Downstairs he moved fast, checking all the doors and windows to make sure they were locked and pocketing the keys before wrenching the main telephone connection out of the wall. In the kitchen he unlocked a door at the back of the room and switched on the light beyond to illuminate a steep flight of stone steps. Like many older houses in Bradfield, this one had a small cellar, built to accommodate a narrow space for regular deliveries of coal through a hatch from above to feed the open fires that used to be the only means of heating, and beyond the coal-hole, another larger room with a stone sink and copper for the household's washing in the days before electric machines took over.

His mother had bought the house after the death of an elderly woman and although she had spent some of her savings on modernising the rest of the property he knew she had done nothing at all to the cellar, beyond boarding up the area window to deter intruders and rodents. Gingerly, he made his way down the steps to find the space much as he had expected, reasonably dry but cold, dusty and lit only by a single low watt bulb dangling from the ceiling. It would do the job he wanted it to do, he thought with satisfaction. It would keep prying eyes and ears away from Anna until he had finished the task he had decided, in the dark hours of the previous night, that he had to complete before he and his daughter would be safe.

He hurried upstairs again and began carrying down cushions from the sofa in the front room, and then as much of the food in the kitchen as he thought they would need, and a couple of bottles of water. On his last trip he met his mother, fully dressed but looking gray and dazed, inching her way down the stairs.

'I want you to look after Anna for me,' he said, brusquely. 'Just for a little while. I've got things to attend to and then I'm going to take her right away from here...' Vanessa made as if to object but Holden's face suffused with colour and she seemed to think better of it, flinching away from his outstretched hand as he offered to help her down the last few steps.

'Where is she?' Vanessa asked faintly.

'In the car. I'll get her in a minute. She fell asleep. You come with me and I'll bring her in.'

He hustled Vanessa into the kitchen and to the top of the cellar steps and at that point she realised what he intended.

'Not down there,' she said in horror.

'Not for long,' Holden said. 'I don't want you ringing Julie. I need some peace to finish things off here. You and Anna will be safe enough down there, no problem.'

Ignoring her protests he hustled her down the stairs into the cellar and pushed her down roughly onto the cushions he had arranged in one corner of the small stone-floored room, knowing that she would find it very hard to get to her feet again. He glanced around and waved towards a cardboard box.

'There's food and drink here. You won't starve. What about a bucket for you-know-what? I'll get you a bucket, just in case it takes longer than I think.'

He bustled back up the stairs, located a bucket and placed it in the small coal cellar.

'Not quite all mod cons but I'm sure you'll manage. I won't keep you long, I promise.'

Within minutes he had carried his sleepy daughter, fully dressed and wrapped in a blanket, into the makeshift prison he had constructed and put her on the cushioned floor beside her grandmother.

'Daddy,' the child wailed, looking around her in astonishment. 'Where am I?'

'I want you to stay here for a bit and look after your nanna, sweetheart,' Holden said brusquely. 'And Nanna will look after you. I won't be long, I promise. I'll come and get you very soon and then we'll go away together, somewhere warm and sunny, maybe. Not bloody miserable and cold and wet like Blackpool. We'll be fine, I promise.'

And without looking back at woman or child, he strode back up the cellar steps and they heard the door being closed and locked behind him. Anna gazed at her grandmother in horror and saw silent tears streaming down her wrinkled face.

'Don't cry, Nanna, please,' she said taking her hand. 'Please don't cry. He'll be back soon. He always does what he says.'

But it was that certainty which filled Vanessa Holden with terror as she wondered exactly what business her son intended to complete before he came back to release them. But that was speculation she did not dare share with the child at her side. She sniffed back her tears and put her arm round Anna.

'We'll have to think of some games to play until your daddy comes back,' she said. 'I'm sure he won't be long.' She glanced at her watch and shivered slightly. It was half past five.

After carefully locking up his mother's house, Holden eased his car out of its parking slot and drove a hundred yards to the end of the street and turned into a narrow alleyway that led to a row of lock-up garages, where his mother kept her little used car. He reversed her Nissan carefully out of the garage and put his own four-by-four in, dropping down the door as quietly as he could. He did not think he had been seen. The houses all around were still in darkness. Driving the Nissan circumspectly so as to attract no unwelcome attention, he made his way to his own road and went slowly past his own house, pausing to take in the absence of a vehicle on the drive and the fact that the curtains were not drawn on the window of the main bedroom. He parked a couple of streets away and walked back slowly. In the distance he could see a milk float proceeding at a leisurely pace from house to house but otherwise there was no sign yet that anyone was awake as the faint grey light of morning stole over the rooftops. Glancing around cautiously for one last time he let himself in through his own front door and very quietly began a systematic search of the house.

He sniffed at a bottle of fresh milk in the fridge and smiled faintly, guessing that someone had been there recently but he was not really surprised when he gently opened the bedroom door to find the bed neatly made, and no one there. He pulled back the cover and picked up the pillow on what had been Julie's usual side, and sniffed it. She had been here, and not long ago, he was sure, and therefore might well come back. He went back downstairs and into the kitchen, taking the largest of the cooks' knives from the knife block and then moving into the living room and settling himself into the armchair half hidden behind the door. He could wait, he thought. He could wait for the pleasure of giving her what she deserved. He felt exhilarated by the idea and considered putting some music on the stereo, but then told himself firmly that he could not risk disturbing the neighbours. His silence would have its reward, he promised himself, when Julie walked through the front door.

CHAPTER FOURTEEN

Mohammed Sharif flung himself onto the small, hard bed in the bed and breakfast establishment he had deliberately chosen to be as anonymous a base as possible in the city of Lahore, still jet-lagged by the time difference, enervated by the heat, and aching all over after he had crushed his battered body into an airline seat for so many weary hours. It was mind-blowingly hot and stuffy in the tiny room, with a faint smell that he hesitated to identify, but he had decided to keep well away from the glitzy air-conditioned tourist and business hotels, which were still busy in spite of the country's slightly ambivalent relationship with its friends and neighbours internationally. He could stand the heat, he hoped, for the few days he intended to stay, and although there was little chance of his being recognised in the teeming capital of the Pakistani Punjab, he did not want to take the slightest chance. What he was doing, he knew, would infuriate family members even more in Pakistan than at home in Bradfield, and would not enchant his colleagues and superiors in CID, and he did not want to take the slightest risk of anyone reporting back to anyone at all.

He did not really know the city at all. He had flown into Allama Iqbal airport often enough on family visits, most recently to Faria and Imran's wedding, but his father's custom was to hire a people-carrier at the airport and drive the family immediately out of Lahore, with the children craning through the window to glimpse as many of its famous parks and monuments, and a good proportion of its six million inhabitants, as they could before they headed across the agricultural plains to the family village about one hundred miles away. This time Sharif had taken a taxi straight to the centre and, encumbered only with an overnight bag, asked to be dropped close to the old walled city, where he found himself almost overwhelmed by streets clogged with a maelstrom of cars and vans and technicolour *quingqi*, motorised rickshaws, which swirled in what looked like an intricate and noisy dance of death, and by the sheer number of people milling in the narrow streets. Although he felt hungry, he resisted the enticing smells and noisy blandishments from the roadside food stalls selling every variety of snack and which he knew that his unaccustomed western digestion might reject violently. His grandfather's village still seemed an oasis of timeless tradition to young people born and brought up in

England. This was a metropolis uneasily, it seemed to him, poised between the old and the new: beautiful, glamorous even, but at the same time so seethingly crowded and, in parts, impoverished, as to seem faintly threatening.

He lay on his bed naked, still feeling sticky after what passed for a shower in the communal bathroom – a one-handed contortion because of the need to keep his strapped ribs and bandaged hand reasonably dry, and considered his next move. Two days ago he had driven up to his parents' house after checking that his father would be out and cross-questioned his mother, so gently he hoped that she had not realised quite what was happening. He had felt guilty as he took advantage of her grief over Faria's death to persuade her to get out her precious photograph album and show him pictures of his cousin's wedding to Imran Aziz, pictures in which he himself appeared on the back row, in traditional dress, looking slightly uncomfortable and half hidden by the bride and groom.

'Did you go to Imran's first wedding?' he had asked, hoping that the question sounded like an idle one, but his mother was only too pleased to discuss weddings, anybody's wedding, with her so far unmarried son, no doubt hoping that it would enthuse him in that direction. As he had hoped his mother

272

flicked back through the pages of her album, full of uncles and aunts and cousins and second and third cousins, until she came to a single fading snapshot of another village wedding.

'Only your father went,' she said. 'There he is, look.' But Sharif was looking much harder at the bride, her headscarf thrown back after the ceremonies, and at the same time trying to conceal his surprise. She was not a young woman, nor a particularly beautiful one, and he wondered callously why Imran, who at that time was reputed to be doing well in business in Lahore, should have consented to marry such an unprepossessing bride.

'What was her name?' he asked his mother as casually as he could manage, but she only frowned as she tried to recall. She flicked through her photographs again. 'I remember your father saying that Imran could not attract a young bride because he was too old. He had left it too long. And at that stage of course Faria was too young...' Her eyes filled with tears and she dabbed them with the end of her scarf. 'They couldn't insist on that arrangement then. It is such a pity that it happened later.' She dabbed her eyes.

'Can you really not recall her name?' Sharif persisted, knowing that going to Pakistan to trace a nameless bride would be worse than useless, but very reluctant to try to extract the information from Faria's own parents. His mother shrugged and detached the fading wedding photograph from the album and looked at the back of it.

'There,' she said. 'Imran Aziz and Mariam Gul. That was her name. She seemed a good woman, but not perhaps what Imran's father had really wanted. But Imran was beginning to be the subject of gossip at his age and not married... I don't think Mariam came from a very good family. Perhaps Imran chose her himself, being away from home in Lahore anything is possible...' She glanced at her son slyly. 'Away from home is away from good advice,' she said. 'You should remember that.'

And with that Mohammed Sharif had had to be satisfied, and he flew from Manchester to Lahore two days later without much confidence that he would be able to track down Mariam Gul or her family with the minimal information at his disposal, but determined to try.

The next morning, after a fitful night's sleep in a room where the heat built up to a point where he felt as if he was drowning in the damp air, and still half bemused after the long flight and the painkillers he was still taking, Sharif spent half an hour using the mobile phone he had rented at the airport. His aim was to track down a distant cousin of his mother's who had outraged his father, much as Mohammed had infuriated his, by joining the Pakistan security services after taking a degree in law. Sharif only knew of his existence, not being nearly as well versed in family relationships as his parents' generation, because his name was occasionally invoked by his mother's father and his own as an example of another young man in the family who had unaccountably and outrageously ignored his elders' advice and chosen his own career and, Sharif suspected, his own lifestyle.

In his apparently hopeless quest to find a divorced woman of uncertain age amongst the millions of inhabitants of the Punjab, Ali Hussain, if he could locate him, might be at least a source of advice if not practical assistance, and Sharif was prepared to use the remote family connection on this occasion to the hilt. Official channels, he knew, would be slow and devious and might bring him unwanted attention both in Lahore and back home if anyone felt moved to report back to West Yorkshire about a holidaying British detective playing sleuth in a foreign country. That he could well do without.

Somewhat to his surprise, he eventually tracked Hussain down to central police headquarters, where he had apparently reached the rank of captain in some branch of the service that Sharif had never heard of. After the family politeness of exploring the tortuous connections of blood and marriage that linked the two men, Hussain had suggested that they meet that lunchtime at a branch of McDonald's close to a sparkling new shopping centre and not far from the colonial mansions and administrative buildings of the British Raj on the Mall.

'I didn't know the Big Mac had arrived here,' Sharif said.

'*Halal*, of course,' his cousin said. 'But is there anywhere they haven't arrived? It has the advantage of being quick. I have a busy afternoon booked.'

'Of course,' Sharif said. 'It's good of you to take the time.'

'I heard something about Faria from my uncle. Family news spreads fast here – though not always accurately. The speculation can get red hot. Time for us policemen to keep our heads down below the parapet.'

'I'm sure,' Sharif said dryly. 'I'll see you in an hour then.'

After dressing painfully in khakis and a long-sleeved sports shirt to hide his bruises, although there was nothing he could do to disguise the plaster that still covered the deep cut on his head, and the strapping on his left hand, he ventured out into the crowded street and hired a *quingqi*, plastered with brightly coloured pin-ups and scenes from Bollywood and Lollywood – the fiercely competitive Mumbai and Lahore film industries

– and asked to be taken to the McDonald's he had been instructed to find. The driver veered and swerved through the traffic, while chattering on his mobile phone, but with thankfully unerring accuracy, although more than once Sharif closed his eyes as a truck or bus seemed to be heading straight at them at breakneck speed. The *quingqi* finally deposited Sharif, safe but shaking slightly, outside the familiar golden arches. As he paid the driver, he noticed a tall man of about his own age in a smart uniform heading towards the doors and he guessed this must be Hussain.

The two men waited in line for food and then settled at a table close to the door and exchanged the obligatory family pleasantries, news and information that spanned three continents and three generations from the ancestral village to branches of the family in Bradfield, London and Toronto.

'And you?' Hussain asked, finishing his cola and wiping his mouth, his eyes appraising his cousin. 'You look as if you have been in the wars. What happened?' Sharif told him about the assault he had suffered, but did not go into details. His belief that he had been attacked by members of his own community might spark a political debate, which he did not want.

'You make enemies in this job,' he said. 'I expect you find the same.'

'Oh yes,' Hussain said. 'Here you must watch yourself all the time. But you said your interest was this sad family matter? How can I help with that?' He listened quietly while Sharif told him in detail about Faria's death and the disappearance of Imran Aziz.

'You think he killed her?' he asked when Sharif had finished. 'You think it's a question of honour? She was unfaithful?'

'We know nothing about the marriage or what went on between them,' Sharif said. 'She visited her parents very seldom and not at all for a few months. And I have been taken off the case because I'm too close to it. And now I'm on sick leave, anyway. That's why I came. I thought that here I might find out a bit more about Imran Aziz from his former wife – if I can find her.'

Hussain looked at him consideringly for a moment as if wondering how far he would go even for a kinsman from a faraway country.

'It is possible we could trace her,' he said thoughtfully. 'You know that here divorced women are not always welcomed back by their families? Some of them find themselves alone and in difficulties and it's not unknown for them to become known to the police.'

'They lived in Lahore while they were married,' Sharif said. 'My mother says she was not a woman from a village family. She thinks Imran may have met her in Lahore. She may still be here.'

'She may,' Hussain agreed. 'Give me a day and I'll see what I can discover in our files. Since 9/11 they have become – what shall I say? – a bit more extensive, and a bit more accurate. I'll check her out and give you a call. I've got your mobile number. I'll check out Imran Aziz for you, too. If he was in business here there will be traces of him to be found in the records, more easily than for his wife actually.'

'I'd be grateful,' Sharif said. 'Faria was like a sister to me. Her death, her murder, must be solved. Her killer has to be found.'

'Of course,' Hussain said. 'Of course he must.'

Laura sat hunched in her chair on the other side of the fireplace from Michael Thackeray, grimly aware that what had been planned as a rare evening together was turning into a battlefield. She should not have answered her mobile, she thought, when it had rung soon after they had finished a companionable meal together. Just for once she should have let it ring. She, after all, was not the senior police officer on more or less permanent call. She could have let it ride, but her insatiable curiosity always made it very hard to ignore a ringing phone.

So she had answered it and listened to a

hysterical Julie Holden on the other end of the line, demanding to know what her bloody boyfriend had done today to trace her daughter. Laura had tried to calm the distraught mother down, but she was conscious of Thackeray half listening to the conversation and that he very quickly adopted a stony expression, which presaged nothing but trouble to come as he worked out what was going on.

'Would you like to talk to her,' she had mouthed at Thackeray eventually, but he had shaken his head vehemently, and left her to persuade Julie to calm down as best she could by suggesting she talk to Sergeant Janet Richardson the next morning. When she finally hung up Thackeray had buried his head in that evening's *Gazette* and continued to read it in silence until Laura could bear it no longer.

'She says nobody's been in touch with her,' she said. 'Surely someone's liaising with her. She's beside herself with worry.'

'She's no right to try to get to me when I'm not on duty,' Thackeray said, his voice like ice. 'She's no right to try to get at me through you.'

'Of course not,' Laura said. 'But you can understand how desperate she is, and I have been following her story. She's a perfect right to call me if she wants to.'

Thackeray flung the newspaper to one side with a heavy sigh but Laura ploughed on regardless, ignoring the warning signs.

'Isn't Sergeant Richardson supposed to keep her in touch with developments?' she asked. 'She could be at risk if Holden comes back to Bradfield. She needs to know...'

'As far as I know there are no developments. No one's seen Holden and the child since they left their rented place in Blackpool. He could be out of the country by now. As far as I know Janet Richardson is doing the job she's paid for, which involves dozens of cases like this. Neither she nor CID can devote themselves to Julie Holden full time when there's no obvious risk to her safety or the child's. Get real, Laura. And for God's sake don't give your mobile number to every lame dog in your contacts book. We'll never get any peace. We get little enough time together as it is.'

Laura flushed faintly and turned away. She understood the justice of Thackeray's reaction but she was still concerned for Julie's safety.

'You haven't talked to Julie and her mother-in-law,' she muttered. 'They're both terrified of this man. He's a monster. And there's a child involved.'

Thackeray gazed at her for a moment without speaking.

'You get in too deep,' he said at last. 'All the time, you get in too deep. You should learn to insulate yourself from it, if you're going to insist on writing about these emotional cases. It's the only way to survive. Believe me, I know.'

Laura looked at him sceptically.

'But you don't, do you? You don't insulate yourself. You can't, any more than I can. Is that what this is all about? There's a child involved again so you're trying not to think about it? I watched you when those children were killed in Staveley last year. You hated every minute of that case. It nearly tore you apart. You're just as emotional as I am. You just hide it better.'

Thackeray said nothing as she flounced across the room and poured herself a large vodka and tonic.

'Do you want anything?' she asked, grudgingly and when he shook his head she sat down in the armchair opposite him and sipped her drink, trying to look unconcerned although her heart was thudding uncomfortably. She knew that she was trespassing flat-footed into areas that she had never felt were hers to approach, but with a flash of understanding she knew she was right to venture there at last. She had been happy with Thackeray for months now, as their relationship seemed to have reached a level of contentment they had never previously known. But if it was to go further, she thought, she needed some answers to questions she had quietly buried for years. And perhaps the disintegration of Julie Holden's marriage and what she believed was the threat to her daughter was the catalyst they needed to clear the air. She took a larger gulp of her drink and decided to live dangerously.

'You don't deny it, then,' she said quietly, more a statement of the obvious than a question. 'You hang on in there with the job, on the edge every time a child goes missing or a body is found, but can you hang on in with me when you know how much I want a child? Can you give me that, Michael? Or am I wasting my time with you? I really, really need to know the answer. I have a right to ask. I've waited long enough.'

Thackeray flinched at the directness of the question and for a moment she thought he was going to fling himself out of the flat with all the risk that entailed of his trying to drown his past in a bottle of whiskey. But after closing his eyes for a moment he seemed to come to a decision.

'You have a right to ask,' he said, his voice thick with emotion. 'And you have a right to an answer.'

The silence between them lengthened until, her voice hesitant, Laura spoke again.

'And what is the answer, Michael?'

He crossed the room to her and sat beside her, taking her hands in his, and she could see the pain in his eyes but for once did not regret putting it there. They needed to have this out once and for all.

'You have no idea how the guilt corrodes you inside,' he said quietly. 'It's enough to lose a child and see so many lives wrecked, Aileen's destroyed so slowly over so many years, my parents distraught, her parents distraught, but to know that it was all down to the way you behaved, the crimes you committed... I wonder if your man Holden is going through all that now, you know? Is he thrashing about the way I did? The way I still do sometimes?'

'He's sick, Michael, that's obvious,' Laura said, veering away from their own problems as if the heat was too intense. 'And thankfully someone's decided to stop him abusing women before he goes too far. If you can just find Anna and get her out of his clutches...'

But Thackeray had lost interest in Julie Holden and her problems.

'No one even noticed what I was doing,' Thackeray said. 'There was no one to stop me before I drove Aileen over the brink and she did what she did. I've forgiven her long ago but I don't think I can ever forgive myself. I live with the fact that I effectively murdered my son every day of my life.'

Laura knew better than to argue with his bleak assessment of his own part in Ian's death. It was too close to the truth to be debatable now.

'No absolution, then?' she said softly. 'I thought you were brought up with that.'

'I was brought up with a lot of things, but they died too and were buried with Ian. And now with Aileen.'

'You're too hard on yourself,' Laura whispered, although she knew she was wasting her breath.

'No, I don't think so,' Thackeray said. 'And you want to know why I persist with this job, for all the stress and pain it can cause? Because every time someone's killed, and especially if it's a child, I want to pin the blame where it belongs, however hard it is to do. I want everything out in the open and justice served as it never really was in Ian's case. It wasn't Aileen who should have stood in the dock, it was me. But neither of us ever did, Aileen because she was never fit to plead and me because the blame was indirect and could never be proved. So I plough on, dispensing some sort of justice, knowing all the time that it's a case of the guilty pursuing the guilty, that I'm as culpable as the Bruce Holdens of this world.'

'No, that's not true, Michael. You're too hard on yourself,' Laura said, taking his hand.

'You don't know. You can't know. You weren't there. But maybe it makes me a better copper. Who knows?'

'No, I don't believe that,' Laura said. She kissed his cheek, fighting back the tears, knowing that she had her answer. 'You can't do it again, can you? You can't bear another child.'

He pulled Laura close and clung to her for a long time.

'I love you, Laura,' he said. 'I always will. But no, I don't think I can do that again. I'm too afraid to make myself that vulnerable again. I'm sorry.'

'I'm sorry too,' Laura said. 'You can't imagine how sorry that makes me.'

CHAPTER FIFTEEN

Anna Holden sat on the floor in her grand-mother's cellar trying not to cry. Her nanna was lying asleep on the bed of cushions her father had left for them and Anna had spent the last half hour creeping around the small square room and the coal cellar next to it trying to find some way out of their prison. But the cellar window had been securely boarded up from the outside, and the small metal grill at the top of the coal chute was too small and too firmly wedged in place by years of accumulated dirt and dust for her to move it even when she scrambled up the chute and tried to put her full weight on it from beneath. Hot and dirty, she had sunk to the floor, trying not to cry in case she woke Nanna.

She could see that outside it was daylight again now. Small lozenges of light dimly illuminated the coal cellar through the patterned grating, but in the main room almost no light at all penetrated past the boards attached to the window frame outside. When Bruce had first locked them in her grandmother had tried banging on the window and even shouting to attract attention from the street outside, but after a while both of them had grown hoarse and they had evidently not been heard through the glass and thick boarding. Anna had seen her nanna glancing anxiously at the single light bulb that Bruce had left on and she knew that occasionally bulbs failed. If that happened, she thought, she would be really frightened, especially of the spiders, whose webs festooned the ceiling in great dusty swathes. Anna hated spiders. But there was no way to turn the bulb on or off. The switch, Nanna said, was on the kitchen wall beyond the locked cellar door. They should just be thankful he had decided to leave it on when he left them, she said, trying to reassure Anna, who was not at all reassured but said nothing.

Anna was beginning to panic as the second day of their imprisonment wore on. At first she had believed her father's promises that he would not keep them there long. It had seemed like something of an adventure: she had helped her grandmother, who found it hard to get up from the cushions on the floor, to make picnic meals from the supplies her dad had dumped in a cardboard box. But although he had put in cans of baked beans and ham he had neglected to include a can-opener, so that even Anna began to wonder how long their supplies of bread and cheese would last. She noticed that her grandmother ate and drank very little, and while at first she had tried to fulfil her promise of playing games to keep themselves occupied, she soon seemed to run out of energy and as night fell outside she lapsed into a heavy sleep while Anna, cuddling up to her for warmth under the single duvet and blanket, found it hard to close her eyes, anxiously watching for signs of life amongst the cobwebs.

They were both awake by six, while it was still dark outside, and Anna rummaged in the box for a picnic breakfast, noticing anxiously that they had already eaten more than half of the bread and cheese and that their two bottles of water were going down fast.

'Daddy will be coming back soon,' she said, trying to keep her own spirits up as much as Vanessa's after her grandmother had struggled into the coal cellar to use the bucket he had left there. 'He can't be much longer.'

Vanessa had nodded vaguely as she lowered herself back into a sitting position with a groan.

'Shall we play I-spy again?' Anna asked, but Vanessa had lain back on the cushions, clutching her arms around herself and beginning to shiver.

'It's so cold,' she whispered.

'I'm not cold, Nanna,' Anna said cheerfully.

'You jump up and down a bit,' Vanessa said. 'That'll keep you warm'

'P'raps you should do that too.' But Vanessa just sighed and closed her eyes again and Anna realised, as she had not quite done before, that although Vanessa was supposed to be looking after her, in these circumstances their roles had insidiously reversed themselves. She picked up the blanket from the floor and laid it over her grandmother gently and watched as the old woman fell back to sleep, her bruised and stitched face relaxing as she did.

'Poor Nanna,' Anna whispered. 'It'll be all right. He'll be back soon. He loves us, you know.' But somewhere at the back of her mind she was beginning to doubt all the protestations of undying love her father had made to her over the last few days when they had been alone together. His parallel insistence of how much he hated her mother for what she had done to him suddenly took on new significance, and as she sat watching her grandmother's shallow breathing tears rolled down her dirty cheeks. What, she wondered, was her father doing now? And would he ever come back to release them? Suddenly frightened she shook her grandmother's arm, but there was no response. Very quietly, Anna began to sob.

Half a world away, Mohammed Sharif was

riding beside his cousin in an official car, heading towards the far suburbs of Lahore where, Hussain had assured him, they would be able to speak to Imran Aziz's ex-wife, who was, to Sharif's horror, incarcerated in a women's prison on the outskirts of the city.

Sharif had spent the previous day anxiously filling in time while waiting for Hussain to call him on his mobile. He had pushed and pummelled his way through the crowds of the Inner City near his hotel, admiring its small shrines and palaces, walked through the Elephant Gate into the Lahore Fort and persuaded a friendly caretaker to take him to the underground summer rooms where the Sikh rulers of the Punjab had sheltered from the blazing heat, and ended the day watching Sufi dancers at the shrine of Shah Jamal, sitting in the separate seating area for women and foreigners. But his mind was not on sightseeing. He felt hot and jet-lagged and anxious, even as he tried to relax watching the kite flyers in the Lawrence Gardens just off the magnificent Mall. Eventually he gave up, risked buying a frugal, piping hot meal at one of the many small food stalls close to his hotel and went to bed early, hoping that by morning Hussain's researches would have born fruit.

His phone shrilled soon after breakfast and Hussain announced that he had tracked down Mariam Gul and that she was in fact in gaol, serving a six month sentence.

'For what?' Sharif had asked, horrified.

'Theft and immorality.'

'She's a prostitute?'

'She's a prostitute,' Hussain confirmed. 'With divorced women it sometimes happens. If their families don't want to take them back, all sorts of bad things can happen. It is hard for a single woman on her own to make a living.'

'Maybe we can help her,' Sharif breathed, without much confidence but he did not think that Hussain heard him. Or if he did, he chose to ignore him, instead making arrangements to pick him up and take him to see Mariam.

The prison consisted of low white buildings surrounding a central courtyard where, once through security, Sharif was surprised to find the prisoners free to wander and chat in animated groups. The two men were taken to a small-white walled room furnished with a bare table and chairs and eventually a puzzled looking Mariam Gul, in faded blue *shalwar kameez* and a white headscarf, was brought to them. She was a small woman and much older that Sharif had expected, her face creased and her eyes tired. For a moment she looked at the two men without speaking, and then sat meekly on one of the chairs with her hands in her lap, evidently waiting for them to speak. Hussain introduced them both and as Mariam took in Sharif's relationship to her former husband a flicker of understanding crossed her face but she said nothing.

'Are you the former wife of Imran Aziz?' Hussain asked, not unkindly. And this time, for a second, a flash of anger showed in her eyes. But she quickly looked down as if to veil it, and when she met their eyes again she looked bland as she nodded silently.

'He divorced me three years ago,' she said. 'As you must know.' She directed her last remark to Sharif, who nodded.

'And what happened after that? Did your family not take you back into their home?'

Mariam shook her head.

'I have unmarried sisters. There was no place for me there. And my father regarded my divorce as a disgrace.'

'Why? Were you unfaithful?' Hussain asked, without much sympathy.

'No, I was not,' she said quietly.

'But the marriage was unhappy and they blamed you? Because there were no children?'

'The blame should not have been on my side as there was no marriage in any real sense, anyway,' she said. 'There could be no children because the marriage was never complete. Imran Aziz did not want me except to disguise his own lifestyle, to escape from his parents' pressure to marry.'

The two men stared at her for a long moment in silence and Sharif could feel his stomach tighten.

But now she had started Mariam seemed to decide to tell them everything.

'Imran's father had pressed him to marry and now they seemed to be pressing him to have a family. But I am getting old. The chance of children has passed me by now. I think Imran would have been happy to continue as we were but his father wanted grandsons, it was obvious, and grandsons meant a younger wife. And then Imran's business ran into some difficulties so I think he too began to feel a new start was necessary, in England, if possible. And there may have been other reasons for him to want to leave the country. I don't know.'

'What other reasons?'

'You really don't know, do you?' Mariam asked. 'About his tastes?'

Sharif's mouth was dry and he struggled with the question.

'What tastes?'

'He prefers boys to women,' Mariam said quietly. 'That is what I was supposed to conceal from his family. And his new wife in England, too, no doubt. Here in the city it was easy enough for him to follow his inclinations. And maybe even easier in England. I don't know. But I think maybe the family of one of his boys had discovered a liaison and threatened him so he decided he must leave. He divorced me and married your cousin within a month, had left the country within two.'

'Leaving you with nothing?' Sharif asked.

'Oh, I got by,' Mariam said with a shrug. 'I got a job in a factory for a while, but there were always men willing to offer more money for a night than I could earn in a week there.'

Sharif stood up and pressed his head against the barred window from which he could see the women in the courtyard outside, drifting from group to group, chatting as if it was some village market place.

'How long are you in here?' he asked, his voice thick with anger.

'Another month,' Mariam said.

'And then?'

'Back to work,' she said, as if it was the most normal thing in the world.

'Will you let my cousin here know when you are released?' Sharif said. Mariam shrugged and looked at him wide-eyed.

'If you wish,' she said.

'Come on,' Sharif said to Hussain. 'Let's go.'

In the corridor outside Hussain looked at his companion curiously.

'There's nothing you can do for her, you know. Officially, these women don't exist. To their families they no longer exist. The chances are she's already HIV positive and she'll be dead within a couple of years.'

'And homosexuals don't exist either?' Sharif asked furiously. 'The family here must have done all this to cover up Imran's unacceptable sexuality, the divorce and remarriage, everything. We knew nothing about it in England but they must have known what they were doing here. They owe that woman something.'

'You may be right,' Hussain said. 'But I'd be very surprised if they repaid the debt.'

'We'll see about that,' Sharif said.

'Do you want to talk to Imran's business partner?' Hussain asked. 'We have records of him and Aziz. They ran an import/export business together for ten years, mainly textiles to Europe, but it collapsed just before Imran divorced his wife. It was apparently fairly openly known in his circle that Imran was a homosexual but Lahore is quite liberal in that respect if you are discreet. No one seems to have taken much notice anyway. The wife spent a lot of her time in the village with his parents. But when that relationship broke up the business seems to have collapsed as well. I can give you his partner's address if you like.'

Sharif pulled a face, knowing that he was revealing his own prejudice, deeply ingrained since childhood when he had first asked his father what 'gay' meant and seen his face suffuse with rage.

'I'll give him a miss,' he said, 'so long as you're sure there's no political dimension to all this. That's what they're worried about at home.'

'No,' Hussain said. 'There's nothing like that, unless there are security files I can't get access to. But I've no doubt your people will have made inquiries about that already.'

'Will you keep me in touch if anything else crops up?' Sharif asked.

'Of course,' his cousin said.

'I'll see if I can persuade the family to help Mariam.'

'I wish you luck,' Hussain said. 'I doubt very much that anyone will want to know.'

As Sharif sat on the plane the next day heading back to Manchester and gazing down at a cloud-shrouded Europe below, his mind was still whirling with fears that he had not even broached with his cousin. If Imran had followed the same pattern with Faria as he had with his first wife, he thought, pursuing a sexless marriage of convenience, then it seemed extremely unlikely that he was the father of the baby she was carrying when she died. And if he was not the father, then DCI Thackeray would undoubtedly wish to find out who was, with all the implications that line of inquiry implied for Sharif himself and his entire family in Bradfield. The trip to Pakistan had seemed like a good idea at the time, Sharif thought as he tried to accommodate his still painful ribs to the narrow airline seat without much success. But the closer he got to England the more he became convinced that it might have been a terrible mistake, a mistake Faria's father and his own would never forgive him for as it inevitably exposed their family secrets to the public gaze.

'Guv?' Sergeant Kevin Mower put his head round his boss's door the next morning and found Thackeray with his chair turned round towards the window, apparently oblivious to the interruption as he gazed out at the wind-torn trees tossing in a wintry and almost deserted town hall square, a cigarette clutched unlit in one hand.

'Morning, guv,' Mower said more loudly, closing the office door behind him. 'A few developments overnight for a change.' Thackeray swivelled his chair round towards the sergeant, who tried not to allow his concern to show as he realised how ill the DCI looked. His face was ashen and he had dark circles under his eyes, and as he lit his cigarette, Mower could see that his hands were shaking.

'Health and safety haven't got you yet,' he said as lightly as he could, nodding at the smoke that wreathed around the office as Thackeray exhaled deeply. Thackeray merely shook his head irritably.

'What are these developments then?' he asked. 'Have we traced Imran Aziz?'

'No, not that,' Mower admitted. 'But we are getting a clearer picture of what had been going on in that house. Slower than we might like because the spooks took so much stuff away, but they're feeding the inform-ation back to us now. In fact, I get the distinct impression that they've lost interest in Imran Aziz as a potential terrorist. There's no evidence of that, apparently.'

'I'll check personally with Doug Mc-Kinnon later,' Thackeray snapped. 'If he's not a terrorist they're just getting in the way of our investigation of his wife's murder.'

'That's what I thought, guv,' Mower said. 'Anyway, what they have found are traces of Class A drugs.'

'Drugs?' Thackeray could not hide his excitement.

'Heroin, to be precise,' Mower said. 'Just a single wrap hidden in some of Aziz's paper-work, which suggests a user rather than a dealer. But interesting, even so.'

'Especially in the light of what forensics say about Faria having narcotics in her bloodstream. Talk to the drug squad, Kevin, and see if they have any knowledge of his involvement and of his most likely source. Did anyone find a syringe or any other para-phernalia?'

'No, not yet, but I'll ask for everything to be checked again. It might be worth asking Amos Atherton if he's found anything further as well. He did say he would have a another look, didn't he?'

'I'll chase him,' Thackeray said. 'We could ask the police in Pakistan if there's any record of Aziz's involvement in narcotics, though I don't understand how he would get a visa to come here if anything like that was on record, even if he had married a British woman.'

'Well, perhaps he picked up the habit after he arrived,' Mower said. 'It's pretty obvious he wasn't making the success of his life here that he'd hoped. He'd not got a business off the ground, his wife was working, possibly needing to work to keep them going, which doesn't go down too well in that community, and he'd only had factory jobs himself. Perhaps he was more desperate than anyone's letting on.'

'I think there's a lot going on in that family that no one is telling us,' Thackeray said. 'Do we have a photograph?'

'A couple,' Mower said.

'Right, let's get them on TV and into the press. I want Imran Aziz found. Have you spoken to DC Sharif since he got out of hospital?'

Mower looked at his boss warily for a moment.

'I thought you didn't want any contact,' he said.

'Come on, Kevin. I know you'll talk to him if you think he has anything to offer. Have you done that?'

But Mower shook his head.

'I did give him a bell to see how he was but I got no reply. His mobile was switched off. I might try to contact his girlfriend...'

'He's got a girlfriend, has he?' Thackeray asked. 'One his parents would approve of?'

'Almost certainly not,' Mower said, with a tight smile. 'She's called Louise.'

'Check he's OK. That's legitimate enough,' Thackeray said. 'That was a nasty beating he took. Any witnesses turned up?' Mower shook his head.

'Well, if Omar offers you any further thoughts about Aziz, let me know.'

'Right, guv,' Mower said.

'Is there any further news on Bruce Holden? Any sightings?'

'Nothing's come in overnight,' Mower said. 'He seems to have vanished off the face of the earth.'

'I had David Mendelson bending my ear first thing this morning,' Thackeray said. 'The wife is staying with them for the time being, though I told him I didn't think that was a very good idea. Can you tell uniform she's there and ask them to keep a close eye? We know he's made one attempt to break in and he might try again. I'd rather his wife got right out of the area, really, but David says she won't move until she finds out where the daughter is. She's in a bad way, apparently.'

'I'm not surprised,' Mower said. 'I'll pass it on.'

When Mower had gone, Thackeray ground out his cigarette in the overflowing ashtray that, according to the rules, had no place in his office any longer, and sighed heavily. He glanced at the phone, wondering whether he dare call Laura, who had left the flat early that morning with barely a word, and then decided against it. She would, he thought, either come to terms with what he had said the previous night or she would not, in which case he knew their relationship would probably be over. But he felt that there was little he could say to convince her that she should give up the prospect of being a mother for his sake. To ask her to do that, he thought, would be grossly unfair. It was a decision only she could make, and he feared the worst.

Angrily, he picked up the phone and punched in Amos Atherton's number, but the pathologist was not available, intent, no doubt, on his delicate dissection of some new and fascinating cadaver. But he did succeed, at the second attempt, in making contact with Doug McKinnon, who admitted, cautiously, that his investigators had found nothing at all to link Imran Aziz with fundamentalism or violence of any kind.

'He seems to be clean, from our point of view,' McKinnon said. 'As far as any of the bastards are clean. He's all yours. It looks like a simple domestic to me.'

'We'll see,' Thackeray said coldly and made to hang up just as McKinnon spoke again.

'There was one thing I bet you don't know, though.' The man sounded faintly triumphant, Thackeray thought, and his heart sank. 'Your DC Sharif. What do you call him? Omar? Spent the weekend in Lahore, didn't he? You might want to ask him what he thought he was up to out there, mightn't you? Blood being thicker than water with that lot, after all. I'll let you know if anything else crops up.'

'Do that,' Thackeray said, hanging up angrily. He punched in Mower's internal number.

'Find Sharif and get him in here now,' he said. 'And don't take no for an answer.'

CHAPTER SIXTEEN

Mohammed Sharif knocked at his uncle's front door before his young cousins had left for school that morning. Faisel let him in without a word, almost as if he had been expecting him to call. Sharif glanced at Jamilla and Saira, coats already on over school navy blue *shalwar kameez* and headscarfs pulled over their hair.

'I need to speak to you privately,' he said to his uncle. The girls glanced anxiously at their father but obeyed as he waved them out of the front door before closing it firmly behind them.

'I've been to Lahore,' Sharif said without preamble as he followed his uncle into the living room. He could hear his aunt in the kitchen but knew she would not interrupt if he closed the door on their discussion. His uncle looked gaunt and distant but he said nothing in reply.

'I was very disturbed by what I discovered there,' Mohammed said quietly. 'I was very unhappy, in fact.'

Faisel stared impassively at his nephew, still saying nothing, his deep-set dark eyes blank, waiting for the younger man to continue, but Mohammed hesitated himself, unsure where to begin. Finally he decided he had to tackle Faisel head on.

'Did you know that Imran Aziz was a homosexual when you persuaded Faria to marry him?'

Faisel glanced away but Mohammed could see no sign of the shock that might have been expected if the allegation had come as news to him.

'Did you know?' he repeated, more angrily this time. 'Did you knowingly marry Faria off to a homosexual to get him out of Pakistan? Or what, exactly?'

'No,' Faisel said hoarsely. 'She was married for the reasons I explained to you before. She was married as had been arranged when she was a child, for family reasons. Her grandfather and his brother, my uncle, wished it. She agreed. She met Imran and she agreed to marry him.'

'So did she discover his tastes later and tell you about them? His previous wife was under no illusions about his preferences when I spoke to her the other day. Though she seems to have been deceived into marriage as well. And abandoned by our family afterwards. I found her in prison after working as a prostitute. Did Faria find out as well?'

'No, Faria never said anything to me about her marriage. She seemed happy enough.'

Mohammed Sharif got to his feet and walked angrily from one end of the room to the other, his unbandaged fist clenching and unclenching as his uncle watched him apprehensively.

'But you knew about Imran?' he asked. 'You weren't surprised when I told you?'

'I found out later,' Faisel admitted. 'I was told quite recently by someone from the mosque in Milford. Aziz had made approaches to a young man ... he was outraged and told the imam.'

'The imam said nothing of this to me,' Sharif objected. 'I spoke to him last week.'

'There is a new imam. He may not have known. It was the previous imam who told me.'

'And what did you do about it? It's not illegal in this country.'

'I told Faria what I knew and then I spoke to Imran privately. I asked him to divorce her. To set her free. God willing, she could start again. We could find her another husband. Perhaps she could go to university, which is what she had wanted earlier... I tried to put things right.'

'Did you really not know she was pregnant? That would make your plans for her more difficult, to say the least.'

'No, I didn't know that,' Faisel said. 'Not until Jamilla told me, after her body was found.'

'Did you tell DCI Thackeray any of this, about Imran?' Sharif asked.

His uncle shook his head.

'No,' he said. 'I was too ashamed.'

Sharif flung himself into a chair with a groan.

'Did Faria agree to this plan? Did she find this acceptable? You spoke to her about it?'

'She did not object when I asked her if that was what she wanted. She seemed happy to divorce.'

'And even then she didn't tell you about the baby?'

'No,' Faisel said.

'And Imran? Do you know where Imran is now?'

Faisel shook his head and Mohammed sighed.

'The imam said that under sharia law ... well, you know what would happen.'

'Is that what's happened?' Sharif asked, his face betraying his horror.

'I don't know,' Faisel shouted. 'I don't know what's happened to Imran. He deceived us all but I don't know what's happened to him.'

His nephew took a deep breath to calm himself before he felt able to continue.

'You must go to DCI Thackeray and tell him the truth, the whole truth,' he said. 'If Imran was known to be gay there are enough angry young men at that mosque to try to do something about it. To be honest, I think I've run into some of them myself.' He nursed his bandaged hand thoughtfully before going on. 'We've been assuming that Imran disappeared because he was involved in some way in Faria's death. But perhaps he's in danger too. Perhaps he's been murdered. You must talk to Mr Thackeray and be completely honest with him. You could be arrested yourself for concealing information. Do you understand me, Uncle? You must do it and do it now, or you will find yourself a suspect in Imran's disappearance, or even Faria's death. They will think the worst.'

'Will you come with me?' Faisel asked and Mohammed knew how hard the question was to ask. But he shook his head vehemently.

'I am not involved in this case,' he said. 'I have been told that I can't be involved. Nor did I know anything about this deception. I don't want my officers to think that I knew anything about it. You must take the responsibility. It's nothing to do with me.'

'It is a family matter,' Faisel Sharif said angrily. '*Your* family. You have a duty.'

'No,' Mohammed snapped back. 'I want nothing to do with it. I'll tell Mr Thackeray later what I discovered in Lahore. That duty I can't avoid. But I won't take any responsibility for what the family did to Faria, and your involvement in it, tricking her into that marriage. It may not have been illegal but it is shameful and I've no doubt that it has something to do with her death.'

He got up and moved towards the door. He felt cold and sick and he knew that he would not be forgiven for what he was about to say.

'I will ask to see Mr Thackeray this afternoon,' he said. 'If you haven't been to see him by then I will tell him everything you've told me this morning and everything I discovered in Lahore. I don't know what the consequences will be for you. But I do know what the consequences would be for me if I remained silent. I have no choice. I'm sorry.'

And he closed the door behind him quietly, and left the house. He was unlikely, he thought, ever to be invited into it again.

Sharif met DS Kevin Mower in a coffee shop close to the central police station that lunchtime. Mower had called him on his mobile soon after he had left his uncle's house and insisted on the meeting. Sharif had not been surprised to discover that DCI Thackeray wanted to talk to him at two, regardless of his own intentions, and was grateful that the sergeant was prepared to fill him in on what had been happening while he had been away.

'You look rough,' Mower said as the younger man joined him at a corner table with an espresso in his good hand and a pack of sandwiches tucked awkwardly under his arm.

'Jet lag,' Sharif said dismissively. 'I'm fine.'

'Yes, I heard you'd been away. Interesting trip, was it?'

Sharif shrugged.

'Not the word I'd choose,' he said. 'I uncovered stuff about my family that I can still barely believe.'

'You'll tell the boss?'

'Oh yes, I'll tell him,' Sharif said heavily.

'You must,' Mower said. 'Your uncle came in this morning and passed on a lot of stuff about Imran that he hadn't bothered to mention before. Mr Thackeray wasn't best pleased.'

'Well, at least he turned up. He wouldn't have done if I hadn't threatened to shop him earlier this morning.'

Mower looked at Sharif appraisingly. He knew very well how hard that conversation must have been for the DC.

'You've burnt your boats with the family, then?'

'I don't think my uncle will ever speak to me again,' Sharif said. 'I don't know about my own parents. I haven't seen them yet.'

'You have to know which side you're on in this business,' Mower said. 'There's no room for divided loyalties.'

'I never thought mine were divided until

this case,' Sharif said, still uncertain how far he was willing to go to help locate the men who had assaulted him. 'I had no idea what was going on with Faria and Imran. I'm appalled.' He pushed his sandwiches away with his bandaged hand after a single mouthful.

'You may have difficulty persuading the boss you knew nothing about it,' Mower said. 'The spooks are already asking why you shot off to Pakistan so suddenly. They didn't miss that.'

'Bastards,' Sharif said. 'What do they think I went for after being beaten to a pulp? A bit of weapons training in Afghanistan? They're idiots.'

'Just be careful,' Mower said soothingly. 'I'm sure you can put their minds at rest.' He glanced at his watch. 'You'd better get over there. The boss looked as if someone had pissed in his cornflakes this morning. And believe me, when he's in a strop he takes no prisoners. Personally, I think he came back to work much too soon after he was shot, but there you go. Be warned.'

Anna Holden began to despair that morning. She and her grandmother had slept fitfully under the blankets her father had flung down for them for a second night, but they were barely adequate in the dank chill of the cellar and Anna knew that her grandmother's constant shivering was not good for her. She tried to keep herself warm by singing and dancing around until she ran out of songs that she could remember, then spent some time trying to scramble up the coal chute and hammer on the metal grille in the roof until she was exhausted.

'He'll be back soon, won't he, Nan?' she asked. But her grandmother, huddled under the blankets, simply shrugged.

'He said he'd be back soon,' Anna said firmly. 'I'll get us something to eat. We'll have a picnic.' But by now, as they had consumed the two cans of soup that opened with a ring pulls, she had to be content with dried out sliced bread, and the last of the cheese and a swig from their almost empty bottle of water. She offered food to her grandmother but she shook her head at the bread and took only a sip from the bottle.

'You must eat, Nanna,' the child said, pushing her dishevelled hair away from her battered face. But Vanessa merely turned away from the light and pulled the blanket more tightly around her shoulders.

'What he really should have given us was that little camping stove we used to take on picnics,' Anna said, trying to sound cheerful. 'Then we could have made hot drinks.' Her voice faltered slightly as she realised that her grandmother's eyes were closed and she did not appear to be listening. 'Wouldn't you think he'd have let us make hot drinks, Nan?' she insisted. 'I would be very careful with the stove...'

When they had first been left alone in the cellar her grandmother had taken charge of the situation but now she had subsided beneath the blankets, and this morning, as a little daylight penetrated the cracks at the sides of the boarded up area window, she seemed barely able to make the effort to speak. Anna gazed up at the single light bulb and wondered again how long it would burn for. If it went out, they would be in almost total darkness and that thought frightened her even more. She glanced at the spiders' webs and shuddered. She went back into the small coal cellar, where the bucket her father provided was beginning to smell, and looked around her desperately for something solid to bang against the grating above her head. But someone had emptied and swept out the confined space and there was not so much as a broom handle that would allow her to push upwards. She tried shouting again but her voice sounded thin and outside there was no sound at all. She glanced at her watch and saw that it was not yet eight in the morning, and she wondered what her mother was doing now she was not there with her, getting ready for school, and the thought of the normality she had been swept away from brought tears to her eyes again.

'Daddy, where are you?' she cried. 'You said you wouldn't be long.' At that moment the single light went out and in her sudden panic to get back to her grandmother Anna kicked over the toilet bucket and burst into tears. Finding her way blindly back towards the cushions on the floor she scrambled under the duvet beside Vanessa, but when she cuddled up against her for warmth there was no response and, rigid with shock herself, she began to wonder if her grandmother would ever wake up.

Michael Thackeray listened to Mohammed Sharif's description of his trip to Lahore and what he had discovered there in silence. His head ached and he was distracted both by thoughts of Laura and by occasional jabs of pain from the scars his brush with death had caused so recently. But he fought off the distractions determinedly, knowing that what his anxious looking young DC was telling him was crucial not only to the murder investigation but to Sharif's future in the police force. When he had finished Thackeray said nothing for a time and Sharif himself felt impelled to break the heavy silence.

'Did my uncle come in to see you as I advised him to?' he asked, his mouth dry.

'Yes, Kevin interviewed him,' Thackeray said. 'You were right to encourage him to come in.' Thackeray hesitated before going on, knowing that what he had to say would be unwelcome.

'I asked you in for a word in private,' he said at length. 'That, rather than taking my worries higher, which is where they will inevitably go very soon. I can't protect you from the implications of what you've done by dashing off to Pakistan like that, even less from the fact that your close family will inevitably become the focus of this inquiry now, and however much you think you've distanced yourself from them, you are still part of that family.'

'You mean my uncle is a suspect?' Sharif asked, his mouth dry.

'Inevitably,' Thackeray said. 'He hasn't been frank with us and his response to what seems to have happened will be a line of inquiry we have to follow. But he's not the only person we will need to investigate. You must know that.'

'You mean I could become a suspect?'

'I hope not,' Thackeray said. 'But it's possible, isn't it? Tell me honestly what the traditional reaction might be if the circumstances of your cousin's marriage to a homosexual man became widely known in your community? Would anyone feel bound to take some action, and if so, who? And what action would they feel impelled to take?'

Sharif gazed at the DCI for a moment in silence, aware that his whole career stood on a knife-edge and there was very little he could do to influence the course of events one way or the other. He had walked out on his uncle, and by implication, the rest of his family, but even that might not save him, he thought bitterly.

'You must talk to me, Mohammed,' Thackeray insisted. 'I know it's difficult.'

'Yes,' Sharif said. He took a deep breath. 'You have to understand that it is all a question of family honour and traditional values,' he said reluctantly. 'There seem to be two problems here. Imran is evidently gay. That is a sin in Islam, but it is tolerated here and in the big cities in Pakistan like Lahore, so long as it is not flaunted in a way that brings disrepute on the family. He seems to have kept a low enough profile, but ran into problems in Milford where there are some zealots at the mosque who seem to have discovered his tastes and taken exception to them.'

'Would they kill him?' Thackeray asked. Sharif shrugged, hesitated and then made his decision.

'I think the same people took exception to my lifestyle,' he said. 'I have an English girl-friend. When I was attacked someone called on Allah as they hit me. I don't think white racists were involved at all.'

Thackeray looked at the younger officer for a moment in silence, his mind racing.

'Now you've remembered that, perhaps you can add it to your statement?' he said carefully.

'Sir,' Sharif said.

'So let's get back to these zealots from the mosque, now we've one more reason to interest ourselves in them. Would they kill Imran Khan when they uncovered his homosexuality?'

'They might not kill him, but they might well threaten to expose him to the rest of the community.'

'And that would upset your family?'

Sharif swallowed hard, and nodded.

'That would upset my family,' he said quietly. 'Very much.'

'And Faria? Who has she upset? We've been concentrating our attention on Imran as a potential suspect for her murder, but maybe that's all wrong. Maybe he's a victim too, and someone else entirely hated both of them enough to kill.'

Sharif ran his hands over his face and shrugged.

'I don't know what to think,' he said.

'You do know,' Thackeray insisted, not unsympathetically. 'And I need to know. Is the baby Faria was carrying likely to be Imran's? I'm having DNA checks done but I've not got the results back yet, so tell me what you think. Is the reason she wanted a divorce because she was carrying a baby that was not her husband's?'

'A divorce?' Sharif said, evidently shocked. '*She* wanted a divorce? I knew nothing about that. I thought that was my uncle's idea.'

'She made inquiries some months ago, apparently. Did your uncle not know that?'

Sharif shook his head wildly.

'He said nothing to me, but then he would not be broadcasting the news. Divorce – for a woman – is difficult in our culture. Not forbidden but difficult. My uncle said he was considering the possibility of divorce because of Imran's ... predilections. But he implied it was his idea – and a very recent one.'

'And he still says he didn't know she was pregnant before she died?'

'Jamilla says she never told him,' Sharif said.

'But if the baby is not Imran's? Would that make a difference to what he thought about her marriage, or a divorce?'

'That would create a huge scandal,' Sharif said very quietly. 'You must know that.'

Thackeray sighed.

'So could she have had a boyfriend, do you think? Could the baby be another man's? An Englishman's perhaps? I know this is all speculation but I need to know how likely that is.'

'His former wife in Lahore thinks it's un-likely Imran would sleep with her,' Sharif

318

mumbled. 'So if there was a baby coming...' he shrugged.

Thackeray took a deep breath.

'You were obviously very fond of your cousin. Did it go any further than that?'

Visibly shaken, Sharif shook his head, his eyes full of tears.

'No,' he said.

'Good,' Thackeray said. 'You understand why I had to ask?'

Sharif swallowed hard and nodded.

'So, do you know anyone she might have been having a relationship with?'

'No,' Sharif said again, this time letting his anger show. 'You don't understand how horrified I am by all this. I try to be modern, western, all that, but the old ways run deep. I've lost my beautiful young cousin and now it appears her reputation is to be ruined too. It's unbearable.'

'I'm trying to understand,' Thackeray said. 'That's why I'm taking the time to fill you in on what's going to happen next. The forensic results will clarify some things, but in the meantime, I'm going to have to interview most of your family to discover who knew what about Imran and Faria's relationship. In Milford, I'm going to want to know who knew what at the mosque about Imran's activities, and we will have to look at Faria's possible relationship with someone else. All this will, I'm sure, be very upsetting, but it

319

has to be done. You understand that.'

'Sir,' Sharif said, his expression impassive now. 'And what do you want me to do?'

'Firstly, I want you to make a formal statement about your trip to Pakistan. Naturally, we'll want to check with the police there officially, to find out as much as we can about Imran Aziz at that end. Then I want you to take some leave, go away somewhere if you like, but keep me in touch with where you are. Special Branch may want to talk to you. They were jumping up and down yesterday when they discovered you'd flown out, but before they could set up any sort of hue and cry they found out you were already on the plane back. You know how twitchy they are.'

Sharif got to his feet and moved towards the door but before he opened it his anger got the better of him.

'It's just not tenable any more, is it?' he said. 'You try to integrate, you try to do a useful job that needs doing, you make every effort, but then suddenly you're under suspicion, your kids go to the wrong mosque, your wife has the wrong relations in the wrong country, you take an unexpected trip abroad, and suddenly you're a suspect; your face doesn't fit, all your efforts go for nothing because you're the wrong colour and the wrong religion. Do you want me to resign now, sir? Or should I wait until someone finds a reason to charge me with something? I'd just like to know.'

Thackeray winced as his back wrenched his body with pain but he got to his feet anyway.

'No,' he said quietly. 'I don't want your resignation. I want you to come through this unscathed and continue what looks like a very promising career. I know how difficult this must be for you, but give me the help I'm asking for and I promise you, if you're honest with me, I'll do my best to protect your position. You have my word on that.'

Sharif took a deep breath.

'Thank you,' he said.

CHAPTER SEVENTEEN

Laura Ackroyd found it almost impossible to concentrate that morning. Thackeray had not come home the previous night, retreating, she supposed, as he sometimes did, to the small flat on the other side of town that he resolutely refused to sell. He saw it, she thought, as a bolt hole, and this time she feared he might have bolted there for good. She sighed as she gazed blank-eyed at her computer screen. She had precipitated this crisis, she thought, and now she had got her answer she was not sure what to do. She needed to talk to someone else, she decided, and she dialled Vicky Mendelson's number in the hope that she might be able to go up to her house for lunch and some friendly counselling. Naomi would be home from nursery school and she guessed that seeing a child she loved would crystallise her feelings and make some sort of decision easier. She had always adored Vicky's children and she simply could not decide whether living without children of her own was possible. But nor could she get her mind round the equal impossibility of living without Michael. She knew why he could not commit to starting a new family with her, but she resented it bitterly just the same.

To her surprise, a voice she recognised as Julie Holden's answered her call.

'Is Vicky there?' Laura asked, only to be told that she was out collecting Naomi from nursery.

'I was thinking of inviting myself to a quick lunch,' Laura said, irritated by the other woman's presence when she wanted some time alone with Vicky.

'I'm sure she won't mind,' Julie said. 'She'll be back soon. Daniel is off school with a cold so I'm baby-sitting. Have you heard anything more about Bruce and Anna? The police haven't been in touch for a couple of days.'

'I don't think there's been any trace of them,' Laura said, slightly impatiently. 'You should ring Janet Richardson. She's supposed to keep you informed.'

'Yes, maybe I'll do that,' Julie said, her voice dull, and Laura felt guilty about her impatience.

'I'll see you in about half an hour,' she said. 'We can talk about it then.'

Less than half an hour later, Vicky Mendelson opened the door with her daughter in her arms, and for a second Laura struggled to hold back her tears as she kissed them both.

'You look rough,' Vicky said, taking in her

friend's pale face and the purple circles under her eyes. She led the way into the kitchen, where the table was laid for three adults with a high chair for Naomi, and Vicky strapped the child in with a plate of vegetable and fruit fingers in front of her. Julie was already sitting at the table waiting for them.

'No turkey twizzlers, then?' Laura said, with a grin. Vicky's passion for feeding her children healthy food was becoming a joke amongst her friends.

'You must be kidding. Could you take this in to Daniel for me?' She handed Laura a plate of sandwiches. 'He's in the sitting room with the latest Harry Potter. But keep your distance. He's got a streaming cold.'

Laura did as she was asked and was rewarded with an attempt at a smile from the Mendelson's elder son, who was huddled under a duvet with his nose in his book.

'Hi, Laura,' he said between snuffles.

'Good book?' she asked.

'Yes, great,' he said. 'Better than school.'

To Laura's frustration, but not her surprise, lunch turned out to be a silent affair, at which neither she nor Julie raised their burning concerns over tuna salad and wholemeal bread. But when they had finished, Julie seemed to become more aware of the long silences between the three of them and left the kitchen to sit with Daniel.

'So?' Vicky asked quietly. 'You look as if you've lost the crown jewels and found a Ratner's ring. Is Michael being difficult again?'

Laura managed a smile at that.

'I may have lost not just a wedding ring but a whole future,' she said, and told Vicky the gist of how her partner had rejected any prospect of having another child.

'Bloody man,' Vicky said, lifting her own daughter down from the table so she could run off to see her brother. 'Bloody, bloody man. Why couldn't he have told you this before? It seems wickedly late now.'

'Yes,' Laura said. 'And I don't know whether I can bear it.'

'Oh, Laura,' Vicky said, putting her hand over her friend's. 'It's difficult to talk now with Julie here. Officially she's moved back to the hostel but this morning I asked her to come and keep an eye on Daniel while I did some shopping and fetched Naomi from nursery. She was glad to make herself useful and that refuge she's staying in is like a prison. But she's going back later. Why don't you come back to supper tonight and we'll have a proper talk. If Michael's not coming home, that is.'

'I don't know whether he is or not. He's up to his eyes in a murder case, as you know. And I don't even think he should be at work at all. He's still not really fit. He's still getting a lot of pain. Oh, Vicky, I really, really don't know what to do.'

At that moment Julie came back into the room, holding her bag and her mobile phone in her hand.

'Are you OK, now, Vicky?' she asked. 'I really want to go up to my house to get one or two things and then I've an appointment with my solicitor at four.'

'Yes, thanks, Julie, it was very good of you to help out.'

'Don't mention it,' Julie said dryly. 'I've nothing else to do but sit and worry myself sick.' She turned to Laura. 'I took your advice but Sergeant Richardson had no news,' she said. 'They seem to have disappeared off the face of the earth.'

'Where are you going now?' Laura asked. 'I'm going back to work but I can give you a lift if you like.' She knew that Bruce Holden had disappeared in the family's only car.

Julie took up the offer with alacrity and Laura drove quickly the half mile or so from Vicky's house to the Holdens' and parked outside.

'Do you want me to come in with you?' she asked as Julie made to get out of the car.

'No, you get back to work,' Julie said. 'Bruce is obviously not here. There's no sign of the car. Anyway, he'd be a fool to bring Anna back to Bradfield, let alone home. The neighbours must know now what's been going on from what appeared in the *Gazette*. He's miles away by now, with no intention of coming back.'

'If you're going into town, I'll wait for you,' Laura said.

'Can you? Are you sure?' Julie hesitated but she looked relieved. 'I'll be ten minutes, maybe. I'll try to be quick. I just want to collect some stuff from my bedroom.' She slammed the car door and Laura watched her walk slowly to the front door, open it and close it behind her.

The ten minutes passed slowly as Laura wrestled with her own dilemmas, which her lunch had in no way resolved, and when she next glanced at her watch she realised that Julie's ten minutes was more than up, and she began to worry about getting back to work herself on time. She locked the car up and went to the front door and rang the bell. There was no response and, after waiting for a minute or so, she tried the handle and was surprised to find that the door swung open. Hesitantly, she stepped inside and called out to Julie.

At first there was no reply, but then she heard a sort of half-strangled gasp coming from the back of the house.

'Julie?' she called again, walking very quietly down the hall to the door that she guessed opened into the kitchen. 'Julie, are you there?'

The door was not closed and when Laura pushed it swung open and she found herself face to face with Bruce Holden, who had an arm round Julie, pinning her arms to her sides, and was holding a large kitchen knife to his wife's throat.

'You again? Come in, why don't you?' he asked. 'Let's make a party of it.'

'He called me on my mobile,' Julie gasped. 'He said he had Anna here and I could see her if I came round. What else could I do?'

'Come in, I said. Come bloody well in!' Holden's voice was harsh and Laura could see his grip tighten on the knife as he pressed it harder against the flesh underneath Julie's ear. She swallowed hard and closed the kitchen door behind her and stood leaning against it, one hand in her pocket clutching her mobile phone, wondering whether she could dial 999 without his noticing.

'Where's your daughter?' she asked quietly. 'We've all been very worried about her.'

Holden responded by moving Julie at knife-point towards Laura and pushing himself and his wife between her and the door to the hall, effectively closing off that escape route. Close up Laura could see that Julie was not only white-faced but that there was already a smear of blood on her neck where the knife had creased the skin. Laura felt herself shivering and could see that Julie was in much the same state. But she could think of no way to remove the knife from Holden's fist without his finding the seconds it needed to cut Julie's throat before she could pull him off.

'Sit over there at the table,' Holden instructed, and Laura did as she was told, knowing that the worst possible thing would be to provoke him. But with one hand still in her jacket pocket she ran a finger gently over her phone keypad, trying to work out which was the number 9.

'Why don't you let Julie go and then you can talk sensibly about Anna. She wouldn't want either of you hurt, would she? Her mother *or* her father?'

'Don't you worry about Anna,' Holden snarled.

'Where is she?' Julie asked, with a sob. 'What have you done with her?'

'I told you, she's safe. She'll come to no harm with me, you know that, you bitch. You've been telling people I would hurt her, but that's a filthy lie. I'd never hurt my own daughter.'

'Don't you think you've hurt her already, putting her through all this stress?' Laura asked, reckoning that maybe provocation would distract him from Julie and allow her a chance to break free, but he was evidently not to be distracted. He gripped his victim even more closely and screamed back at Laura, his face contorted with rage.

'Shut up, you interfering cow! I told you I would never never hurt my daughter.'

'You will hurt her if you hurt her mother,' Laura said, angry herself now. 'You must have hurt her, every time you hit Julie.'

'Fuck you!' Holden screamed, twisting Julie's head back so hard that Laura could see that she could barely breathe. 'You're all the same, you fucking women – my bloody mother, my bloody wife, my bloody wife's nosy friends. A man doesn't stand a chance with you, any of you. You gang up on us, you nag and nag and nag until we go de-mented...' And suddenly he seemed to lose control of his thought processes entirely, turning purple and flinging Julie across the kitchen, past Laura, who took the chance to pull her phone half out of her pocket under the shelter of the table and finally punch in three nines.

Julie hit the worktop next to the cooker hard and stood there, apparently stunned, half slumped across the surface with her shoulders shaking. But suddenly she spun round with a knife from the knife block in her hand and launched herself back across the kitchen at her husband to stab him in the chest repeatedly in an eerie silence that was broken only by a strangled choking sound as Bruce Holden slid slowly down the door onto the floor, dropping his own knife from limp fingers with a clatter, leaving a smear of bright red blood behind him.

Laura sat where she was for a moment, too stunned to move or speak, until she realised that someone was calling repeatedly to her on the mobile phone she still held in her hand.

'Which service?' the voice asked again. 'Are you there? Which service do you require?'

'Police,' Laura said, her mouth dry. 'And ambulance.'

DCI Thackeray faced an urgently summoned briefing of his detectives early that afternoon, unable to disguise his weariness. Sergeant Kevin Mower watched him from the back of the room with barely concealed anxiety. Since the incident in which the DCI had been shot, he had rarely looked well, he thought. But now he appeared to be positively ill, his shoulders bowed as if he carried the troubles of the world on them, and his face grey and creased with tiredness, and he wondered, not for the first time, if the DCI was back on the bottle. How many years until he could retire? the sergeant wondered dispassionately. Too many, by the look of it.

'There have been some developments,' Thackeray said quietly. 'Developments from forensics and more information about the relationships between Faria Aziz, her family and her husband. Everything seems to confirm our conclusion that she was murdered and gives us a much clearer picture of the means and the motive for this crime. But they also throw our assumption that her husband is the prime suspect into some doubt. In fact, they leave me wondering whether Aziz himself is not another victim and we should be looking for another body. However, one lead at a time. Kevin, will you go through the latest forensic reports for us?'

Mower moved to the front of the room while Thackeray sank into a chair, leaning forward, his hands clasped between his knees.

'Right,' Mower said briskly. 'Following the discovery of heroin in the victim's body and then at her home, we asked for a further examination of her body on the off-chance that there might be evidence that she was a user. The pathologist has managed to pinpoint a single puncture mark on her arm – not exactly evidence of a habit, but enough to confirm that she might have been under the influence of drugs when she went into the river.' Mower indicated a photograph of a discoloured area of flesh on the whiteboard behind him, with a circle around a small wound that might easily have been dismissed, as Amos Atherton had initially dismissed it, as an insect bite or the result of damage during the time the body had been swept miles in the waters of the Maze.

'That, of course, followed the toxicology tests that revealed a significant amount of heroin in her blood stream. Not enough to kill her, maybe, but she might have been semi-conscious or unconscious when she went into the water. Of course, it's a pity we didn't know this earlier, but no one had any reason to suspect that Faria might have taken – or been given – drugs.

'That's the first thing. The second forensic result is even more significant. We knew she was pregnant. What we didn't know until the DNA results came through this morning, is that her baby was not her husband's. There's no match with Imran Aziz. So somewhere out there is a man who is the father of her child. Top priority, obviously, is to find him. This is hugely significant because it implies she was in another relationship. We have no idea which, if any, members of her family knew about this. But we need to find out. As you know, adultery is seriously frowned on in Muslim families. It could be a motive for murder.'

Thackeray got to his feet again and faced his slightly startled-looking team.

'The rest of this is getting even more difficult,' the DCI said. 'You all know, because its been drummed into you at every training course on race and community relations you've ever been on...' There was a faint groan from the back of the room, which

Thackeray quelled with an angry glance. 'You all know very well,' he repeated coldly, 'that honour is of great importance to Muslim families, especially the honour of their women folk. Whether or not Faria's situation provides us with the motive for her murder, and it's looking increasingly likely, it will undoubtedly cause her family great distress.'

'You're not going all politically correct on us, are you boss?' another voice asked from the back of the room.

'Soft-pedal, should we?' a different voice asked.

Thackeray scowled.

'This is a murder case,' he snapped. 'We put every ounce of energy into finding out who killed this young woman, just as we would in any other case. That's been true from the beginning and is even more true now it has become even more complicated. But I do expect you to treat everyone we interview with respect, particularly Faria's close family. I don't want the water muddied with accusations of racism or cultural insensitivity. It isn't helpful, in fact, it's a serious distraction, even if in the end we have to arrest one, or more, of them. That's all.'

There was a moment of silence while the assembled team absorbed this warning.

'You think they won't cry racism anyway?'

a young detective at the front of the room asked.

'Of course they will,' Thackeray said. 'Their lawyers will jump on us if they think we've put a foot wrong and even if we haven't. But when, rather than if, they do, I need to know that there's absolutely no justification for the complaint. If there's no justification, I can deal with it. So play it by the book. Understood?'

There was a murmur of assent from the meeting.

'Right. Now we'll deal with new and crucial information that has come back to us about the family from Pakistan. Kevin.'

But as Mower stood up again, to pass on essentially what Mohammed Sharif had discovered in Lahore, a uniformed constable came into the room and handed the DCI a note, which he read quickly, his face becoming a shade paler and even grimmer as he nodded for Mower to continue and walked out of the room. He made his way quickly down the stairs to the control room, where he took hold of the duty sergeant's arm fiercely.

'This incident in Southfield? Was anyone else hurt?' he asked.

'One fatality, according to the paramedics. Male. Two women at the scene. No one else hurt. Is CID on its way, sir?'

'I'll fix it,' Thackeray said.

Mower drove Thackeray to Southfield faster than the law allowed and pulled up outside the Holdens' modest house, which was already hemmed in by an ambulance, two squad cars and a group of concerned neighbours. Thackeray shouldered his way past the uniformed constable on the door to be met by a sergeant, barring the way inside to unauthorised visitors.

'The body's in here, sir,' he said, standing aside, and Thackeray glanced cursorily into the kitchen, where the body of Bruce Holden lay where he had fallen, surrounded by blood, which was liberally spattered and smeared on the floor and walls around him.

'Weapon?' he asked.

'Two knives, one heavily bloodstained, on the floor,' the sergeant said, waving towards them.

'Secure the scene for the SOCOs,' Thackeray said. 'And the women who were here?'

'In the front room, sir. They're both in shock. The paramedics have had a look at them. We're not sure whether they should go to hospital...'

'I'll talk to them now. Then decide,' Thackeray said, turning, with Mower on his heels. Opening the door to the living room, he found Laura on the settee supporting an almost comatose and shivering Julie Holden whose hands and clothes were stained with blood. Laura looked up at Thackeray, her eyes full of tears.

'Are you all right?' he asked.

'Yes, I'm not hurt or anything,' she whispered. 'I'll be fine. He took us by surprise...'

'Wait,' Thackeray said sharply to Laura. 'Mrs Holden. I'm DCI Thackeray. Can you hear me?'

Julie Holden turned dull eyes towards the two police officers.

'Where's my daughter?' she asked. 'Where's Anna? What have you let him do to her?'

'Mrs Holden, I want you to go to hospital now for a check-up,' Thackeray said, knowing that the two women had to be separated before they could discuss what had happened, and reckoning this was the least contentious way to do it. 'The ambulance will take you. And we will talk later about what has happened when you're feeling better. Do you understand?' Julie nodded and Mower slipped out of the room to summon the paramedics, who helped Julie into a wheelchair and took her out.

'Go with her, Kevin,' Thackeray said. 'We'll want her clothes. And if they don't want to keep her in, I want her at HQ straight away.'

'Guv,' Mower said, turning on his heel but not without flashing Laura an encouraging smile.

When they had gone, Thackeray closed

the living room door firmly on the increasingly congested crime scene outside, and flung himself down beside Laura, putting his arm round her shoulders, where she collapsed in tears.

'This isn't the sort of support witnesses are supposed to get,' he murmured, kissing her wet cheeks. 'I thought you'd put yourself at risk again... Are you sure you're all right?'

'I'm fine, just a bit shaken,' Laura said. 'I don't think I was at risk. That was a purely domestic battle. He wasn't really interested in me.' She dried her eyes.

'Sorry,' she said, sniffing. 'It's the shock.'

'Do you need to see a doctor?'

'No, I'll be fine. This is a story I can't wait to write, and I guess you're not going to like it very much. I think the police let Julie down very badly. This should never have happened.'

'Hang on, Laura,' Thackeray said. 'We haven't even established what did happen yet. And you're going to be our main witness. Ted Grant will have to take his turn on this one.'

'Oh, phooey,' Laura said, her eyes sharp again. 'That bastard tried to kill her. He would have done if she hadn't grabbed a knife herself...'

'Save it for your statement,' Thackeray said. 'We'll need a blow-by-blow account but we'll do it at the station, not here. What possessed the two of you to come up here to meet Holden anyway? You must have known it was a terrible risk.'

'I didn't know he was here. She told me she just wanted to come and collect some of her stuff. But he called her, apparently, and told her she could see Anna...' Laura stopped, realising the implications of what she had just said.

'She lied to you?' Thackeray said quictly. Laura nodded.

'You'll charge her, won't you?'

'Inevitably, I should think,' Thackeray said. 'Though what with remains to be seen. But what about the child? Was she here?'

'No.'

'Did he say where she is?'

'No.' Laura stared at Thackeray, her eyes wide with shock again. 'You don't think he's killed her, do you?' she asked.

'I don't know what to think,' Thackeray said. 'But we need to find her.'

'This shouldn't have happened, should it?' Laura asked, angry again now. 'It really shouldn't have happened. If you'd given Julie and Anna more protection, if you'd arrested Holden when he was making all those threats, if the police in Blackpool had bothered to find them when they were holed up there... You all had so many opportunities and they were all wasted. It's low priority stuff, still, isn't it? Domestic violence? Low level, low priority, even though it's well known that men who bash up their wives are likely to hurt their children as well. Kill them even...' Laura stopped suddenly and Thackeray froze.

'Is that what you're afraid of?' she whispered. Thackeray stood up abruptly, policeman, not lover, suddenly.

'I want you to go down to HQ and make a full statement about everything that's happened this morning. Someone will be waiting to look after you. I'll tell them you're coming. I have a search for a missing child to supervise.'

Laura stood up too, and straightened her clothes, glancing in distaste at the faint spray of blood on her shirt sleeve.

'I'll go home and change first,' she said, her voice matter-of-fact. 'Will I see you later?'

Thackeray shrugged, and Laura turned away without another word and left the house, where the SOCOs were now busy in the blood-spattered kitchen.

CHAPTER EIGHTEEN

Sandra Wright wriggled in embarrassment as she faced Sergeant Kevin Mower across her desk at the travel agency where Faria Aziz had worked.

'A boyfriend?' she said. 'She never said anything about a boyfriend. I didn't think that was allowed for Muslims. They're a bit strict, aren't they, about that sort of thing? Playing away?'

'It wouldn't be something she would want widely known,' Mower said dryly. 'But we have some evidence for it. She gave you no hint?'

'No way,' Sandra said. 'I'm amazed actually.'

Mower sighed. His ears were still ringing from a tongue-lashing Thackeray had doled out earlier when he realised that the statements which had been taken from Faria's colleagues did not include one from her boss, Mark Harman, the manager of the agency. Mower had been dispatched to Milford to fill in the gap, only to find that once again he was not at his desk.

'Did Mr Harman say when he would be back?' he asked Sandra. 'I really need to see him.'

Sandra flashed a glance at her colleague Damien at the other end of the counter.

'He's been out a lot lately. You don't think he...'

'I don't think anything,' Mower said sharply. 'It's just that he was out the last time we came and I need to catch up with him in case he can add anything to what we know about Faria.'

'Here he is now,' Damien said as the door opened and a tall young man in his thirties, with an anxious-looking, pale face but fashionably cropped fair hair and a sharp suit, came in.

'Can I help?' he asked, pleasantly enough, though when Mower introduced himself his face fell and Mower thought he saw a flicker of fear in his eyes.

'You'd better come into my office,' he said, leading the way into a small room at the back of the premises, and closing the door firmly behind him on his staff. 'I suppose you're here about Faria. I was devastated, you know? Absolutely devastated.' He took off his coat and sat down behind his desk, but did not seem to know what to do with his hands as he waited for Mower to continue. In the end he settled for pushing his chair back and hiding his hands in his pockets.

'Was she a good employee, Mr Harman?

Reliable, all that?' Mower asked, sure that he had hit gold here.

'Absolutely,' Harman said enthusiastically, as if let off a particularly unpleasant hook. 'She was an excellent employee, very useful in an area like this because she spoke Asian languages, you know? Very good for some of our clients... They fly back to ... wherever they came from a lot, for holidays and weddings and all that.' But Mower was impatient to get to the nub of the matter.

'Did she discuss her private life with you at all?' he asked sharply. 'Her family life? Did she tell you, for instance, that she was pregnant and presumably might be leaving her job, at least for a time?'

Harman hesitated for a moment and Mower watched impassively as a red flush spread from his neck to suffuse his face. This was not a man who would ever be able to hide his feelings easily, the sergeant thought happily, and Harman seemed to realise just how clearly he had given himself away.

'Sandra's been chattering, has she? I did wonder if she guessed. Some women seem to have a sixth sense for these sorts of things, don't they? I knew I should come to see you but...' He shrugged. 'My family wouldn't have liked it if they'd known. They're not BNP or anything, but they wouldn't have liked it. And...'

'And?' Mower prompted.

'I was scared, if you must know. I was scared of her family finding out. Right from the beginning, but even more when she disappeared. I expected her husband or her father to come storming through that door. You hear things about them, don't you? Muslims, I mean, especially where woman are concerned. She was a married woman, though she said she wanted a divorce. The marriage was no good...' He trailed off miserably.

'You were having an affair with Faria Aziz?' Mower said flatly, and the other man nodded.

'Yes,' he said. 'For the last six months or so. I was crazy about her. We loved each other. I'm not ashamed of that.'

'There's no reason why you should be, Mr Harman, but I'm not sure my boss will be very pleased to hear you've been concealing vital information in a murder inquiry.'

'It was all concealed,' Harman came back angrily. 'She was terrified of it coming out because of what her family's reaction would be. Then, when she got pregnant, she said she would get a divorce. Definitely.'

'You assumed the baby was yours?'

'Oh, yes. She said she wasn't sleeping with her husband. She said her husband had never wanted to sleep with her though I took that with a pinch of salt. I thought she was trying to please me, you know? Though

344

when I think back...' He hesitated. 'I think she maybe was a virgin. It could have been her first time when we first slept together. I wasn't sure. She was very ... modest in what she did. I liked that. It made a change from the little slags you meet on a Friday night. But if that's really true, her husband must have known the baby wasn't his.'

'A DNA test will establish the paternity of the baby,' Mower said. 'We would have tracked you down in the end that way.'

'I'm sure you would. I don't mind. I loved her very much and I want you to find out who killed her. I'll help you any way I can.'

'Do you know if she told her husband she was pregnant?'

'I don't think so. The only people she confided in were her sisters. I never met them but I know they were very close to Faria. It was the men in her family she was afraid of. They still seemed to think they were living in some medieval village in Pakistan, rather than Yorkshire in the twenty first century. The men in her family, the men at the mosque. It's bizarre the way they carry on.'

'Did you know her husband was gay?' Mower asked.

'Gay?' Harman sounded genuinely surprised. 'Faria never told me that. She just thought ... well, I don't know what she thought. She said the marriage had been

345

arranged for family reasons and I think she just thought he didn't fancy her. He was much older than she was. At first, when she started telling me things when we were on our own here in the office, I just felt sorry for her. But things developed from there.'

'She must have been afraid of being seen with you,' Mower said.

'We spent most of our time at my place. I've got a cottage out at Broadley. We went there mostly. Or if we wanted to do anything else, we went to Leeds. We took great care not to be seen in Milford or Bradfield. Neither of us wanted that.'

'I'll have to ask you to come to police headquarters to make a full statement about all this, and answer more questions,' Mower said. 'You've seriously hindered our inquiry by not coming forward before and you need to understand that we'll be checking out everything you tell us.'

Harman flushed again.

'You can't imagine that I could have harmed her,' he said, his voice shrill. 'You can't imagine that.'

'I don't imagine anything, Mr Harman, but I assure you we'll want to be certain that you're telling us the truth now we've found you. We won't be taking anything on trust.'

'Do you believe him?' Thackeray asked Mower when he reported back on Mark

346

Harman's statement, which he had completed after a couple of gruelling hours in an interview room.

'I think so,' Mower said. 'He's given us a DNA sample voluntarily to check the paternity of the baby. He seems genuinely shocked and upset by what's happened and there doesn't seem to be any reason why he should have killed her.'

'But no shortage of motive now for either the husband or the father to have taken exception to what Faria had been up to. That's clear enough. It all comes down to who knew she was pregnant and exactly when they found out.'

'And who knew Aziz was unlikely to have been the father,' Mower added.

'Well, the fact that he was gay seems to have become fairly common knowledge at the mosque in Milford, and it was not very popular with some of the worshippers there, so it's not impossible the news got back to Bradfield on the grapevine some time ago. Have we traced the previous imam in Milford?'

'He's in Pakistan,' Mower said. 'Visiting his family. He's an old man, so that's not an unlikely story.'

'Right. I'll talk to the super about liaising with the police in Pakistan. We need to check out what Sharif uncovered there, and ask them if they can trace our imam from

347

Milford and see exactly what he knew about Aziz, who he told, and what, if anything, the young militants at the mosque might have thought to do about it, if anything. Meanwhile, keep up the hunt for Aziz – dead or alive.'

'Guv,' Mower said.

'Any news on the Holden child?'

'Not yet,' Mower said. 'We've not traced the father's four-by-four, which is odd. He must have got to the house somehow. Mrs Holden's still at the infirmary under observation. Not fit to be questioned, they say. I thought I would go up to her mother-in-law's place to see if she's had any contact with Holden since he left Blackpool. It's a bit unlikely after what he did to her before he buggered off, but she might have some ideas that would help.'

'Good idea,' Thackeray said. 'I hope to God we're not looking for another body. We'll be pilloried again for not taking domestic violence seriously enough, even if Julie Holden does get away with pleading provocation. Laura's already threatening to crucify us in the *Gazette*, as it is. She says she's sure Holden would have killed Julie if she hadn't grabbed a knife herself.' The memory of Laura's anger when he had seen her briefly at the Holdens' house still felt raw.

'She'll say that in court, will she? You two

must have some interesting exchanges of view around the fireside,' Mower said lightly, and was shaken by how quickly Thackeray's expression changed to a mask of fury, quickly suppressed.

'Thank you, Sergeant,' he snapped, and Mower turned and left without a word. There was something very wrong there, he thought, as he went back to his desk to pick up his coat. And it did not seem to be getting any better.

Sergeant Mower parked outside Vanessa Holden's neat Victorian house and glanced up at the façade. It was a dark afternoon, drizzling with rain, but there was no sign of any lights inside, and when he unlatched the gate he noticed that there was still a bottle of milk on the doorstep and a morning paper, soggily wet, protruding from the letterbox. Feeling anxious now, he knocked on the door, but no one responded. Glancing around, he noticed the curtains at the bay-window of the next door house twitching slightly. Nosy neighbours, the policeman's best friend, he thought with a faint smile, and sure enough, as soon as he opened the next door gate, the front door was flung open and an elderly woman, warmly clad but wearing her slippers, squinted out at him.

'I'm looking for Mrs Holden,' he said conversationally. 'Is she away, do you know?

Her milk's still on the step.'

'I've not seen her for a day or two,' the neighbour said. '*He* were here the other day, though. The son, Bruce. I thought he'd left after what he did to her before, but he were back with the little lass for a while. I'd not have let him in the door if he were my son.'

'When did he leave?' Mower asked. 'Did you see him go?'

'No,' the neighbour said. 'I didn't notice him leave. D'you think there's summat up? D'you think we should call the police?'

'I am the police,' Mower said grimly, flashing his warrant card. 'You don't happen to have a spare key to Mrs Holden's house, do you?'

'I do,' the neighbour said, more cheerful now. 'I have hers, and she has mine. At our age you never know, do you? Summat can go wrong.'

'Would you open the door for me?' Mower asked. The woman agreed and bustled off, coming back with her shoes on, and a thick coat round her shoulders, to lead an increasingly impatient Mower back to her neighbour's front door. She picked up the milk.

'I'll put it in her fridge,' she said, as she inserted the key into the lock.

The narrow hallway smelt slightly musty and all the internal doors were closed, but there was nothing to spark a panic in

Mower's suspicious mind. One by one, he opened the doors, and inspected a neat and tidy front room, a kitchen where a modest amount of washing-up lay drying on the draining board, before going upstairs and repeating the process to discover two empty bedrooms and a bathroom where the bath and basin looked dry and unused.

'She's not here,' he said unnecessarily to Vanessa Holden's neighbour, who was waiting for him in the hall. He felt massively relieved not to discover Vanessa's body, or worse, that of her granddaughter, decomposing in the house. 'Did she not mention that she might be going away?'

'She didn't,' her neighbour said, with faint disapproval in her voice. 'She usually let's me know. Asks me to keep an eye out, you know. There's so many little yobs about these days.'

Mower went back into the kitchen and tried the back door. It was locked on the inside.

'Where does that door lead?' he askcd, seeing a further door at the side of the kitchen for the first time.

'Down to the cellar. All these houses have an old wash-cellar down below, and a coalhole. The young couples are opening them up and modernising them for extra space, but I've never bothered and I don't think Vanessa has either.'

Mower tried the door handle only to find again that the door was locked, but this time there was no key in the lock.

'She'll not be there in a locked cellar, will she?' the neighbour asked. 'Stands to reason.'

'Sssh,' Mower said urgently. 'I thought I heard something.' He banged on the door and shouted against the wood panel.

'Hello. Is there anyone there?'

This time a voice responded, young and faint, and Mower, with a huge sense of relief, knew that the DCI's worst nightmare had not come to pass this time.

'Is that you, Anna?' he shouted. 'Do you have a key?'

'No, no. Let us out please. Please, please let us out.'

Mower glanced round the kitchen angrily, looking for something with which to force the lock, and when nothing obvious presented itself, he took several paces back from the door and charged it with his shoulder. After a couple of attempts the elderly door gave way and he almost toppled down the stone steps into the smelly, gloomy depths below. Grabbing the door frame just in time, he steadied himself and tried the light switch, without effect, before going down circumspectly in the dim light. At the foot of the steps he found the girl he recognised as Anna Holden waiting for him, clutching a blanket around herself and shivering uncontrollably.

'I thought no one would ever come,' she said, grabbing his hand in her small, icy one. 'Daddy said he would come back but he didn't. And my Nanna's asleep now and she won't wake up. She got very cold.'

Mower put his arm round the child and guided her up the steps quickly to where the neighbour was waiting.

'Make her a hot drink,' he said curtly. 'She's half frozen.'

Then he went quickly back down to the room where he had half-glimpsed in the faint light which filtered down the steps what looked like a bundle of rubbish in one corner. There, curled up on a bed of cushions and covered by a blanket, he found Vanessa Holden, icy cold and stiff and undoubtedly dead.

'Oh, shit,' he muttered, pulling out his mobile phone to call for reinforcements. This was a case, he thought, that had gone more than pear-shaped. It was rapidly turning into a catastrophe.

Mohammed Sharif was pacing up and down the living room of his small flat waiting for Louise to finish work. He had exhausted his stock of DVDs, read a morning paper from cover to cover, and gone shopping, and it was still only lunchtime, and he could find neither the enthusiasm nor the appetite to eat. What he really wanted to do was talk to as many members of his family as he could, to try to tease out who knew what about Faria's death. He was, he believed, in a far better position to do that than any of his colleagues were, but he knew that not only would that compromise his position with Thackeray, but would aggravate the abyss that had already opened up between him and his uncle. He was condemned, he thought, to this agonising inaction, which meant waiting in silence for an axe to fall.

But just when he began to think he might catch Louise on her mobile as the school day ended, there was a buzz on the intercom, and he was surprised to see his cousins Jamilla and Saira downstairs outside the main doors to the block. He buzzed them in and waited anxiously, certain that they could be bringing nothing but bad news.

The girls scuttled in when he opened the door to them and flung off their top coats, sitting themselves side by side onto the sofa, almost like twins in their dark blue school *shalwar kameez* and white headscarves. He could see the nervous tension in their expressions and the reluctance, even though they had made the effort to come to see him, of either of them to break the silence.

'We need to talk to you,' Jamilla said eventually.

'Well, here I am,' Sharif said, with a feeling of foreboding wrenching at his guts. Both the girls looked more worried than he had ever seen them before.

'We think we should have told someone before,' Jamilla said. 'But we weren't sure what it meant. Or who to tell.'

A single tear ran down Saira's cheek, and she wiped her eyes with the corner of her headscarf.

'We thought you would know what to do,' she whispered.

'It's about Imran Aziz,' Jamilla said. 'He came to our house.'

'When?' Sharif asked. 'I thought you said that you hadn't seen him or Faria for months'

'We didn't actually see him,' Saira said. 'I heard him, one night, talking to my father. A couple of weeks ago. I went downstairs for a glass of water and overheard them talking.'

Sharif's mouth was dry as he looked at the two girls, trying to keep his expression calm.

'What were they talking about?' he asked.

'My father was very angry. He was telling Imran that he should know what he had to do. He should know, and he should do it.'

'Did he say what he should do?'

Saira shook her head.

'No, but then Imran said he didn't have the money for a plane ticket, and my father said he would see to that, so I thought maybe Imran and Faria were going to Pakistan. That's what it sounded like.'

'But this was when? How long ago?' Sharif asked. 'Was it before Faria disappeared?'

'Just after she told us on the phone she might be having a baby,' Saira said.

'But she wasn't sure about it then? Did she say she had told Imran?'

'She said she hadn't told anyone else. It was too early,' Jamilla said firmly.

'And you didn't tell your parents?'

Saira glanced at her sister for a second before she spoke again.

'I told my mother,' she whispered. Mohammed Sharif suddenly felt very cold, knowing with absolute certainty that anything Saira told her mother would reach her father's ears too.

'You were right to come and tell me,' he said, keeping his voice calm. 'But I don't think any of this is very important. I'll pass it on if I think it's useful.'

The girls looked relieved and Jamilla struggled back into her coat and handed her sister hers.

'We'd better get home. We'll be late and our parents will think we've been chattering to boys.'

'And that would never do,' Sharif said, his expression desolate. 'Will you tell your father I may be round to see him later on? There's something I need to talk to him about.'

'You won't tell him that we told you?' Saira asked anxiously.

'No, I won't tell your father,' Sharif said. But the knowledge that he had to tell someone hung like a lead weight around his neck. He sat for a long time, contemplating his own future and that of his shattered family, before he pulled out his mobile and speed dialled Sergeant Kevin Mower's number.

'I need to talk to you,' he said.

The early winter dusk was falling when a countryman out walking his lurchers failed to bring them under control as they ran off and started eagerly exploring amongst the rubble and tumbled rock at the foot of a small quarry on the scrubby moorland above Milford.

'Come here, you silly beggars,' he commanded. Annoyed that two normally well-trained dogs were taking absolutely no notice of him, he strode over to the pile of rubble they were scattering in all directions with manic zeal, only to stop dead a foot or so from where they were digging, swearing virulently to himself.

'Come here, you beggars,' he said, pulling the dogs' leads out of a deep pocket in his camouflage jacket and clipping them to their collars. He pulled them away roughly and wound the leads around an old fence post, where they stood straining and whining in high excitement. Gingerly, he approached the rocks again and kicked away a few more to make sure that what he thought he could see in the fading light was actually what he suspected it was. But there was no doubt, and he swore again as he uncovered a human hand, filthy with mud and blood, and the side of a human head, the dark hair matted and the skull distorted like no human head he had ever seen before.

He thought himself a hard man but this sight turned his stomach and he turned away quickly. He untied the dogs' leads and dragged them away, back down the track towards the lights of the nearest houses in the valley below. Let the police deal with it, he thought. That's what they were paid for. And he made his phone call without leaving his name.

Michael Thackeray sat in his car outside the flat he had shared with Laura, gazing up at the darkened windows, and wondering if it was still in any sense his home. He should have been feeling elated at the conclusion of a difficult murder case, but when he had watched Faisel Sharif being taken from the interview room to be charged with the murder of his daughter Faria, he had felt only a deep discontent, and he had not joined the rest of the CID team, who were celebrating in the pub at this moment. He and Mohammed Sharif, who had been waiting in the CID office for the conclusion of the interview with his uncle, had left police HQ quietly side by side.

'There was nothing you could have done,' Thackeray had said to the younger man as their paths diverged. 'You mustn't blame yourself.'

'I had no idea he could ever, *ever* contemplate something like that. He was not a fanatic... He seemed like a good man.'

'If the last few years have taught us anything, it's that you simply can't tell. Take some time off, Mohammed. Help the rest of your family to come to terms with what's happened. Come back to work when you feel ready.'

'You want me back?' Sharif muttered.

'Of course I do,' Thackeray said.

He had gone to his car, feeling limp and exhausted, and then driven, in defiance of common sense he knew, towards Southfield and Laura's place, not his own, only to discover that she was not there. Rather than call her, he had slumped back into the driving seat, eyes closed, reliving and trying to make sense of the rollercoaster of an evening that had left him with almost as big a problem as he had managed to resolve.

They had picked Faisel Sharif up from his home soon after Mohammed had poured out his horrified suspicions to Sergeant

Mower. The older Sharif had not seemed unduly surprised to find a posse of policemen on his doorstep, and while Thackeray and Mower had waited for his legal representative to arrive before they began their interrogation, they found that they already had sufficient evidence, accumulated that day, to tear holes in Sharif's almost half-hearted protestations of innocence.

Imran Aziz's telephone records showed that he had been in touch with his father-in-law's house several times during the period when Sharif claimed he and Faria had lost contact, including the day on which Saira had overheard the two men together. Sharif did not deny that he had been furiously angry, nor that the cause of that anger was the confirmation Imran brought that Faria was pregnant with another man's child.

'So when you told Imran to do what he knew he had to do, you expected him to kill her?' Thackeray had asked at last. Sharif gazed at him with sorrowful eyes and then nodded slightly, in spite of his solicitor's warning hand on his arm.

'I did not want that shame brought on my family,' he said. 'Here, or back in Pakistan, it was too much to bear, for me, for my father, for everyone. She had become a whore.' He stared angrily at Thackeray, as if daring him to contradict his indictment of his daughter.

'So Imran killed her? With your encouragement?' Thackeray pressed him.

'He called me one night a few days later. He said he had given her an injection and that he needed help to move her. We took her to the river in his car and threw her in. She did not know what was happening to her.'

'And where is Imran now? Did you give him a plane ticket to go back to Pakistan?'

'No,' Faisel said. 'I don't know where he is now. He never came back to me for the price of a ticket.'

But no sooner had Faisel Sharif signed his confession, than that final question was answered when news of the discovery of a body in a quarry to the north of Milford filtered back to CID in Bradfield. Identification was easy, it turned out. Imran Aziz still carried his driving license and his wallet in his blood-stained jacket. Faisel Sharif, now in a cell, took the news of his death quietly, almost indifferently.

'You found him?' he said, resignedly.

'We found him,' Thackeray had snapped. 'So now we know why he never came back for the plane ticket. And now, perhaps, you can tell us how he died.' Sharif shrugged, looking old and tired and gray.

'There were people at his own mosque anxious enough to kill him. He caused outrage there.'

'He seems to have been beaten to death.

He was found on the moors beneath a pile of stones. Are you saying you think the young militants at the mosque did that because he was gay?'

Faisel hesitated, and then he shrugged.

'The traditional way can be by stoning,' Sharif said, evidently unmoved by Thackeray's horrified expression at the equilibrium with which he seemed to accept what amounted to an execution.

'You encouraged this?' he asked. Sharif nodded imperceptibly.

'I did it,' he said very quietly. 'If I had let him live it would have made a mockery of Faria's death and brought endless shame to my family. Imran had to die too. It was inevitable.'

'No,' Thackeray had said, containing his own anger. 'In this country it is not inevitable. It is a murder like any other, and we will always track down those who did it. There are no excuses for murder.'

The two men's eyes locked in mutual incomprehension.

'You did this alone? No one helped you?' Thackeray asked at length.

'I did it alone,' Sharif said, though Thackeray did not believe him. But if he had help from the angry young men at the mosque in Milford, he knew he might never prove it, and by the end of another hour Sharif had signed a new confession, taking full responsibility for the death of his son-in-law.

For a few minutes Thackeray slept in the car, exhausted by everything that had happened, until he wakened again with a start that sent a stab of pain across his back. He took a moment to work out where he was, and then pulled out his mobile and called Laura. The phone rang for so long that he almost despaired of reaching her, expecting to be switched to voicemail, when at last the familiar voice answered, noncommittally, but a sound so welcome that he could hardly speak.

'Where are you?' he asked.

'At Vicky's,' she said. 'We've been working out how to get Julie bail tomorrow. And if we can't, who's going to look after Anna?'

'I should think she'll find a sympathetic judge,' Thackeray said. 'We're not on opposite sides in this, you know.'

'You've charged her with murder!' Laura's outrage almost made his ear burn.

'David will explain why,' he said quietly. 'The CPS will make the final decision, anyway.'

Laura seemed to take a moment to digest this and in the background Thackeray could hear the sound of a child crying, a sound that triggered an almost physical pain somewhere deep inside him.

'Are you coming home?' he asked.

'Is that where you are?'

'I wanted to see you,' he said, knowing how inadequately that conveyed the desperation he felt. 'It's been a God-awful day for families. I've been doing a lot of thinking and wondered if maybe we couldn't do it better. We could hardly do it worse.'

'D'you really mean that?' Laura asked, her voice almost inaudible.

'I think so,' he said.

'I was trying to get Naomi back to sleep when you rang. She's been disturbed by all the noise.' Laura laughed. 'I'm not very good at it,' she said.

'You'll learn,' Thackeray said.

This Large Print Book, for people
who cannot read normal print,
is published under the auspices of

THE ULVERSCROFT FOUNDATION